SLOW BURN

A COLORADO HIGH COUNTRY NOVEL

USA Today BESTSELLING AUTHOR

PAMELA CLARE

SLOW BURN

A Colorado High Country Novel

Published by Pamela Clare, 2016

Cover Design by © Carrie Divine/Seductive Designs

Photo copyright © avmedved (Andrei Medvedev)/Depositphotos.com

Photo copyright © Hot Damn Stock

Copyright © 2016 by Pamela Clare

ISBN-10: 0-9903771-8-0

ISBN-13: 978-0-9903771-8-4

Dedication

This book is dedicated to Colorado's first responders, who take on the dangers of the mountains to keep us all safe. You saved my life once. Thank you for that and for all you do.

Acknowledgments

Many thanks to Michelle White, Jackie Turner, Shell Ryan, and Benjamin Alexander for their support while I wrote this book.

Special thanks to Rick Dirr, chief of the Nederland Fire Protection District, for generously giving of his time and experience. I learned so much from him. I couldn't have written this book without his insights and his willingness to answer questions. Any mistakes in this work are my own.

Additional thanks to Benjamin Alexander for his insights as a county seasonal ranger and filmmaker; to Reid Miller, for helping me understand more about the work of EMTs and paramedics; to Jana Reffel for her help with the Colorado casino scene and blackjack; and to author Julie James for answering questions about Chicago.

Personal thanks to Chris Wu, who is like a son to me, and Lisa Marrs for including me in their lovely wedding ceremony, which inspired parts of the wedding in this story.

Last but not least, thanks to the many readers who wrote to me, messaged me, tweeted me, and otherwise got in touch, asking when you'd get Hawke's book. Here it is!

Prologue

June 23

Denver, Colorado

*E*ric Hawke parked his blue Ford F-150 on the upper level of the parking garage at Denver International Airport, and then looked up Vic Woodley's flight info on his smartphone. He glanced at his watch.

Shit.

The guy's flight had landed thirty minutes early.

Eric grabbed the little cardboard sign he'd made, climbed out of his truck, and moved in long strides toward the terminal, the late afternoon heat stifling.

Well, he couldn't have gotten here any sooner. Traffic coming down the canyon had sucked, and it had only gotten worse when he'd hit Highway 36. Besides, picking this Woodley guy up hadn't been on his list of things to do this morning. He wished Woodley would mind his own business and fly back to Chicago. From what Taylor had told Eric, the bastard was here to convince Lexi to leave Scarlet Springs and Taylor behind and return to Illinois with him.

Yeah? Well, let him try.

Austin Taylor had been Eric's best friend since preschool, and Lexi Jewell was the woman Taylor had loved since he was seventeen. Eric wasn't about to stand by while some slick, big-city hipster dude tried to convince Lexi that staying with Austin was wrong for her. She and Austin were crazy in love, and they'd been through too damned much to put up with more bullshit.

Eric was only picking the guy up as a favor to the two of them. They were still dealing with the aftermath of Lexi's near-death ordeal. Lexi couldn't drive because of her broken leg, and Taylor couldn't pick Woodley up because he was taking Lexi to a follow-up visit with her orthopedic surgeon. Eric had offered to dump Woodley in a ditch somewhere, but Taylor had been against the idea. In fact, he'd seemed awfully chill about the thought of another man coming to visit Lexi.

"I can handle the competition," he'd said. "Besides, if Lexi stays in Scarlet, it needs to be because she wants to live *here*, not because we murdered her friend."

Okay, so Taylor had a point.

Eric stepped into the crowded terminal, air conditioning blasting him, bringing relief from the heat. He glanced around, fairly certain Woodley would have made his way to baggage claim by now.

How was Eric supposed to recognize the guy?

He had planned to stand at the top of the escalator in the main lobby holding the little cardboard sign with Woodley's name on it so that all new arrivals would have to pass by him. Woodley would have seen his name, and that would have been it. Nice and easy. But now Woodley could be anywhere—sipping chardonnay in a restaurant, getting his nails buffed, waiting for his baggage.

Ah, hell.

Eric walked over to a white service telephone, dialed Paging Services, and asked the woman who answered to page Vic Woodley. She told him the airport had switched to a visual paging system and said his page would be visible within the next five minutes.

Left with nothing to do but wait, Eric ended the call and headed down the center hallway toward the coffee shop in the lobby. He'd spent most of the day working a controlled burn and was thirsty enough to drink a water tender dry. He hadn't even had time to take a shower or put on a clean T-shirt and probably reeked of sweat and smoke.

He reached into his back pocket for his wallet—and then he saw her.

Whoa.

She entered the coffee shop ahead of him, pulling two blue suitcases behind her, one strapped to the other. Her thick, dark hair fell in soft layers to below her shoulders, a short black tank dress hugging her curves, strappy black heels clicking on the stone tiles. He walked to the cooler, grabbed a bottle of water, and then got in line, watching as she tried to decide which flavor of bottled iced tea she wanted. Finally, she made up her mind and maneuvered her way through the shop to stand in line behind him.

God, he could smell her, the sweet scent of her skin and the faint musk of her perfume warming his blood.

He turned to the side and looked over his shoulder toward the lobby as if searching for someone. He looked down and found the woman's gaze right where he wanted it—fixed on the Scarlet Springs Fire Department logo on his T-shirt. She had a sweet face. Long lashes, high cheekbones, flawless skin. Her nose was small and slightly upturned at the tip, her lips full and covered with shiny gloss.

She looked up at him through big brown eyes, then leaned in as if to tell him a secret, those lips slowly curving into a smile. "Firemen are my favorite color."

Her flirty words hit him right in the solar plexus.

Jesus!

His brain must have shorted out because all he could say was, "Yeah?"

"What's your name?"

He'd left his name pin and badge in his truck. "Eric. What's yours?"

"Victoria."

"I like it." A classy name for a classy female.

"Can I help who's next?" a voice said.

Eric turned to find the kid at the cash register—a barista with dyed black hair and black plugs in his earlobes—waiting for him to step up to the counter and pay. He closed the distance with a single stride, set the bottle down, and took a five out of his wallet. "Just the water."

"That'll be four dollars and four cents."

It was a sign of how distracted he was that he didn't complain about the price.

He twisted the bottle open and drank, while the kid with the earlobe plugs counted out ninety-six cents in change. "Thanks."

He shoved the change into his pocket and left the coffee shop, stopping just outside the door. Victoria would come over to him. He knew she would.

He raised the bottle to his lips again, finishing it off with big gulps.

From behind him came the clicking of heels and the scrape of suitcase wheels.

"Thirsty?" She stood beside him, iced tea in hand.

He nodded, wishing he'd bought two bottles of water or maybe four. "I spent most of the day working a controlled burn."

She opened her tea, smiled up at him. "I can smell the smoke."

"Yeah, sorry about that. I'm picking someone up for a friend and didn't have time to shower or change."

"Oh, don't apologize. I like it."

Holy shit.

Eric wished he could forget about Woodley and take Victoria out for a drink—and maybe something more. In his line of work, the only relationships he had time for were the casual kind. Still, hooking up with someone he'd met two minutes ago would be fast, even for him. It wasn't going to happen—not in the middle of the airport with Woodley waiting for him somewhere. Besides, he knew nothing about Victoria—where she was going, where she was from, whether she was in a relationship.

He motioned toward one of the nearby tables. "You want to sit for a minute?"

It wouldn't kill Woodley to wait another ten minutes.

"Sure." She glanced at her watch.

"Waiting for your boyfriend?" Eric had to know.

Her little laugh told him she saw right through his question. "I'm not attached."

Wasn't it just Eric's luck? She was beautiful, available, and completely beyond his reach at the moment. Unless she was staying here in Denver...

They walked over to a vacant table and sat.

He tried not to be Captain Obvious. "So are you coming or going?"

"I'm coming."

The word lingered in the air between them for a moment, and Eric could tell by the flash of color in her cheeks that her mind had latched onto the double entendre just like his had. An image of her lying beneath him, lost in bliss, flashed across his mind, the thought sending a surge of raw lust through him.

Oh, didn't he wish.

V ictoria Woodley felt her cheeks burn. She could see in Eric's blue eyes exactly where his mind had gone. Her mind had gone to the same place. She wasn't into casual hookups, but in his case, she might be willing to make an exception.

Good freaking grief!

Lexi hadn't exaggerated when she'd said the men in Colorado were hot.

Well over six feet with thick brown hair, Eric had a rugged outdoorsy vibe she liked. She could see the outline of his pecs through his T-shirt and was willing to bet they came with a six-pack. His biceps, forearms, and even his hands were muscular and so much bigger than her own.

If what they said about the size of a man's hands was true…

Belly flutters.

"You said you came to pick someone up?" She willed herself to quit undressing him with her mind and focus on his face, but even his face was sexy. His brown hair hadn't been cut recently and had a tousled look, as if he'd brushed it out of his eyes with his fingers. His eyebrows were dark slashes against tanned skin, his square jaw covered by a growth of stubble. Long lashes, a full mouth, and a dimple in his chin softened his masculine features. And he was a freaking firefighter.

Some men had it all.

She'd always had a thing for firefighters, but she'd never been this close to one, much less sat down to have a conversation with one.

"Yeah. I've never met him. I think he's here to try to break up my best friend and his girlfriend. I offered to dump him in a ditch, but my friend wouldn't go for it." The grin on his face told her he'd been joking—mostly. "He would have come to pick the jerk up himself, but his girlfriend was almost killed last Sunday, and he's taking her to a checkup with the surgeon."

"What happened?"

"A fugitive took her hostage, dragged her into a mine shaft, and the shaft collapsed. The bastard who kidnapped her died and almost took her with him. We were able to get her out, but she has a fractured tibia."

Vic stared at the man across from her, his story one she already knew. Anger made her face burn. "What's the name of the *guy* you're supposed to pick up?"

He held up a cardboard sign that read, "Vic Woodley."

She found herself on her feet. "That's *my* name."

He gaped at her, astonishment on his face. "You're … ?"

"Lexi Jewell is my best friend."

A look of understanding crossed his face, followed by an angry frown. He muttered something that sounded suspiciously like, "Taylor, you bastard."

"I'll catch a cab." She took hold of her suitcase handle, turned toward the door, and hurried toward the sign with the taxi on it.

He caught up with her in a single stride. "Victoria, hey, I'm sorry. It was a misunderstanding. My buddy let me believe you were a guy."

"Yeah, I figured that part out for myself." But that wasn't the problem.

She stepped through the automatic doors, dry heat hitting her in the face.

Eric followed her to the curb. "It's an hour and a half to Scarlet Springs. Do you have any idea how much a cab will cost?"

She hadn't realized it was that far. Still, she wasn't going anywhere with him, not if he was the kind of man who would try to manipulate Lexi. He didn't really want her here. "That's okay. I can afford it."

She'd been born with more money than she could ever spend.

She stepped out to the curb to hail a cab—only to see that there were no cabs. She turned to look the other way and found herself looking at Eric's chest.

"Come on, Vic*toria*. You can't be that angry with me. It was a simple misunderstanding."

"You think I'm angry because you thought I was a guy?" She bent to the side to see, his broad shoulders blocking her view.

No taxis there either.

What did it take to get a cab in this state?

Eric's eyes were hidden behind mirrored aviator-style sunglasses now, but there was a slight grin on his face, as if he found all of this amusing. "I wasn't serious about dumping you in a ditch, you know. I'm *not* going to hurt you."

Men could be such idiots.

"Before she came to Colorado, Lexi made me promise that I wouldn't let her get stuck in Scarlet Springs. She's my best friend. She tells me everything. I know how much she hates it here."

"I get it. You came to keep your promise."

"You're afraid that spending time with me will remind Lexi how much she loves her life in Chicago, and you and Austin wanted to keep me away from her. That's manipulative and just plain wrong."

His smile vanished. "I was joking. You know, a *joke?* If you think Austin or I can make Lexi do anything she doesn't want to do, you don't know her as well as you say. Whether she stays or goes is up to her. Austin won't stop her, and neither will I. But I'll admit that I wasn't excited about you coming here. Lexi has been through enough. She doesn't need you making things more complicated."

He turned and started to cross the street toward the parking garage.

Vic stood there in the heat, the glare of the sun almost blinding. She glanced left and right. Still no taxis.

Well, hell.

She called after him. "You're just going to leave me here?"

He stopped, looked over his shoulder. "I thought you were going to take a cab."

"Do you see any cabs?"

He turned and strode back to her, reaching for her luggage.

"I can manage."

A muscle clenched in his jaw. "Fine by me."

Vic followed him, dragging her suitcases behind her, her temper as hot as the air. Okay, so maybe she had been planning on campaigning pretty hard for Chicago—the tickets she'd bought for the Adele concert, Taste of Chicago, shopping on Oak Street, the beach, Lou Malnati's deep-dish pizza. But she knew Lexi would be turning her back on so many things she loved if she stayed in Scarlet Springs. What were best friends for if not to keep you from making a big, fat mistake?

Vic followed Eric until they came to a blue pickup with a handful of bumper stickers on the back.

Support Search & Rescue. Get Lost.

Climbing: It rips the screams from your throat.

Firemen find 'em hot and leave 'em wet.

Someone certainly had a high opinion of himself.

"You advertise your prowess on bumper stickers?"

"Bumper stickers? I put them on my truck because I think they're funny, not because I'm advertising."

"I'm surprised you don't have one that just says, 'Hey, I'm a fireman. Want to play with my hose?'"

He laughed. "That's pretty good. Do you want to play with my hose?"

She rolled her eyes in disgust.

"I'm joking! For God's sake." Eric jerked open the passenger side door and stepped aside to make room for her. "Just leave your luggage. I'll put it in the back."

"I'll do it. I don't need some big muscle man to save me."

"Okay." He walked to the rear of the vehicle and lowered the tailgate, then stood a few feet away and watched her, arms crossed over his chest.

She unstrapped the bags, and then lifted the smaller one onto the tailgate and rolled it into the bed of the truck. The bigger one was a lot heavier, however, and she struggled to raise it high enough to get it onto the tailgate. She only needed to lift it a few … more … inches…

Damn.

Eric walked over to her, took the bag, and lifted it into the back of his truck with one hand. He slammed the tailgate shut. "I can see why you and Lexi are friends. You're as stubborn as she is."

Embarrassed that she'd needed his help after all, Vic ignored his comment. She walked to the passenger door and climbed inside, the truck hot and stuffy from sitting in the sun. She opened her tea and drank, the liquid cool and sweet in her throat.

Eric climbed into the driver's seat beside her and jammed his keys into the ignition. "You need to be drinking water. It's pretty dry here. If you don't stay hydrated, you're more likely to get altitude sickness."

Whatever.

"I'll be fine."

"Suit yourself, city girl. I've been a paramedic for a decade. You'd be surprised what altitude and dehydration can do to a person."

So he was a paramedic as well as a firefighter.

And a jerk.

No *way* would she let him come between her and Lexi.

He started the engine, backed out, and drove down a succession of ramps to exit the garage. She took out a few dollars to cover the parking fee, but he refused it, paying with his own money.

She tucked the cash away. "I'm not the only one who's stubborn."

He drove the two of them out of the airport and onto the highway. For a long time, neither of them spoke, classic rock playing from an iPod plugged into his dash.

Vic watched through the window, the cute little cluster of skyscrapers that must be Denver off in the distance to their left, the landscape around them a mix of farms and new residential developments, plains and rivers. "Those are the mountains? They're not so tall."

"You're a good hour's drive away. They'll look a lot bigger up close."

He was right. The longer they drove, the bigger the mountains became. Then, at last, they came to the top of a hill, and a valley opened before them, the mountains rising out of nowhere to touch the sky, snow on their jagged summits.

"Oh!" The breath left Vic's lungs in a rush, and she stared, overcome by a sense of awe. "I didn't know it would be so beautiful."

Eric's lips curved in a grin, his gaze on the highway. "I guess Lexi doesn't tell you everything."

Chapter One

One year later

Victoria Woodley waited with her luggage in baggage claim at Denver International Airport, scrolling through work emails on her smartphone. She looked up from the small screen every few seconds, checking her surroundings. No one had recognized her so far, but she couldn't help feeling jumpy when she was in public.

Welcome to the new normal.

She worked through the emails, answering them as fast as she could, typing with one finger. In the two-and-a-half hours since she'd left Chicago, Abigail had sent her no fewer than seven messages, all of them about the Merced Capital campaign Vic would be spearheading when she got home. Abigail was a decent boss, but she seemed to believe that Vic wanted to spend every waking hour working like she did.

It had been almost a year since Vic had seen her best friend, Lexi Jewell, and more than a year since she'd had any vacation. Now Lexi was marrying her high school sweetheart, Austin Taylor, and Vic was her maid of honor. After the hell of the past year, Vic really needed the time off. Lexi and Austin had planned a week of fun leading up to their wedding, and Vic wanted to spend those days relaxing and celebrating Lexi's happiness, not working.

Vic had just sent the email when a shadow fell over her. Her head snapped up.

"Hey, Vic*toria*. Whoa. Sorry to startle you."

Eric Hawke. Again.

Her pulse skipped. She'd been expecting Lexi.

"You got everything?" He stood there looking hot as hell in a navy T-shirt and blue jeans, hands on his narrow hips, black mirrored Revos concealing his eyes. He hadn't shaved, a day's growth of stubble on his chin. "It's déjà-vu for me, too, city girl."

She'd known she'd see him again. He was Austin's best friend and his best man, so, of course, she'd see him. But it was a long drive to Scarlet Springs. She hadn't expected to spend time alone with him. He might be sexy as sin and a firefighter, but he was cocky, arrogant, and too much of a lover boy.

Last time she'd been here, Lexi had told her that Eric had been with his share of women, but had never been serious about anyone. He'd even asked Lexi out before she and Austin had gotten back together. Vic wouldn't be surprised if he'd left a trail of broken hearts behind him. Regardless, none of it mattered.

Vic was done with men.

You're attracted to him.

Okay, yes. She was. And that *right there* was proof positive that he was bad news. Her ovaries always got her into trouble.

Firemen are my favorite color.

Her own words came back to her, making her cringe inside. She'd only said that because she'd thought she'd never see him again—and, well, because he was smoking hot. What an idiot she'd been!

She would never say anything like that now. She knew firsthand how much ugliness a handsome face and sexy smile could hide.

Her feelings must have shown on her face, because Eric laughed. "Sorry you're stuck with me, but Lexi's dad started having palpitations while he was mowing the lawn. She and Kendra took him to the ER."

"Oh, no." Vic slid her phone into her handbag and got to her feet. "Is he okay?"

"He's fine—just dehydrated."

"Thank goodness!"

Lexi would be crushed if anything happened to her father, especially the week of her wedding. The two of them were just getting to know each other.

"That's what happens when you have whiskey for breakfast." Eric's gaze moved over her luggage—a garment bag and three suitcases. "Exactly how long are you planning to stay?"

With all the arrangements for their wedding under control, Lexi and Austin had decided they wanted to spend the week before the ceremony having a good time with their friends—rafting, hiking, swimming, and horseback riding. Vic had never done most of those things, so she'd had to go shopping. Uncertain what she'd need, she'd brought an entire Athleta shop with her.

She slipped on her sunglasses. "Lexi told me to be ready for anything."

"You sure did take her seriously." He reached for her bags, hesitated. "Are we going to fight about who carries these this time?"

She picked up the garment bag, leaving the others for him. "Knock yourself out—and thanks."

She followed him out the automatic doors into a cool and breezy Saturday morning, not a cloud in the blue sky, the mountains purple in the distance. She couldn't wait to be up there again, to smell the fresh air, to look up at the white summits of the high peaks. Scarlet Springs might exist in a different reality than the rest of the world, but it was beautiful.

Eric's pickup was parked at the far end of the center row, its bumper sporting yet another sticker.

Feel safe at night. Sleep with a fireman.

Had she mentioned arrogant? Because, oh, yes, he was arrogant.

While he settled her bags in the truck's bed, she climbed into the passenger seat and laid her garment bag over the narrow bench seat in the back of the cab. By the time she had her seatbelt on, he had the keys in the ignition.

He turned toward her and held out his hand. "Hey, Victoria, I know we didn't get off to the best start last time, but I hope that's behind us. I thought you were here to pressure Lexi. You thought I was doing the same thing. We were both trying to protect her. As it turns out, she managed just fine without us. I hope we can be friends."

She supposed he was right. She could respect his loyalty. Besides, he was the best man, and she was the maid of honor. For Lexi and Austin's sake, the two of them needed to get along.

"Sure." She took his hand.

Heat arced between them at the contact, unexpected and startling, and she had to fight not to jerk her hand away. But then his lips curved into a devastating smile, and she felt her ovaries begin to purr.

Oh, no. No way.

In that moment, she made herself a promise. No matter what Eric said, no matter how nice he seemed, no matter how good he looked without his shirt, she was *not* going to sleep with him.

*E*ric Hawke drove down the E-470, Joe Walsh playing on the radio. He glanced over at the woman beside him. He'd had the same visceral reaction when he'd seen her today that he'd had a year ago, because …

Damn.

She wore a short, sleeveless dress that hugged her lethal curves, its color caught somewhere between red and hot pink. Her dark hair spilled around her shoulders in long layers, except for where it was pushed away from her face by her sunglasses, which sat perched on her head. Her legs were bare and silky-smooth.

Eyes on the road, dumbshit.

He had no business letting himself get hot and bothered. For starters, she was Lexi's best friend. If things got messy, it could hurt his friendship with Lexi. And then there was the little warning Taylor had given him.

"Be careful with Vic, okay? She's had a hard time lately. She's a little fragile."

Taylor hadn't bothered to explain what he'd meant by that, but Eric had gotten the message loud and clear. Victoria was off-limits.

Okay, fine.

She wasn't the least bit interested in him anyway. Her face was buried in her phone, her fingers tapping out a message. She hadn't said a word since they'd left DIA, but was preoccupied with checking emails or text messages or some damned thing.

What was it with people and their phones? Life was happening around them, but they missed it, their attention focused on itty-bitty screens. What was the point?

She let out a breath, irritation flashing across her features.

"Everything okay?"

She looked over at him, phone still in hand. "It's just work stuff."

"Public relations, right?" He remembered Lexi saying something about that last year when Victoria had come to visit.

She nodded. "I work for Jensen West Communications, the biggest public-relations firm in the city."

"You must love your job to bring it with you on vacation."

She gave a little laugh, looked down at her phone again. "It's not by choice, believe me. My boss works eighty hours a week and thinks everyone else should too. I don't think the word 'vacation' is in her vocabulary."

"That doesn't sound healthy."

"Says the man who runs into burning buildings for a living."

Okay, so she had a point.

He found himself grinning. "But you love the job, right?"

"Does anyone love their job? You go to college, get a degree in something you hope you'll enjoy, then bust your butt to find work in your field. Ten years later, you wonder how you'll be able to stand showing up at the office every day for the rest of your life. You know how it is."

"Actually, I don't."

"Really?"

"I love what I do, and I didn't go to college."

"You didn't?"

"Nope." Her surprised tone of voice made him grin. "I didn't want a desk job, so I didn't see the point of college. I put myself through firefighter academy and got certified as an advanced life support paramedic. I worked on a state hot-shot crew for a few years, traveled a lot, got to see a lot of cool places."

"Weren't they burning at the time?"

He laughed. "Yeah, I guess they were."

So, she had a sense of humor. It was dark and a little twisted, but he liked that.

"How did you become fire chief? Aren't you young for that? You're my age, right?"

"Ah, let's see ..." He took her flurry of questions in reverse order, pleased that he'd momentarily become more interesting to her than her phone. "I'm thirty-three. I'm the youngest chief in the department's history. I volunteered for Scarlet FD until a position opened up. I made shift captain in four years and was promoted to chief two years ago when the old chief retired."

"I've always wondered how it works. Do you live at the fire station?"

"Near enough." He laughed. "We all work forty-eight-hour shifts with four days off in between. I'm at the station on a lot of my off days because I'm chief, but right now, I'm on vacation."

"You're part of the Team, too, aren't you? You helped save Lexi."

"Yeah, I was there." That had been one *hell* of a day. He'd been on a lot of calls, but that one had shaken him to his core. "I've been with the Team since I turned eighteen."

The Team—Rocky Mountain Search & Rescue Team—was an all-volunteer nonprofit that handled searches, technical rescues, and evacuations for the region. It was widely regarded as the best S&R team in the nation. It gave him a chance to put his climbing and paramedic skills to work in high-risk situations.

Yeah, he'd do just about anything to get in some rock climbing.

"How can the Team function with you and Austin away at the same time?"

"There are almost fifty people on the Team. Some are provisional members, not primary members like Taylor and me. Our being away gives them a chance to get into the field a little more and accrue the hours necessary to be primary members." He glanced over, saw she was watching him. "What?"

"I think that's cool—the work you do. I guess I never imagined someone could skip college and still be so successful." She squeezed her eyes shut, opened them again. "Wait. That sounded snobby, didn't it?"

He couldn't help but laugh. "My mom says that the path to success is the one that enables people to feel at peace with themselves, and I can't complain. But there are times when I wonder if I missed out on something."

"Like what?"

He said the first thing that popped into his head. "Computers. I'm not great with all that electronic stuff. We have a volunteer who handles IT at the firehouse, but there are times I wish I could manage more myself. I'm working on a project right now—a video project—and I don't know what the hell I'm doing."

"What are you having trouble with? I have experience doing film editing for video marketing campaigns. I might be able to help."

God, that would make his life easier. But could he trust her?

"Can you keep a secret from Lexi?" He could see that she was curious.

Then her big brown eyes went wide. "It's something for the wedding."

She wasn't slow. He'd give her that.

"Promise you won't tell anyone, especially not Lexi. I know how women are. They tell their best friends everything."

She gave an impatient wave of her hand. "Yes, yes, I promise. Tell me."

"I've done some interviews with people around Scarlet, folks who knew her mother, asking them what they think she'd say to Lexi on her wedding day and how she'd feel about Lexi marrying Austin."

Lexi's mother had died when Lexi was only four, killed by a drunk driver.

"Oh!" Victoria's gaze went soft. "What a sweet thing to do. That will mean the world to Lexi."

Eric had thought the same thing. "Unfortunately, at this rate, I won't be done editing the footage until their first kid goes to high school. The video editing software is *such* a pain in the ass."

"Can I help? I'd love to be a part of that."

"I'd appreciate it." As he turned off E-470 onto Highway 36, Eric couldn't keep the smile off his face. He and Victoria were going to be spending a lot of time together over the coming week.

An hour later, they pulled into the long driveway of the Forest Creek Inn, the historic bed-and-breakfast owned by Lexi's family. The large, three-story Victorian house with its yellow paint and neat white trim stood proudly against the mountain backdrop and was one of the most photographed spots in town.

But Vic's gaze wasn't on the inn. Garment bag in hand, she hopped to the ground, as stunned by the beauty of the mountains as she'd been last year. "God, it's beautiful."

Behind her, Eric unloaded her bags. "I grew up with that view, and I can't say I've ever grown tired of it."

"I don't think I would either." She inhaled the fresh air, the scents of pine and sunshine filling her head.

Scarlet Springs—population 1,448, give or take a few—might not have a Starbucks, but what it lacked in lattes, it more than made up for in scenery. The town sat in a valley at 8,936 feet elevation surrounded by the Indian Peaks, the summits of which gleamed white with snow year round. Lexi had taught Vic their names last year, but Vic had forgotten them.

The door of Rose's New Age Emporium opened, and a woman Vic recognized as Rose stepped out and hurried across the street, all flowy skirts and long silver hair. Austin and Lexi had asked her to officiate at the wedding.

She embraced Vic, kissed her cheek. "It's so good to see you again, Victoria. I'm glad to see you and Eric together."

Vic tried to explain. "Oh, well, we're not—"

"Come by sometime, and I'll give you a free reading. I'm doing that for everyone in the wedding party."

"That's sweet of you. Thanks."

"Vic!" The back door to the Forest Creek Inn flew open, and Lexi ran out, wearing a tank top and shorts, a bright smile on her face, her long red hair pulled back in a ponytail. She gave Vic a big hug. "Sorry I couldn't pick you up myself."

"Eric told me what happened. How's your dad?"

From inside the house came a man's raised voice. "Leave me be, woman!"

Lexi rolled her eyes. "He is himself."

"Too bad the doctors couldn't cure him of that." Eric chuckled at his own joke. "Where do you want her bags?"

"We put her in the Matchless Suite," Lexi answered.

Eric gave a little whistle. "Someone's getting the special treatment."

Vic lifted her chin, teasing him. "I *am* the maid of honor."

She said farewell to Rose, then followed him and Lexi through the door into the Jewell family's kitchen, where Bob, Lexi's father, sat at the table glaring up at his wife, Kendra, Lexi's stepmother, while Britta, Lexi's younger sister, sliced tomatoes. The three of them looked toward the door, their expressions turning to smiles when they saw her.

"Welcome back, Victoria." Bob got to his feet. "How was your flight?"

"It was quick. Thanks. How are you?"

"If the females of this family would quit pestering me, I'd be fine."

"Just ignore my father." Britta glanced up from her slicing. She looked so much like Lexi that they might have been twins, though her hair was strawberry blond rather than outright red. "He scared the bejesus out of us this morning."

Kendra stayed where she was—standing, hands on her hips at her husband's side. "Nice to see you again, Vic. I'm trying to get Bob to lie down, but he won't budge."

"The doctor said to rest. He didn't say to lie down."

"Mmm-hmm." Kendra's eyes narrowed. "And you think that standing on your feet doing dishes counts as resting?"

Bob chuckled, and it was evident to Vic that he was enjoying the attention. "Does that mean you don't want my help doing dishes?"

"Not today."

Bob grinned, settled back in his chair. "Okay. If you insist."

Kendra shook her head. "The man doesn't have a lick of sense. Lunch will be ready in about ten minutes if you want to get settled."

The Jewell family's home was on the bottom floor of the house, while the bed-and-breakfast operated out of the top two floors. Vic had stayed here last year and had no trouble remembering her way around. There were two ways to reach the upper levels—the great staircase just inside the front entrance and a small elevator.

Vic, Lexi, and Eric took the elevator together. If it had just been the three of them without luggage, this would have been easy. But because of Vic's bags, they had to crowd together. By the time the doors closed, Vic stood with her back pressed against Eric's chest, his body hard against hers, the spicy scent of his shaving cream or aftershave teasing her.

Her ovaries sighed.

She ignored them. "It looks like those two are getting along."

Last time she'd been here, Kendra had just filed for divorce and was living somewhere else.

Lexi nodded. "He's drinking again, but, yeah, it looks that way."

Eric chuckled. "Are you kidding? They're crazy about each other."

The elevator stopped, and the doors opened.

Vic had to wait for Lexi to exit first. When it was her turn, she all but ran, following Lexi across the hall to her room.

"The Matchless is our best suite. I hope you'll be comfortable." Lexi pulled a key card from the pocket of her shorts. "It's named after the Matchless Mine, where Horace Tabor made his fortune in silver."

"And where his wife Baby Doe froze to death, alone and penniless, many years later," Eric said.

Lexi glared at him. "Nice."

He shrugged. "Hey, just finishing the story."

Lexi opened the door and stepped back to let Vic enter.

"It's … *beautiful.*" Vic had stayed in plenty of five-star hotels in her life. Her father was a wealthy man, and she had traveled the world with him before she'd left home. But nothing could surpass this little suite for comfort or charm.

"I hope you don't mind, but I thought we could all get dressed here the morning of the wedding," Lexi said.

"Of course I don't mind. It will be perfect for that."

A living area with antique wood furniture led to a bedroom with a fireplace and a king-sized brass bed and, beyond that, a bathroom with modern fixtures, including a tub big enough for two. A large, standing antique mirror stood off to one side, an ornate wooden frame holding silver glass. Everywhere there were beautiful touches that made Vic feel welcome—a bouquet of pink cabbage roses on the coffee table, a coffee mug with a bow on it that said "Keep Scarlet Weird," and a box of …

"Estes Park taffy! You really do love me." Vic had tried it during a trip to Rocky Mountain National Park last time she was here. Handmade the old-fashioned way, there was nothing else like it. She unwrapped a pink one, popped it into her mouth, and chewed. "Mmm. Cherry."

Eric left her bags near the bed. "Why doesn't the best man get digs like these?"

Lexi looked over at him, straight-faced. "Eric, you live here."

"Oh. Right." He took his cell phone out of his pocket, glanced at his text messages. "I need to get going. We're hitching Moretti's boat trailer to my truck. I'll see the two of you at the reservoir in a couple of hours."

That's right. Today was Reservoir Day. Tomorrow they were going up to Rocky Mountain National Park, then on Monday they were going horseback riding at the Cimarron Ranch. That would be fun. Tuesday was set aside for a whitewater rafting trip, which Vic was not looking forward to one bit. The idea of getting tossed around on rough water was scary, not fun. Wednesday they were renting the rock gym for a climbing party. Vic didn't climb, but she would watch. Then on Thursday, it was Casino Night. She had a surprise planned for Lexi and Austin that night and couldn't wait. Friday was Spa Day and the wedding rehearsal. The wedding was Saturday morning.

"Terrific," Lexi said. "See you there."

Eric turned to go.

It took Vic a moment to pry her jaw open, her teeth stuck together by taffy. "Hey, Eric. Thank you."

He gave her a nod. "Anytime."

The door shut behind him, leaving Vic and Lexi alone.

"This is amazing, Lexi. Thanks so much."

"I'm so glad you're here. How are you? I've been so worried about you."

"I'm okay." Vic left it at that. There was no way to talk about it without crying, and she didn't want to open up that emotional Pandora's box this afternoon.

Lexi's gaze hardened. "It's a good thing he's in prison, or I'd hunt him down."

Vic didn't want to think about this. "Let's just pretend for now that it never happened, okay?"

Lexi reached out and gave her hand a squeeze. "We'll have lunch as soon as you get settled in. Then we'll go and have some fun at the res. How does that sound?"

"Can we swing by your new office?"

That made Lexi smile. "Sure. I'd love to show you around."

Lexi had started her own accounting firm in Scarlet last summer, renovating an old Victorian house to serve as her office. She'd sent photos, but photos weren't the same as seeing it in person.

"Terrific. I've missed you so much." A rush of bittersweet joy ambushed Vic, leaving a lump in her throat. "Oh, my God, Lexi, you're getting *married!*"

Lexi gave a little squeal, her face radiant. "I know! Isn't it amazing?"

Chapter Two

$\mathcal{E}$ric stood on the deck in his swim trunks and flip-flops, counting and inspecting floatation vests to make certain there would be one for everybody. He probably ought to be looking for a new living situation rather than hanging out at the reservoir. He'd come home to find an email from his landlord. The guy and his wife were selling their house together with all twelve acres of their property, which included Eric's cabin. They'd wanted him to know in case the new landlord decided to kick him out.

But Eric and Taylor rarely got vacation at the same time. He didn't want to miss this week's fun. Besides, the landlord's house probably cost a couple million. It's not like the guy was going to find a buyer overnight.

He called to Taylor over his shoulder. "Did you say Sasha is coming, too?"

Sasha Dillon was the youngest member of the Team at twenty-three. She was also a world champion rock climber whose success enabled her to live off sponsorships. Petite with a delicate face and long, blond hair, Sasha attracted men by the dozens. Those who didn't recognize her thought they'd found a new belay slave or a little woman they could impress—until she roped in and made them look like amateurs.

Taylor dumped ice into a large cooler, covering cans of soda and bottled water. "Sasha, Lexi, Britta, Vic, you, me, and Moretti. That's seven."

"Did you have to count that on your fingers?"

Taylor laughed. "Hey, at least I *can* count."

Eric couldn't resist. "Hey, Moretti, can this old tub handle seven people?"

You could call Moretti names to his face, but no one insulted his boat.

Moretti's head popped up from below the helm where he'd been tinkering all morning. "Fuck you, Hawke."

"You wish." Eric grinned.

That had been too easy.

One of the newer members of the Team, Jesse Moretti had served as an Army Ranger and had seen combat in both Afghanistan and Iraq. He'd come to Colorado from Louisiana on vacation, discovered rock climbing, and hadn't looked back. Still, he missed fishing and boating on the Gulf, so he'd thrown down a bundle for a fancy speedboat.

"They're here." Taylor waved, a big grin on his face.

Yeah, the guy had completely lost it over Lexi, and Eric was happy for him. Sure, Eric had had the hots for Lexi, too. He'd been the first one to notice her in junior high, but he'd been too damned shy to say anything to her. Taylor had been state ski champion in high school and had been more confident than Eric. When she'd first come back to Scarlet, Eric had thought he might connect with her, but, nah, man. She and Taylor had gotten back together in a matter of days. Anyone could see they were made for each other. They'd been each other's first serious relationship and first lover, and now they were finally getting hitched. It was the perfect happy ending, and it couldn't have happened to better people.

Lexi led her flock of friends toward the pier, the lot of them wearing cover-ups over swimsuits, except for Sasha, who wore a bikini over her slender body as if it were street clothes, wakeboard tucked beneath her arm.

"Hey!" Lexi called to them. "Sorry we're late. I took Vic to see my office and got a little distracted."

"We were about to leave without you," Taylor joked.

He met them at the stern and helped the women aboard, first Lexi, then Vic and Britta, while Sasha climbed onto the starboard gunwale and stuck her wakeboard in the rack before hopping into the boat, a sunny smile on her face.

"*Vamanos!*" she called to Moretti. "Let's go."

Lexi introduced Victoria to Moretti. "Vic, this is Jesse Moretti. He's with the Team. He's also one of Austin's groomsmen. Jesse, this is my best friend and maid of honor, Victoria. She and I were roommates in college."

Moretti looked at Victoria as if she were lunch, puffing out his hairy pecs. "Have you ever been on a boat?"

The big idiot.

She nodded. "My brother owns a boat, and he used to take me out."

"What kind of lakes do you have around Chicago?"

Dear God. Had he truly just asked that question?

Dude!

A smile tugged at her lips. "Oh, lakes like Lake Michigan."

"Right. Yeah, I knew that."

Sure you did.

"Have you gone boating on a *real* lake?" Victoria fired back. "Not that there's anything wrong with this one. It's cute."

Was she flirting with Moretti? And, hey, was she dissing the reservoir? Okay, so it was manmade and wasn't very big, but not everything could be a Great Lake.

Moretti grinned. "I grew up in a house two miles from Louisiana's Gulf Coast. Does that count?"

Irritated, Eric walked over to the starboard side and reached for the stern line. "Are we going to get out on the water, or are you going to stand there talking?"

They got down to the business of unmooring the boat, Eric and Austin handling the lines, while Moretti started the motor and maneuvered the boat into open water.

Sasha walked up to Moretti. "This *is* a speed boat, right?"

"You want speed?" He opened the throttle, and they were off.

Wind hit Eric full in the face, clearing his mind, easing his irritation. What did he care if Vic and Moretti connected? It's not like he had any claim on Vic. She wasn't his type anyway. He was attracted to sporty women, women who didn't waste time on makeup and clothes, women who....

Lust hit him square in the chest, derailing his train of thought.

Victoria had taken off the short white dress she'd worn as a cover-up and was making her way toward him in a black bikini, her hair blowing in the wind.

Holy hell.

He'd known she had a knock-out body, but ... *damn.* His gaze moved from the swells of her full breasts to her narrow waist to the curve of her hips and her gently rounded belly. He wanted to touch every sweet inch of her, kiss every inch, taste …

She turned and bent down to grab a can of soda, her luscious, round ass barely covered by the fabric of her bikini.

X-rated images flashed through his mind—her bent over just like that, his hands on her hips—

"You might want to close your mouth," Britta whispered in his ear.

Eric snapped his jaw shut. Okay, so he'd been staring and thinking things he shouldn't think. But, Jesus, who could blame him?

Vic sat next to Lexi in the stern, cell phone in hand, cheering with the others as Eric did another front flip. "How does he do that?"

"He's had lots of practice." Lexi brushed a strand of damp hair from her cheek. "He and Austin have been wakeboarding for years. It's what they do in the summer when they can't ski or snowboard."

Amazed, Vic watched while Eric swung far outside the wake, then cut back toward the center, gaining speed. He launched himself off the wake, did some kind of complicated backward flip, seemed to land on his feet—and wiped out.

"Oh!" they all said, more or less in unison.

"He's down!" Austin called back to Jesse, a grin on his face.

Jesse cut the throttle to neutral, let the boat drift, then made a slow right turn and idled back toward Eric.

Eric grabbed hold of the tow cable and motioned for Austin to pull him in. When he reached the swim platform, he hoisted himself out of the water, swinging his feet and the board onto the platform in one fluid motion.

Austin stepped back to make room for him. "Humbled by the Whirlybird."

"Bullshit." Eric stood, unlaced his boots, and stepped out of them. "I landed it, then caught an edge."

"Would you listen to this shit? You wiped out, man."

The two men had been ribbing each other all afternoon, and it was evident to Vic that they enjoyed trading insults almost as much as wakeboarding.

Eric picked up his board and slid it into the rack on the boat's tower, then unbuckled his floatation vest and tossed it aside. His broad shoulders made his hips look narrow, water running in rivulets down the tanned skin of his chest and belly, his dark nipples tight from the chill.

A thrill shivered through her.

Oh. My. God.

She'd been right, of course. Those pecs did, in fact, come with a six-pack, distinct ridges of muscle bisected by a happy trail of dark curls. Then again, all three of the men on this boat were ripped. The last time she'd seen this many six-packs in one place, she'd been at a liquor store. Not that she cared. She'd made herself a promise. Besides, she was over men.

Sexy is as sexy does.

Eric walked over to her, dripping wet, each step he took in her direction making her pulse pick up. "It's your turn, city girl."

"My turn?" She shook her head. "I don't know how to wakeboard."

He pinned her with his gaze. "You're a virgin."

"What did you all do when you went boating on Lake Michigan?" Austin asked. "Did you just sit in the boat?"

Lexi answered, which was good because Vic hadn't recovered from hearing Eric call her a virgin. "Vic's brother, James, steered the boat, while she and I drank margaritas and watched guys."

Austin laughed. "So that's what passes for recreation in Chicago."

Eric's gaze was still fixed on Vic as if it were just the two of them and the other conversation weren't happening. "Don't be afraid. I'll teach you."

He was messing with her now, his words and tone of voice deliberately sexual. And, damn it, it was working, because she couldn't think of a single witty response, blood pulsing way too fast through her veins.

She got to her feet. "I'm not afraid."

That wasn't entirely true, but she wasn't about to admit it.

"You're going to love it," Sasha assured her. "It's no more complicated than learning to ride a bike."

Vic hoped that was true, though she seemed to remember that learning to ride a bike hadn't been all that easy.

"You won't need this." Eric took her cell phone, handing her a floatation vest instead. He checked it when she was done putting it on, then set her up with Sasha's boots and board, tightening the laces for her, all the while explaining to her how to get up on the wakeboard. "Are you ready to try it?"

"I think so." Handle gripped in both hands, Vic dropped butt first into the water the way the others had done, the breath leaving her lungs in a shriek. "It's cold!"

Eric chuckled. "This water was snow a few weeks ago."

And she'd thought Lake Michigan was chilly.

He sat down on the swim platform, his blue eyes focused on her with an intensity that made it hard to think. "Remember to keep your knees bent and relaxed. Let the boat do the work. Don't try to stand up or pull back against the boat, or you'll fall. If you do fall, no problem. We just stop and start over. Let's do a few practice tries."

Holding fast to the cable, he pushed the wakeboard away from the boat with his bare feet until Vic was about six feet off the stern. "I'm going to simulate the motion of the boat, and let's see how you do. Ready?"

She wasn't ready, and she probably never would be. "Yes."

He pulled on the cable, drawing her through the water, lean muscle shifting as he moved. Vic tried to come up onto the board but found herself sinking. How was she supposed to concentrate on anything with a mostly naked man watching her?

"You tried to stand up. Just let the boat bring you up." He pushed her away from the boat again. "Ready?"

"Yes." She drew a deep breath, adjusted her position, let her knees relax.

"Point your toes toward the boat," Britta called out. "That's what helped me."

This time when Eric pulled her forward, Vic did her best to let the boat pull her up, staying in the water, toes angled toward the boat.

"Good. Perfect. Just like that. Now let's try it for real." He motioned to Jesse, who idled the boat forward and away from Vic. "When you're up and on your feet, make sure you distribute your weight evenly. Keep your eyes up and on the boat. It will help you keep your balance."

Oh, shit, was she truly doing this?

She felt the cable go tight, heard the boat's engine begin to accelerate.

Eric called out to her. "You got this!"

Vic wasn't so sure. She tried doing what she'd just done and was surprised when the boat slowly drew her out of the water and to her feet. She felt a single moment of triumph before falling backward with a splash.

She sputtered to the surface, still gripping the tow handle.

"Oh, you almost had it!" Lexi shouted.

"That wasn't bad." Eric motioned to Jesse again. "You pulled against the boat there. Just hold on to the handle, and keep your arms straight."

Three more times they tried it, and three more times she got to her feet and then fell, each time going a little bit farther than the last.

"You can do it!" Sasha shouted. "Don't be afraid."

Vic wasn't scared now. She was ticked off. *No way* was she going to be the only person on this boat who couldn't stand up on a wakeboard.

Pull it together.

Legs relaxed, knees bent, arms straight, weight balanced.

This time when she made it to her feet, she found herself flying along behind the boat. "Woohoo!"

Eric let out a whoop, did a fist pump, Lexi, Austin and the others cheering, too.

Vic couldn't help but laugh, exhilarated by the feel of the wind on her face, blood rushing through her veins, water spraying up behind her.

My God, she'd done it!

When was the last time she'd had so much fun?

Vic looked over the dinner menu, foot tapping to the band. It was almost nine o'clock in Illinois, and she was starving.

"Hey, Victoria. Welcome back to Scarlet."

Vic looked up to see a server with long blond dreadlocks, a nose ring, and tattoos of roses, ivy, and skulls on her arms. "You're Rain, right?"

"That's right." Rain smiled. "It's good to see you again. What can I do you for?"

Vic was touched that Rain remembered her. She'd only been here for a few days. "I'll try the personal deep-dish pizza. Give me the Jackpot, but hold the onions."

"You got it. One Jackpot, no onions. What to drink?"

"Ooh. I'll have one of your margaritas." They were strong, but Vic felt like celebrating. She'd just learned how to wakeboard. "Ice, no salt."

"How about you, Lexi?"

Vic looked around while the others placed their orders, taking in the scene that was Knockers. Jesse was over at the climbing wall, holding the rope for a friend. Men and women with pool cues in hand laughed and talked and drank beer. A man in a tank top noodle-danced his heart out in front of the stage, while a handful of couples bobbed and swayed together on the dance floor.

The first time Vic had been here, she had assumed that Knockers was nothing more than some local version of Hooters—skimpy tops, short shorts. She'd been wrong. The name referred to tommyknockers, mythical spirits that the town's original inhabitants believed lived in the mines. Some locals still believed in tommyknockers, and Lexi was one of them. She was convinced that a tommyknocker had helped save her life last year when that bastard bank robber had almost gotten her killed.

Vic didn't know what to think about that.

"So, city girl, now that you've learned how to wakeboard, are you going to try climbing?" Eric took Vic's menu and handed it to Rain, who half-walked, half-danced away with their orders.

"No way! I've had enough adventure for one day." Already, the muscles in her arms and shoulders were starting to feel sore.

"I thought you did a great job." Lexi ran a hand through hair still damp from her shower, working the tangles with her fingers.

"You stuck it out," Austin said. "Way to go."

"I thought you learned fast." Britta's face was sunburned. "It took me six or seven tries to stay on my feet."

Sasha gave her a high five. "You were a total badass today."

"Thanks." Vic was more than a little amazed with herself. In the span of an afternoon, she'd fallen in love with wakeboarding. "When I get back to Chicago, I'm going to buy a board and take some lessons."

But who would go wakeboarding with her?

The question took her mood down a notch. None of her other friends enjoyed the sport. Her brother certainly wouldn't be interested.

Austin grinned. "The next time she comes back, she'll be doing tricks."

Vic laughed at the very thought. "No Whirlygigs for me."

Eric laughed. "That's 'Whirlybird.'"

"Don't worry about getting the name right," Austin said. "Hawke here won't be doing any Whirlygigs anytime soon either."

"Hey, I landed it, then caught an edge."

Rain brought everyone's drinks on a tray, ending that argument.

Vic had just taken a sip of her margarita when she heard a familiar voice quoting the Bible somewhere behind her.

"If there is a poor man with you, one of your brothers, in any of your towns in your land which the Lord your God is giving you, you shall not harden your heart, nor close your hand from your poor brother, but you shall freely open your hand to him, and shall generously lend him sufficient for his need in whatever he lacks."

She looked over her shoulder, saw the man everyone called Bear standing just inside the doorway, preaching with battered Bible in hand. He was big and shaggy like his namesake, with a long beard and buckskin jacket. He lived alone in a cabin west of town. No one knew where he'd come from, how old he was, or what had happened to make him the way he was. They simply did their best to watch out for him. Their kindness toward him had touched Vic deeply.

She motioned to Rain, who hurried over. "What can I get for you?"

Vic took a twenty-dollar bill out of her handbag and slipped it into Rain's hand. When she spoke, it was for Rain's ears alone. "For Bear."

Rain smiled. "Lexi knows how to pick her friends."

She walked back over to Bear, handed him a menu, and whispered something in his ear that had him looking straight at Vic. He walked over to the table.

Vic felt suddenly on the spot. She hadn't bought him dinner because she wanted attention or even gratitude.

He stood beside her, towering over her in his buckskin jacket. "For I was hungry, and you gave me something to eat. I was thirsty, and you gave me something to drink. I was a stranger ..." His voice trailed off. "You're Lexi's pretty friend."

Vic swallowed, a lump in her throat. "It's nice to see you again, Bear."

Bear smiled and scratched his beard, ducking his head like a shy schoolboy. "God bless you, Victoria Woodley."

Then he turned and walked away, following Rain like a puppy to a table.

Vic found Eric watching her, just the hint of a smile on his face, his blue eyes warm. "You know what, city girl? You're alright."

Chapter Three

"What do you mean the pizza wasn't good?" Eric followed Victoria up the sidewalk, his laptop tucked under his arm. "First you make fun of our reservoir, and now you don't like the pizza?"

Victoria swiped her key card, buzzing them in through the inn's private guest entrance. "Have you ever had real Chicago deep-dish pizza?"

Of course, he hadn't. "How could it be that much different from what Joe serves up? Put toppings on dough with sauce and cheese and bake it. That's pizza."

She smiled. "If you don't know the difference, there's no way I can explain it."

They stepped into the elevator together.

He pushed the button for the third floor. "If Chicago-style pizza is so much better, why don't you make some and prove it? Or don't you cook?"

"Are you kidding? I love to cook." Her chin came up—proof he'd set off her stubborn streak again. "Okay, you're on—*if* I can find the ingredients somewhere."

The elevator doors opened.

Victoria stepped out, walked to her door, opened it with another swipe of her card. "Do you think Lexi and Austin suspect anything?"

Eric followed her inside, locking the door behind them. "Nah. We're good."

That wasn't entirely true. Eric had seen the pissed-off look on Taylor's face when he had offered to drive Vic home. Taylor thought Eric was ignoring his warning and trying to get naked with her.

Would Eric like to have sex with Victoria? Hell, yes. But he wasn't actively working to make it happen. He'd heard what Taylor had said. Besides, Victoria was Lexi's best friend, and if he slept with her, it might blow up in his face. He wouldn't risk his friendship with Lexi and Austin for anything.

Okay, so that wasn't entirely true either. Eric wouldn't initiate anything, but if Victoria started it, he would sure as hell finish it.

He stopped and looked around, dresses, tops, and pants lying haphazard on the sofa. "Did one of your suitcases explode?"

"Sorry about the mess. I couldn't figure out what to wear."

Eric couldn't understand that problem. A clean shirt and a pair of jeans, and he was good to go. "You shouldn't stress. You'd look great in anything."

She grabbed the clothes and disappeared into the bedroom. "You wouldn't say that if you saw me in sweats and a T-shirt on a Saturday morning."

Oh, he most certainly would—though he wasn't complaining about the wispy little spaghetti strap number she was wearing now. It had taken no small amount of willpower to keep his gaze on her face and away from the deep V neckline.

Her feet were bare when she stepped out of the bedroom, her toenails painted a sexy shade of red. "Where do you want to set up?"

"How about over there?" He pointed to the small dining table near the window.

"Perfect. Are you thirsty?"

"Water would be nice. You'd better be drinking lots of water, too, after spending all that time in the sun. You just got here from the flats." He carried his new laptop over to the small table, plugged it into the nearest outlet, and then booted it up.

She walked over with two glasses of ice water. "Here you go."

"Thanks."

From nearby, her cell phone buzzed—again.

Her body stiffened, her head snapping around toward the sound.

"Your boss again?"

Victoria hurried toward her handbag, which sat on the coffee table, and pulled out the phone. "Yes. Another email. It's midnight in Chicago."

"It's eleven on a Saturday night, and you're on vacation. Ignore her."

"I can't." She typed a quick response.

Eric shook his head. "You work too hard. You should throw your phone in a drawer and leave it there until it's time to fly home."

"That would get me fired."

"You say that like it's a bad thing." He turned the computer so that she could see the screen, too. "So how should we do this?"

Still holding her phone, she crossed the room and sat in the seat next to his. "Why don't you show me what you've done so far?"

And, God, he could smell her again.

He willed himself to focus on the job at hand, opening up the video-editing program and showing her the folder where he'd saved the imported footage. "I also imported a bunch of photos of Lexi and Austin as kids. I thought I could edit them in somehow."

She rested her chin on her hand, her gaze on the screen. "That's a fun idea."

"I started going one by one through the interviews, trying to edit them down, but it's taking forever."

She nodded. "Video can be extremely time-consuming. Why don't you show me how you were doing it, and I'll see if I can teach you some shortcuts?"

Eric found the interview he'd done with his mom in the footage bin and opened it, his mother's face appearing on the viewer. "I had Mom repeat a few answers because her neighbor was revving his car engine."

"This is your mom?" Victoria looked over at him, seemed to study his face. "You have her eyes."

"Lexi's mom was her best friend. She took care of Lexi and Britta during the day until Bob married Kendra."

"It's so sad—Lexi and Britta losing their mother when they were so little."

"What about your folks?"

"My dad lives in New York."

Eric waited, and when she didn't go on, he asked. "What about your mom?"

She shrugged. "Last I heard, she and her Italian boyfriend were lying on a beach in Greece. That was four or five years ago."

Okay, so she wasn't close to her family and didn't want to talk about them.

She got down to work. "The faster way to edit clips is to select your in and out points for the clip and then drag the footage you want onto the timeline. See?"

She turned the laptop toward him. "You try."

"Like this?" He'd just dragged another segment onto the timeline when his pager went off, one call-tone following the next—county sheriff, his fire station, the Team, Flatirons Emergency Response.

Something big had gone down.

"Shit." He pulled the pager from his waistband, scrolled through the message.

CAR IN BLDR CRK AT MM31

He was on his feet, the video forgotten.

She stood, too, concern on her pretty face. "Is something wrong?"

He pulled his keys out of his pocket. "A car went off the highway and rolled into Scarlet Creek at mile marker thirty-one. The water's still running pretty high with snowmelt. If the driver and passengers survived the crash, they're going to drown if we don't get them out quickly."

"I thought you were on vacation."

"I'm fire chief, and I'm with the Team. I'm pretty much always on call."

She crossed her arms over her chest. "Now who works too much?"

He shrugged. "When I lose sleep or free time because I'm out saving someone's life, I feel pretty damn good about it. It's a good use of a few hours, no?"

Then he remembered. "Can I leave the computer with you?"

"Sure." She smiled sweetly. "I won't even read your emails."

He glared at her. "You'd better not."

Victoria hurried to the door to see him out. "Good luck. Stay safe! I hope everyone's okay."

So did he. "See you tomorrow."

This time, Eric took the stairs, leaping down two at a time.

By the time Eric arrived on the scene, the eastbound lane was closed, and emergency response vehicles were parked along the shoulder—squad cars, his station's rescue apparatus, and Rescue One, one of the Team's two rescue vehicles.

He grabbed a yellow Team T-shirt out of his back seat and changed into it, then grabbed his headlamp out of his backpack, and climbed out of his truck.

Brandon Silver, his B-shift captain, hurried over to him, dressed in swiftwater gear. "Sorry to bust up your evening, chief."

Eric slipped the headlamp over his head, turned it on. "Find anyone?"

"Not yet."

"Is Flatirons on the scene?"

"Downstream. They've been watching all the snags, bends, and bridges, but haven't seen anyone yet."

Eric climbed over the railing and started down the rocky slope toward the vehicle, which lay on its roof in Scarlet Creek, a handful of Team members searching the banks downstream, three others belaying three of his volunteer firefighters, who waded through thigh-deep whitewater looking for submerged bodies. "How's the water, boys?"

A head turned.

Jenny Miller.

Oops. Not a boy.

"It's fucking cold, sir," she shouted to him. "Care to join us?"

"Thanks. I'll pass." He walked over to the vehicle, looked inside.

The airbag had deployed, and the windshield was shattered. Water three feet high swirled through the vehicle, but there didn't seem to be blood that he could see. He leaned down, tried to locate the ignition.

"No one's home." Megs came up behind him. "No keys, either."

Maggie Hill, called Megs by her friends, was a legend in the climbing and rescue communities. One of the first women to break the gender barrier in rock climbing back in the late 1960s, she'd helped launch the Rocky Mountain Search & Rescue Team after a friend of hers had frozen to death as the result of an accident. In her early sixties and still climbing, she now served as the Team's director.

"Looks to me like the driver took off, unless the car fell from the heavens or jumped into the water all by itself." Megs had her own unique sense of humor.

"Right."

Still, they had no choice but to keep up the search. They couldn't afford to make assumptions. For all they knew, there might have been multiple people in the vehicle, any one of whom could have washed away. Or perhaps the driver had self-rescued and then collapsed of injuries along the embankment somewhere.

"Let's keep looking."

Something buzzed.

Vic's eyes shot open, her heart giving a hard kick.

She reached for the phone.

Abigail.

"For God's sake." It was just after seven.

What was so important that Abigail had to get in touch with her at seven in the morning on a Sunday while Vic was on vacation?

Grumpy from lack of sleep, her head aching, Vic read her boss's email—more questions about the Merced campaign. She forwarded it to Jeff, who was supposed to be covering for her, then put the phone on Do Not Disturb and tossed it to the foot of the bed. She was going to have to find a way to put limits on her boss, or Abigail would be calling her in the middle of Lexi's wedding.

She tried to drift off again, but her headache made sleep impossible, the throbbing ache like a migraine. That margarita must have packed more of a punch than she'd realized. What she needed was coffee.

She crawled out of bed and walked into the bathroom, flicking on the light and staring in dismay at her own reflection. "Great."

She looked like she hadn't gotten enough sleep—which was true. She's stayed up far too late watching the interviews Eric had taped, a few of which had made her cry. She'd made a few obvious cuts, then organized all of the photographs into folders so they'd be easy to find.

She showered, dried her hair, and then put on her makeup. The pain in her skull was unrelenting, her muscles sore from yesterday. When she was satisfied that her appearance wouldn't scare anyone, she followed the scent of fresh-baked croissants and coffee down a flight of stairs to the inn's dining room, where a buffet breakfast was being set out for guests.

"Good morning." Sandrine, the inn's French pastry chef, greeted her with a basket of croissants, her accent charming. "Did you sleep well?"

"Yes, thank you." Vic went straight for the coffee, leaving room in her cup for cream, which sat nearby in a little porcelain pitcher. "This smells delicious."

She wasn't truly hungry, but she ate anyway, the coffee helping to clear the fog from her head. If only it would chase away her headache…

By the time Lexi called an hour later, she was feeling a little better.

"Be sure to dress in layers. It's cold up there."

In June? Okay.

"See you in about fifteen minutes."

Vic changed out of the skirt and blouse she'd been wearing into a pair of jeans, a tank top, a fleece jacket, warm socks, and hiking boots. She had just stepped out of the inn's front door when Austin's SUV drove into the parking lot, Eric's truck behind him.

She waved. "Hey."

Lexi waved back, an excited smile on her face. "We're taking two vehicles in case the guys get called out. Britta's riding with Eric this morning, so hop in."

Vic climbed into the backseat behind Lexi, doing her best to be cheerful despite her aching head. "Good morning."

Cheyenne, Austin's younger sister, sat in the backseat, too. Tall like her brother, she wore her dark blond hair in a messy bun, sunglasses covering her eyes. She hadn't wanted Austin to get back together with Lexi and had been a real bitch to Lexi at first. She'd eventually come around—which was good news because Vic didn't have the energy to scratch her eyes out this morning.

"I heard you kicked ass at the res yesterday," she said.

Vic pushed a smile onto her face. "It was a lot of fun."

Lexi pivoted in her seat. "Did you get a good night's sleep?"

"Yes." Vic didn't want to worry her with something as stupid as a headache. "I stayed up a little too late."

She didn't see the look that passed between Lexi and Austin.

They drove from Scarlet Springs along the Peak-to-Peak Highway, the scenery taking Vic's breath away—snow-capped peaks, aspens with their white bark and tiny green leaves, meadows filled with wildflowers. Lexi, Chey, and Austin pointed out landmarks and named the peaks for her, the landscape something they knew well.

Then it dawned on her. "This is your office, isn't it, Austin?"

He grinned. "Not bad, eh?"

"Pretty fantastic, I'd say." What would life be like if she never had to set foot inside an office building again? She couldn't even imagine it.

Almost an hour later, they drove through the entrance of Rocky Mountain National Park, stopping so that she could get out of the car and take photos—and gawk at a herd of elk that had taken up residence in the middle of the road.

"A Colorado traffic jam." Eric came to stand beside her. "Check out that rack."

Was he messing with her again, or was he talking about the elk's antlers?

She refused to let Eric bait her. "He's huge."

"You should come back in the fall. During the rut, the bulls bugle and fight to establish dominance over harems of cows. You can stand here and hear bugling coming from all over this valley."

"How like males to strut and brawl and make a lot of noise to get attention."

He chuckled. "How like females to fall for that shit."

She started to object, but hadn't she done that with Stewart? Yes, she had. Stewart had put on a show and lured her right in. He'd had her like a fish on a hook the first night she'd met him. How could she have been so stupid?

She changed the subject. "How did it go last night?"

"It was just someone running the Scarlet Midnight Triathlon."

"There was a triathlon last night?" Something didn't make sense here.

Or maybe that was just her headache, which was getting worse.

Eric laughed. "The Scarlet Midnight Triathlon is made up of three events. First, you get drunk in Boulder. Second, you roll your vehicle into Scarlet Creek. Third, you run away."

It was supposed to be a joke, but she didn't find it funny. "Someone rolled their car into the creek and ran away?"

Eric nodded. "We found him hitchhiking a couple of miles up the road."

"He's lucky he wasn't killed. What a stupid thing to do."

"Honey, if we could cure stupid, I'd be out of a job."

ric parked at Forest Canyon Overlook, the parking lot overrun with tourists, snowflakes drifting lazily from an overcast sky. He glanced over at Britta, who was wearing only a tank top and shorts. "You want my jacket?"

Britta laughed. "I'm the idiot who didn't bring a coat. I'll be fine."

They climbed out of the truck and met Lexi, Austin, Chey, and Victoria at the trailhead that would take them over the tundra to the actual overlook.

Vic snuggled into a purple fleece jacket, her hands in her pockets.

"Even the city girl had enough sense to bring warm layers," Eric teased.

He got a laugh out of Britta, but Victoria didn't even look up.

They headed up the trail, now above eleven thousand feet elevation. Lexi, Austin, and Chey were in the middle of a conversation about the wedding reception and didn't seem to realize that Victoria was falling behind.

Eric held back. "Hey, are you okay?"

"Yes." She was winded—not unusual for a flatlander. "Woke up ... with a really bad headache. I shouldn't ... have had that margarita. I don't want to ... ruin it for everyone."

"You're not going to ruin anything, and it wasn't the margarita." He walked her to a bench. "Sit down. Stay here."

"I'm not ... a dog."

He ignored that, jogging to catch up with Austin and Lexi. "I'm taking Victoria down. She's got altitude sickness."

They stopped in their tracks.

"Really?" Lexi turned to look back at her friend. "God, why didn't she say something?"

"What's going on?" Austin was a paramedic, too.

"Bad headache, shortness of breath. She thought she had a hangover and didn't want to complain. I'll take her down and get her hydrated. We'll catch up with you later."

He turned and left them staring after him.

Victoria was right where he'd put her, but now there were tears on her cheeks. She pressed fingers to her temples. "Sorry to be a baby … but it really hurts."

He knelt down, wiped away her tears with his thumbs. "You're not being a baby. You've got altitude sickness."

"Altitude sickness?"

He didn't feel like taking the time to explain. "How long has it been since you've had a piggy-back ride?"

She got to her feet. "I can walk."

So, she was going to be stubborn again.

"I know you can, but I'm not going to let you." He knelt down, her arms going around his neck as he caught her legs and lifted her weight onto his back.

She gave a startled squeak as he got to his feet. "Where are we going?"

"I'm taking you to a lower elevation until you're better." He ignored the curious stares of tourists on their way up the trail. "Are you okay back there?"

"Oh, my God!" she whispered. "I'm being carried by a fireman!"

"I'll take that as a 'yes.'" If only the women of Scarlet were as impressed with his profession as Victoria was…

He set her on her feet beside his pickup, unlocked the door, and helped her into the passenger seat. Then he reached into the back and grabbed a bottle of water. "Drink. Lots of little sips. Got it?"

He headed back down Trail Ridge Road, hazarding the occasional glance her way. "Keep sipping."

Her eyes were closed, her face tight with pain. "This didn't happen last time."

"Last year, Lexi had a broken leg, and you spent most of your time sitting indoors with her. You didn't spend a day in the sun wakeboarding. I'll bet money you're dehydrated. That makes it worse."

It took about thirty minutes to drop to nine thousand feet, the road crowded with tourists in RVs, campers, and family sedans.

"Do you feel any better?"

"No."

He kept going all the way to the park's entrance, but he didn't have to ask to see that she was still hurting. "How do you feel about taking a little drive to visit my mother down in Boulder?"

Victoria didn't even answer.

Chapter Four

Vic opened her eyes, stretched, glanced around her. Late afternoon sunshine spilled through homemade drapes adorned with images of balls—baseballs, footballs, soccer balls, basketballs. Posters of pickups and cars competed for wall space with posters of rock bands—Led Zeppelin, Boston, Journey, Metallica, U2.

Where was she exactly?

Eric's bedroom.

Not his real bedroom, but the bedroom he'd had as a kid.

She'd had altitude sickness, and he'd brought her to his mother's house, given her ibuprofen, taken her pulse, made her drink a lot of water, then told her to rest.

It had worked.

She sat up, both relieved and amazed to discover that her headache was gone. Then again, she was close to a mile lower in elevation than she'd been when Eric had carried her back to his truck.

Oh, God!

She'd been carried by a firefighter.

And, of course, she'd been in too much pain even to think of taking a selfie.

Damn.

She glanced around again, the innocent boyishness of the room putting a smile on her face. This is where teenage Eric had hung out back when he and Lexi and Austin had been in high school together and—

Lexi!

She must wonder what in the world was going on.

That thought had Vic out of bed and on her feet. She reached for her handbag, which sat on the small desk in the corner, and searched inside for her cell phone. It wasn't there. It wasn't in the pockets of the jacket she'd been wearing either. Maybe she'd left it in Eric's truck.

She opened the bedroom door and followed the sound of voices down the hallway and through the living room, snatches of conversation drifting through the front screen door. Outside, Eric's mother, Robin, was talking with her son, who was lying on his back beneath an old SUV, only his legs and a strip of bare abdomen visible.

"They cracked the cap on your transmission tank. Probably screwed it on too tight when you got the fluid changed. That's where the leak's coming from. I'll run to the auto supply store and get you a new one and then top off your transmission fluid. That ought to take care of it."

Vic stepped outside. "Hey."

Robin's head came around. "Hey, there. How do you feel?"

"Much better. Thank you."

"I should thank you." Robin looked down at her son, who was wriggling his way out from beneath the car. "I haven't seen Eric for a while. You brought him home."

A tall woman in her mid-fifties, she had a gentle demeanor that Vic had found instantly soothing when they'd arrived a few hours ago. Like Eric, she had brown hair, though hers was now streaked with gray. Apart from that and her eyes, there wasn't much of a resemblance.

"It's only been two weeks, Mom." Eric's head appeared, the muscles of his bare chest and belly shifting as he sat up. "She just likes to put me to work."

Robin laughed, a happy twinkle in blue eyes that were so much like her son's. "Don't let him fool you. He puts himself to work when he comes here, doing things I can't do by myself. I'm very lucky."

Wiping his hands on a rag, Eric got to his feet, the damp hair at his temples and the beads of sweat on his chest telling Vic he'd been working outdoors for a while. He walked over to her, those blue eyes studying her, concern pulling his brows together in a frown. "How's your head?"

"I feel fine. Thanks." She tried to keep her eyes on his face and not his pecs with their dark curls. It wasn't easy when his chest was even with her eyes. "Um … Do you know where my cell phone is? I need to let Lexi know what's going on."

"She knows. I've been keeping her posted." He opened the front door for her.

"Oh. Thanks." She walked indoors, following him back toward the kitchen.

"Your phone is in the fridge. The damned thing wouldn't quit buzzing."

"You put my phone in the refrigerator?" She hurried after him.

He walked into the kitchen, jerked open the refrigerator door, and pulled out her phone. "I didn't want it waking you up."

"Thanks … I think." She took it from him and entered her password, her stomach sinking at the sight of the half dozen messages that waited for her.

It's not him. He's in prison.

Relief and irritation chased through her one after the other when she saw the emails were all from Abigail.

"Hey, if you don't mind, I'd like to mow my mom's lawn before we head back up to Scarlet." He grabbed two glasses, filled them with ice and water. "It will only take about twenty minutes. Is that okay with you?"

"Of course." She took the glass he gave her, looked up from her phone—and froze, her email inbox momentarily forgotten.

The muscles of Eric's throat worked as he drank, a rivulet of sweat trickling slowly down his neck, his sun-kissed skin radiating heat. He finished drinking, set the glass down on the counter, and walked outside, leaving Vic standing like a statue, glass raised halfway to her lips.

"He likes you."

Robin's words took Vic by surprise, her gaze jerking from the window to the woman who sat beside her at the kitchen table. "What do you mean?"

"He's never brought a woman home before."

"Wait. You think …?" Heat rushed into Vic's cheeks. "It's not like that. He didn't bring me *home* home. I'm just here. I was sick and … Eric and I … We're just friends. Yeah. We're not even good friends."

"I can tell when my son is attracted to a woman." She dropped this bombshell, then took a sip of her iced tea. "You're attracted to him, too."

"Well…" What could Vic say to this?

"Most women see the muscles, the badge, the bunker gear. What they don't see is the man who still mows his mother's lawn, who fixes her car, shovels her sidewalk in the winter, puts up her Christmas lights, and cleans the gutters on her house." Robin's love for her son was palpable, her blue eyes soft as she spoke about him.

"You two are close, aren't you?"

Robin nodded. "He's my only child. For a long time, it was just the two of us against the world. His daddy left Scarlet the day after I told him I was pregnant, so I raised Eric on my own."

Vic supposed she ought to feel awkward hearing Eric's life story. She didn't know him that well. But there was something about his mother that put her at ease, that made her feel safe and at home. "That must have been tough for both of you."

"It was tougher on him, I think. It's hard for a boy to define himself as a man with no man in the house to act as a role model."

Vic had to bite back a laugh. If there was one thing Eric did not seem to lack, it was a sense of his own masculinity. "He seems to have figured that out."

This made Robin smile. "His friendship with Austin helped fill in the gaps. He spent a lot of time at Austin's house, hanging with Austin and his father. They're like brothers, those two."

Altitude sickness must have scrambled Vic's brains. There was no other way to explain what she said next. "Why is he still single?"

Robin glanced out the window into her backyard, where Eric was pushing the mower from one side to the other. "He had a lot of responsibility placed on his shoulders at a young age. Being fire chief, volunteering for the Team—that's a lot of responsibility, too. Can you imagine having someone's life in your hands?"

Vic shook her head. "That would scare me to death."

"I know what some people say about him—that he's a playboy, that he'll never settle down, that he's afraid of responsibility because he was forced to work too hard as a boy." Robin's brows knit together in a frown, hurt behind her blue eyes. "But a man who's afraid of responsibility doesn't spend his days off helping his mother. I think it's the reverse. I think some part of him is afraid he'll let a woman down, given his schedule. He's seen a lot of firefighters end up divorced. It's just another hazard of the job."

"I didn't know that."

Robin's eyes narrowed. "So tell me your story. I've wanted to know more about you since you set tongues wagging during your first visit."

*E*ric brushed his arm across his forehead to wipe away sweat, opened the front screen door, and stopped with one foot inside, the door still open.

Someone was crying.

"It's not your fault, Victoria." His mother's voice was calm and soothing, the tone she used when someone was upset. "Men like him are always looking for an opportunity to hurt women."

Some bastard had hurt Victoria?

Sweat trickled down Eric's back and chest as he listened, rooted to the spot.

"I can't believe I trusted him." Victoria sniffed. "He used me. He humiliated me, and he enjoyed it. He almost destroyed my life."

"He's in prison now, and that's right where he deserves to be."

Prison?

What the hell?

What had the bastard done?

A dozen ideas flashed through Eric's mind, none of them pretty.

If she wanted you to know, she'd have told you.

Taylor and Lexi knew. That's why Taylor had warned him about her.

"I don't think I'll ever be able to trust myself when it comes to men again. I was so *stupid*." Victoria spat the last word out, her rage at herself palpable.

"No, you weren't. There's no way you could have known what kind of man he truly was. But you know what? I don't hear the lawnmower. Eric will be back inside in a minute."

Another sniff. "I don't want him to see me like this."

Well, shit.

His mother had always been someone that people trusted, someone they confided in, someone they turned to for support, so it didn't surprise him that Victoria had opened up to her. But Victoria needed more time, and Eric knew how he could give it to her.

He stepped inside, let the screen door slam good and hard behind him. "Hey, Mom, I'm heading to the auto-parts store to get that cap for your transmission fluid tank. I'll be back as soon as I can be."

"Okay, son. Thank you!"

He grabbed the T-shirt he'd tossed onto the floor a few hours ago, yanked it over his head, and stepped outside again, cutting across the yard to his pickup, which sat parked at the curb. He jerked open the door, threw himself into the driver's seat, then jammed the keys into the ignition. Only when he nearly missed the stop sign at the end of the block did he realize how tense he was.

No, not tense. Angry.

He was pissed off that Taylor hadn't trusted him with the whole story. He was pissed off that all he had to go on were the ideas his imagination was churning up one after the other. Mostly he was pissed at the son of a bitch who'd hurt her.

Damn it.

He had no tolerance for men who abused women.

Then again, why was he so worked up over this? Sure, he felt compassion for Victoria, but then he felt compassion for anyone who was suffering. But what was with the rage? He was getting primal and protective over her, and he barely knew her. She was the friend of a friend who happened to cross his path. Next Sunday, she'd get on a plane and fly back to Chicago. He'd see her now and again when she came to Scarlet to visit Lexi, and that was it.

You're falling for her.

A laugh burst from between his lips.

That was loco. Absurd. Completely insane.

Hell, yeah, he was attracted to her. She'd been on his mind a lot since she'd arrived. But there was no chance he and Victoria were going to get together. He didn't do relationships. He didn't even have time to get laid these days.

That was it. He was horny.

You're always horny.

No, seriously. He hadn't been with a woman in … hell, months? After the wedding, he'd have to do something about that.

Relieved to have worked that out, he drew in a deep breath, turned up his music, and let U2 blast his thoughts away.

*E*ric had his head on straight and his hormones under control by the time he and Victoria headed up the canyon toward Scarlet, where Austin and Lexi were hosting a cookout for the bridal party. He cranked the music and the AC. "Are you cool?"

"Yes, thanks. It's so much hotter down here than it is in Scarlet Springs." A slight puffiness to Victoria's eyes was the only sign she'd been crying.

"That's the altitude."

"I should have guessed. Here, everything is about altitude."

That made him laugh. "Just about."

"I like your mom."

He couldn't argue with that. "She's good people. She did right by me, even when it wasn't easy. She raised me by herself, you know."

Victoria nodded. "She told me."

So they'd had that conversation. It figured.

"Have you ever met your father?"

"Yeah, but I wouldn't use that word to describe him. A father is a man who stands by his kids and their mother. That guy was a sperm donor— nothing more. He dumped my mom when she told him she was pregnant and never gave her a dime."

"You don't have any relationship with him?" She seemed to catch herself. "Sorry. That's just me being nosy. I shouldn't—"

"It's okay." Eric didn't mind. He'd worked through that shit ages ago. "No, I don't have a relationship with him. I tracked him down when I was seventeen, introduced myself, and found myself looking at an older version of my own face. He told me he had no sons and slammed the door. That was it."

"God! I'm so sorry." Those brown eyes went wide and soft. "I can't imagine how you must have felt."

"That day pretty much sucked, but I had good friends, a mother who loved me, lots of people who cared. Austin's dad took us camping that weekend. He even let us drink a few beers." He glanced over to find Victoria watching him. "When people make fun of small towns or talk down Scarlet, what they don't get is that we're a community. We might not always get along, but we've got one another's backs. How many of your neighbors do you know? I know all of mine. Every last one."

"That must be wonderful."

"Most of the time. In my line of work, it also has its downsides."

Silky, dark brows drew together in confusion. "What do you mean?"

"Well, there are fewer than fifteen-hundred people in Scarlet. About seventy percent of our calls are for emergency medical services, not fires. When someone has a heart attack or gets into a serious injury accident or shoots himself in the head, there's a good chance I know him *and* his family."

She was still watching him. "How do you cope with that? It must be hard enough to deal with people's suffering when they're strangers, but when you know them …"

"Yeah." Faces and names slid through his mind—the living, the maimed, the dying, the dead. "People come up to me in the grocery store and on the street. They want to say thank you. Some have questions. They want to know if they could have done something differently. They're searching for peace. I used to find that awkward. It made me uncomfortable. Now, I feel honored to play that role in their lives."

He wasn't sure that made any sense.

He glanced over to catch the hint of a smile tugging at her lips. "What?"

"You are your mother's son."

"Yeah?" He'd take that as a compliment. "The two of you seemed to hit it off."

"She said I set tongues wagging last time I was here."

"She told you that?" It wasn't like his mother to gossip.

"Is it true?"

"Yeah, I suppose it is."

"What did I do? Why would people talk about me?"

How was Eric going to explain this? He didn't want her to think he was hitting on her, especially not after what he'd overheard this afternoon. "I hate to break it to you, Victoria, but you're an incredibly beautiful woman."

That hadn't been creepy, had it? He hoped not. He considered it a feat of self-control that he'd managed to stop with that and hadn't raved on.

She stared at him, disbelief on her face. "*That* is what people talked about?"

"Yeah. Is that so strange? 'Hey, have you seen Lexi's friend, Victoria? She's gorgeous.' You know—that sort of thing." When she said nothing, he doubled down. "Come on. You know you're above average in the looks department."

He expected her to blush or smile or look at him from beneath those long, sooty lashes and say something flirty.

Instead, she looked away. "Thanks, I guess. A lot of good it's ever done me."

What the hell did she mean by that?

They got back to Scarlet Springs to find the group hanging out at Austin and Lexi's place. Vic had seen it last year before Lexi had moved in. A large two-story log home, it had floor-to-ceiling windows in the living room, a sleek kitchen, and an enormous back deck with a hot tub.

Lexi met Vic in the driveway with a big hug, Mack, Austin's black lab, bounding at her heels. "Why didn't you say anything?"

Vic shrugged. "I thought it was the margarita."

Eric came around the front of his pickup. "She needs to rest and drink lots of water. No alcohol—at least not tonight. And speak up if that headache comes back."

Lexi hugged him, too. "Thanks for realizing what was happening."

"That's my job." He headed for the back of the house, leaving Vic with Lexi.

Lexi turned to Vic again. "I saw him carry you to his SUV. Is something going on between you two?"

First Eric's mother, and now Lexi.

"Of course not! I'm done with men." Vic must have been flustered because her mouth took off without her. "The last thing I want right now is to hook up with some sexy, handsome, strong, single firefighter who carries women with altitude sickness off mountains and mows his mother's lawn."

One red eyebrow arched. "If you were trying to convince me, you blew it."

On the back deck, Austin was grilling steaks on a big gas grill, a large cooler full of beer and soda nearby. "You made it just in time. How are you feeling?"

"I'm much better. Thank you." She inhaled, the scent of sizzling beef making her mouth water. "That smells so good."

Britta stepped out of the kitchen followed by Winona Belcourt, both women carrying large salads. They set the salads on a long wooden picnic table that was already laden with food, bowls covered with cellophane to keep out bugs.

"Hey, Victoria." Winona reached to hug her, her dark hair hanging around her shoulders. "I heard the altitude got you. How are you?"

Winona was a veterinarian who ran a sanctuary for injured wildlife and the daughter of a hereditary Sun Dance chief. She had come to Colorado on the heels of her older brother, Chaska, who was also a Team member and one of Austin's groomsmen—and perhaps the most handsome man Vic had ever met. Brother and sister had both fallen in love with the mountains and stayed. Lexi had volunteered for the sanctuary for about a year now, and she and Winona had become good friends. Lexi even got along with Winona's big pet wolf, Shota.

"I'm better now. Thanks."

Voices came from above, jerking Vic's gaze toward the roof.

Eric stood up there, together with Chaska and Jesse.

"They climbed the chimney." Lexi said this as if it were the sort of thing one did at a cookout. "Chaska's testing a new self-belaying device he designed."

The expression on Vic's face must have been amusing because Winona laughed. "Climbing is a sickness you can't cure. Have you met my brother?"

"Yes." Vic's gaze returned to the roof in time to see Chaska, his long dark hair tied back in a ponytail, drop over the other side of the house, while Jesse stood on the roof in a climbing harness, rope in hand.

Eric peered over the edge to watch, a big grin appearing on his face. "It works."

By the time everyone was off the roof, Austin was pulling steaks off the grill, and it was time to gather around the table.

Vic found herself sitting next to Eric, the press of his hard thigh against hers more than a little distracting. She scooted closer to Lexi.

"I don't bite," he whispered, then added in a louder voice, "You got water?"

"Yes, Mom." She held up her ice water as proof, just as Austin tapped a beer bottle with the blade of his steak knife.

"Before you dig in, I just wanted to thank you all for agreeing to stand with us."

"Hey, I signed on for the beer," Jesse joked.

"Your support has meant so much to us over the years, and it's going to mean a lot on Saturday. Cheers!"

"Cheers!"

And there it was—that lump that formed in her throat every time she thought about Lexi getting married. She needed to knock it off, or she'd be a blubbering mess at the ceremony.

They had just started in on dessert—strawberry shortcake—when a *boom* shocked the air, stopping the conversation and turning everyone's heads toward town.

Eric got to his feet, pager in hand before the tone sounded.

"They're playing your song," Austin said.

"Well, shit. It looks like Hank blew up his house. I told him to do that shit outside." He slid his pager back onto the waistband of his jeans, his gaze shifting to Vic. "Want to come with me and see my team in action?"

Was he serious?

"Do you really mean that?"

From the distance, came the sound of sirens.

"You'll have to stay in the truck—no getting out and getting me into trouble. Also, we have to leave *right now*."

Excitement had her on her feet. She followed Eric as he hurried down the steps, calling over her shoulder to Lexi and Austin. "Thanks for supper. It was delicious."

"Bring water!" Eric shouted back to her.

Chapter Five

By the time Vic had fastened her seatbelt, Eric was backing out of Austin and Lexi's driveway, chatter coming over his radio, most of which she couldn't understand.

He drove the quarter-mile stretch of dirt road down to the highway, stopping to wait for traffic before taking a left. "Hang on."

He accelerated onto the road, reaching down to flick a switch on his dashboard.

Flashes of red, blue, and white light danced on the hood of his truck.

"Your truck has lights?" She hadn't seen anything on the roof.

"They're hidden behind the rearview mirror. There's a set on the back window and one on the grill out front."

"Clever." She leaned forward to look behind the mirror, amazed that something so bright could be so small.

"I've got a siren mounted on the grill, and I'll probably have to use it in town." He glanced over at her, his serious demeanor disappearing for a moment behind a grin. "You've been riding around in a fire truck this entire time, and you didn't know it."

"I'm not going to lie. That's pretty freaking cool."

When they rounded the next curve, she saw it—the glowing orange of flames, black and white smoke rising skyward in a column. "Oh, God."

Eric saw it, too. "Damn it, Hank."

He turned up the radio, his brow creased as he listened.

Vic listened, too, but she understood only snatches of the conversation.

"Scarlet FD on the scene."

"It's fully involved now."

"We've got an exposure on the Bravo side."

"The RP is the homeowner. We're all clear."

Eric let out a relieved breath. "I'm going to kick Hank's ass."

Questions chased one another through Vic's mind, but she didn't want to distract Eric, so she kept them to herself. Why did he think the fire was Hank's fault? How could he help at the scene if he didn't have gear? How did they know for sure no one was trapped inside?

They came to the long downhill that led into town.

"Son of a …"

A stream of red taillights stretched out ahead of them, vehicles stopped bumper to bumper on the road all the way to the roundabout in the center of town. Some people had abandoned their cars and stood on the shoulder of the road, filming the column of smoke with cell phones.

"It's human nature to want to watch shit like this, but why can't they pull off the road first?" Eric reached down and flicked a switch, the wail of the siren making Vic jump. "God, I hate tourist season. The traffic is terrible, and the crime rate goes up."

When people failed to get out of the way, he had no choice but to slow down and eventually stop. Twice he blasted the siren's horn before drivers began to make way.

Vic couldn't believe it. "What is wrong with people?"

"If I had the answer to that, I'd be filthy rich."

Slowly, they made their way to the roundabout at the center of town, but rather than turning right and heading toward the fire, he moved through the roundabout, heading up the hill on the other side and making a left into the firehouse parking lot. Vic recognized it because Lexi, in a moment of pure evil, had arranged for Eric to give her a tour of the place last summer.

"Keep the doors locked. I'll be back in a few."

"Why lock the doors?"

He called back over his shoulder. "Tourists."

Vic watched him jog inside the building, her gaze shifting to the column of smoke, which seemed thinner now. Did that mean the fire crews had almost put it out? Not even two minutes had gone by when Eric reappeared.

Oh … *wow!*

Her heart skipped a beat.

He wore full bunker gear, helmet beneath one arm, air pack hanging from one hand. His yellow coat made his shoulders seem even broader, a look of determination on his face. He put the air pack in the back of his truck, then opened the door, climbed into the driver's seat, and held out his helmet. "Can you hold this?"

"Of course." She took it from him, surprised at how heavy it was.

They had to fight traffic again going the other direction, but people gave way more readily this time. The blaze was a couple of blocks away, so it was just a matter of minutes before Eric pulled up behind a big fire engine and parked. He silenced the siren, but left his lights flashing.

Ahead and to her right, a small white house was completely engulfed, flames lapping at the roof through shattered windows. Two teams of firefighters sprayed water on the blaze through two hoses, while another firefighter stood by himself, hosing down the neighbor's roof to keep it from catching.

She rolled down the window, got a blast of hot air on her face. "Oh, man! I can feel the heat from here. How can anyone possibly get close to this?"

"That's what the fancy suits are for." He took his helmet from her, climbed out of the truck, walked around to her window. "You can keep the window down, but stay in the vehicle. Got it?"

"Yes, Mr. Fire Chief." She saluted.

His lips quirked in a lopsided grin. "Damned straight."

She watched him move through the scene, talking first with his crews, then with a sheriff's deputy, then heading back her way. He walked over to a small, thin man with a scraggly ponytail and mustache who stood in the shadow of the fire engine. The man wore nothing but faded jeans, every vertebra and rib visible.

"Sorry to see you in this sad situation, Hank."

So that was Hank. Vic had thought him just a spectator, maybe a neighbor who'd come down the street for a better view.

"Do you think they can save it?"

"Save your house? No, buddy. I'm afraid it's gone." Eric spoke in a voice that held both compassion and a sense of authority. "Are you hurt? If you are, we need to check you and get you patched up."

"I'm fine." Hank gave a little laugh. "You shoulda seen me, man. I jumped about twenty feet in the air and ran like a deer on speed."

"When the fire is out and I walk in there, please tell me I'm not going to find a bunch of butane canisters and a big pile of weed."

Hank's gaze dropped to the ground.

"Damn it, Hank, I warned you. I told you that if you were going to break the law, at least do it outdoors. You're damned lucky you're not burned to a cinder."

"I know. I know."

Eric rested a hand on the man's shoulder. "They're going to arrest you, buddy, and there's nothing I can do about that. You understand?"

His concern for Hank made Vic's heart melt. He wasn't just trying to ensure Hank's safety and protect property. He was doing what he could to shepherd the man through this ordeal, even though it was of Hank's own making.

"You think I should run, go to Mexico maybe?"

"No, I don't. I think you should stand your ground and face the consequences. That's the only way to move forward."

"I'm afraid I'll get pounded in the ass. I'm not like you, Hawke. I'm weak and small for a man. I'll end up being some guy's bitch."

"Jesus, Hank. Prison isn't what you see on TV. Besides, you don't know that you're going to prison. Take it one day at a time. I'll make a few calls, get you a lawyer. I'm not going to let you face this alone." He put his arm around Hank's shoulders, the smaller man making him seem huge by comparison. "Are you sure you're not hurt?"

"I'm pretty shook up, but I'm okay."

"I'm going to get you a shirt." He walked to his truck, opened the door, and grabbed a shirt out of the back—a Team T-shirt. "Megs will have my hide if she hears you wore this to jail, so let's turn it inside out and just keep it between us, okay?"

And Vic's heart melted again.

Hank pulled it over his head, the shirt far too big for him. "Thanks, Hawke. I'll get this back to you one day."

"I'm going to turn you over to Deputy Marcs now." Eric motioned to someone.

"Hey, Hank." A woman in uniform stepped into view. "Remember me? I'm Deputy Marcs. I'm glad you're okay. I'm here to arrest you and take you in. I promise no one is going to hurt you tonight. We don't run that kind of jail."

By the time Hank was cuffed, searched, and headed down the street in the back of a squad car, the fire seemed to be under control, smoke rising from the gutted remains of the house.

Eric walked to the truck, grabbed his air pack out of the back, and then came to stand next to her open window. "I'll give you one guess: Whose job is it to investigate fires in Scarlet?"

"Yours."

He chuckled. "Brains *and* beauty. You're the total package."

If another man had said those words, it probably would have made Vic feel uncomfortable, but coming from Eric, it made her laugh. She watched while he donned his air pack and disappeared through the charred front door.

Five minutes went by. Another five.

Boom!

Flames flared out of one window, then vanished.

Vic's heart leaped into her throat, her pulse taking off at a sprint.

Eric.

When the firefighters around her didn't react, she figured everything must be okay. Eric was their chief. If he were lying there wounded or burned, they would be running inside to help him, not calmly going about their work.

When he emerged a few minutes later, she let out a sigh of relief.

And to think he did things like this every day.

"Butane hash oil extraction," Eric climbed into his truck, his bunker gear stashed in the bed of his vehicle so that it wouldn't stink up the cab.

Between smoke from the fire and the stench of burning weed, it reeked. "That was the cause of the fire."

"I've never heard of that."

He slipped the keys into the ignition, started the engine. "It's illegal to do at home—and dangerous as hell. I counted ninety-four butane canisters. They were sitting right next to a big, old pile of weed. It's a wonder Hank wasn't incinerated."

A woman on a bicycle cut in front of the truck's headlights, headed straight for Hank's place, what looked like a fat wad of twenties gripped in her right hand. When she saw a sheriff's deputy squad car, she turned her bicycle around, cash disappearing into her fist.

"Jesus! Did you see that?" Eric couldn't help but laugh.

Vic nodded. "Was she on her way there to buy drugs from him?"

"That's what it looked like." Eric nosed his truck into the street and headed back toward the station house. "Sometimes life in Scarlet feels like a bad Hollywood flick. Christ! You can't make this shit up."

"But isn't it legal to buy marijuana here?"

"It is—if you buy it from a licensed seller. Hank doesn't even have a driver's license." He glanced over at Victoria, found her watching him, a mysterious smile on those lips of hers. "What now? Did I say something funny?"

"You took good care of him."

Eric shrugged off the compliment. "There wasn't much I could do. Sometimes you've got to sleep in the bed you make."

"Isn't that the truth?" Something in the tone of her voice made him remember the conversation he'd overheard this afternoon.

Could he help it if he wanted to know the whole story?

He changed the subject. "Hey, do you mind if we stop at the station first so I can drop off my gear?"

"Whatever you need to do."

"Are you still drinking?"

She held up an almost empty bottle of water. "No headache."

"Good."

Back at the firehouse, he returned his gear to his locker and dropped the cylinder from his SCBA off in the compressor room. The initial response crew pulled in as he was leaving, men and women piling out of the apparatus, all of them reeking of ganja.

Silver passed him, air cylinder in hand. "The firehouse is going to have a skunk funk tonight, chief."

It sure as hell would. "Great job, folks. Get your showers, and get the gear cleaned. And someone open a damned window."

Back in the truck, he realized that funk had settled on him, mixing with smoke and sweat from doing yard work earlier today. God, he needed a shower.

But first, he needed to get Victoria back to the inn.

He started the engine again. "So, what did you think?"

"It was really interesting—except for the moment when I thought you were dead. After you'd gone into the house, I heard a *boom*, and flames shot out of the window."

Oh, yeah. That.

"A box of butane canisters blew. That's why I tell my crews always to wear full bunker gear when overhauling a scene like that, even when the fire seems like it's out. You never know what kind of surprises might lie in store for you."

"It scared me to death."

Really?

"Sorry about that." He reached over, took her hand, gave it a squeeze.

What the hell?

The moment his skin touched hers, he felt it—raw current arcing between them.

He drew his hand away, tried to act like he hadn't felt a thing. "I'd say we should work on the video, but it's already ten-thirty. You need to rest up."

Tomorrow, Lexi and Austin were taking them horseback riding at the Cimarron, and he'd hate for to miss out on that, too.

"Are you kidding? I couldn't sleep now if I tried. Besides, I got a three-hour nap in the middle of the day. If you want to work on the video for a while, that's fine with me. I can show you what I got done last night."

He pulled his shirt away from his chest. "I'd be up for that, but I need a shower."

"I've got lots of extra towels in my suite, and there are unopened bars of soap and little bottles of shampoo in the bathroom. I'm sure Bob and Kendra wouldn't mind if you took a shower there, considering the circumstances."

"You sure?"

She nodded. "We've only got until Friday to finish this."

"Okay, then."

V ic stood in the middle of her bedroom, her gaze on the bathroom door. For the first time in her life, she was jealous of a bar of soap. Eric was in there, completely naked, washing that amazing body of his without her.

You are losing your mind.

She crossed her arms over her chest, as if that could somehow ward off the unwanted emotions inside her—desire, sexual hunger, loneliness. She could *not* get involved with him. She couldn't hook up with a man who'd once hit on her best friend and who made love with women without actually loving them.

Oh, but it would be so worth it.

That's what she'd thought when she'd met Stewart. She'd been wrong, and she'd paid for it with months of grief, fear, and humiliation. The sex hadn't even been satisfying. The whole nightmare had proved to her that her man-picker was broken. Like a compass that didn't point north, hers had led her to choose a man who had tried to destroy her.

Eric isn't Stewart.

No, he wasn't. He was nothing like Stewart. Stewart was interested only in himself, while Eric took care of his entire community. Images from the day drifted through her mind. Eric giving Hank a T-shirt. Eric carrying her back to his truck. Eric handing her ibuprofen, taking her pulse.

No, he was nothing like Stewart, but Eric's own mother had admitted people thought he was a bit of a playboy. Besides, Vic had made herself a promise.

She closed her eyes and let herself imagine what it would be like to kiss him, his hard body pressed up against hers, his mouth coming down hot and hard on hers, his tongue teasing hers. Maybe he would cup her breast, tease her nipple with his thumb.

Belly flutters. An ache between her thighs. Wetness.

God, she wanted him.

But could she handle it?

There'd been a time—oh, say, yesterday—when she would have sworn she'd never be able to let down her guard and trust a man with her body again. Now here she was staring at a closed bathroom door and fantasizing about a man she barely knew.

You know enough. You've seen what kind of a man he is.

Inside the bathroom, the shower stopped.

What was she doing here? If he opened the door …

Jolted from her fantasy, she hurried out of the room.

"I looked through all the clips last night and made some obvious edits. Then I organized the photos into folders so that we can find what we're looking for quickly." She ran the cursor over the list of folders. "Lexi. Lexi with her parents. Lexi and Austin together. Austin by himself. Those historical shots of the inn. Scenery."

"Aren't you the organized one?" He leaned for a closer look, his damp hair combed into place, the clean scent of his skin like a drug. "What's on the timeline?"

Keep your mind on the job.

"I haven't made any changes there. I cut out dead space, all those spots where your mom had to stop because of the guy revving his engine, and that segment where you dropped the camera onto the floor."

"Oh, that." He ran a hand over his jaw with its day's growth of stubble. "Sorry. Steven Spielberg I am not."

"I think you did a great job." She wasn't just saying that. "I got pretty choked up watching these last night."

"Yeah?" That seemed to please him. "You think Lexi will like them?"

"I don't think there will be a dry eye in the room."

"What do we do now?"

"Now you come up with a narrative."

"A narrative? Okay. Great." It was evident from the confusion on his face that he didn't understand. "How do we do that?"

"You want the video to tell a story so the viewer can take a journey with you." She clicked on a document file. "I made a list of all the interviews and jotted down some keywords for each interview. So what you need to do is decide how you want to order the them—which clip goes first, which goes second and so on."

His brows drew together, and he blew out a breath. "I was just going to put them all together. I hadn't thought about it as a story. It's been so long since I've listened to most of these. Do you have any ideas?"

She liked seeing him like this—a fish out of water, uncertain of himself, needing help rather than giving it. "I think we should start with your mother. She talked about Lexi's mom finding out she was pregnant."

"Okay." He nodded. "That's good."

They got to work, selecting portions of interviews and dragging them onto the timeline. Once he'd grasped the concept of narrative, Eric had no trouble deciding which segment should come next. Vic knew all the keyboard shortcuts, so she did the actual pushing of buttons. After about an hour, they had cobbled together a rough assembly of clips.

"Should we add the photos now?"

"No." Vic rubbed the ache in her neck. "I think we should make sure we're done editing the video first."

"Getting tired?"

"My muscles are sore from yesterday."

"Let me." He moved his chair so that he sat behind her now, his strong hands replacing hers. "Just relax."

"Ow! Oh! *Ahhh*."

He chuckled. "Better?"

"Yes." What he was doing felt *so* good, the skilled motions of his hands chasing away the stiffness in her neck and shoulders. "You're really good at this."

His voice was deep, his words slow, when he answered. "Becoming a paramedic means studying a lot of human anatomy."

Human anatomy? Good grief!

She should stop him before this went in the wrong direction. Yes, she should, but she couldn't because it was already too late.

Oh, yes.

Warmth licked through her blood, desire that had been on a slow burn since yesterday kindling into something more. She couldn't remember being so affected by a man's simple touch. It wasn't just the fact he was touching her; it was the fact that *he* was touching her. Electricity made her tingle everywhere his skin made contact with hers, the heat sending little shivers down her spine. "*Mmm.*"

Had she just moaned aloud?

His hands slowed, his touch sensual now, callused fingers curling at her nape, caressing her cheek. Then he shifted, his lips pressing against her temple, his breath hot against her skin. "God, Victoria."

She turned her head to the side, lifted her chin. "Kiss me."

Chapter Six

*E*ric heard her whispered invitation and damned if he could resist. He slid his fingers into her hair, angled her head to give him better access, then brushed his lips over hers. The jolt of heat took him by surprise, shot straight to his cock. "*Victoria.*"

He closed his mouth over hers, wanting more, but this was no good. Sitting behind her, he couldn't really kiss her, not the way she deserved to be kissed.

He turned her chair, then, in a single motion, scooped her into his arms and stood.

"*Oh!*" She gave a little gasp, but there was no mistaking the thrill in her brown eyes as he carried her toward the sofa, her pupils wide and dark.

He hadn't gone two steps when she caught his face between her palms and kissed him. His eyes closed, and his feet stilled, his awareness shifting to the hot feel of her mouth on his, the pressure of her lips, the sharp edges of her teeth as they nipped his bottom lip, the taste of her tongue as it searched for his.

Jesus!

As much as he'd love to stand here holding her all day, they weren't going to get very far like this. He opened his eyes and staggered forward, the beautiful woman in his arms refusing to break the kiss, her fingers sliding into his hair, holding his mouth right where she wanted it. He struck his shin on the coffee table, adjusted his trajectory, stopping when his knees bumped the sofa. He lowered her to the soft cushions and stretched himself out above her.

If touching her had felt electric, full-body contact nearly blew his mind, the heat between them threatening to make him spontaneously combust. He tore control of the kiss from her, felt her yield, a sound halfway between a sigh and a moan catching in her throat as he plundered her mouth.

God, she tasted good.

She turned her throat to the side, exposing sensitive skin. He took what she offered, licking and kissing her just beneath her ear, breathing in the scent of her, savoring the rapid thrum of her pulse beneath his lips. She shivered, her hands sliding beneath his T-shirt to caress his abs and pecs, the feel of him seeming to turn her on. It wasn't hurting him. That much was sure.

But two could play at this game.

He tore his lips from her skin, slid the spaghetti straps off her shoulders, and tugged down her dress, exposing a low-cut bra of blue satin and the sweet, creamy swells of her breasts. Willing himself not to rush, he kissed the line where satin met skin before releasing the center clasp, hunger for her pounding in his chest like a heartbeat.

She watched him through eyes gone black as he pushed the satin aside to reveal two beautiful natural breasts, their dark tips already puckered.

He knew what she expected him to do, so he didn't do it, but kissed, licked, and nipped the skin of her breasts, moving closer to her nipples without touching them, letting her anticipation build. She whimpered in frustration, her nipples drawing tighter. Still, he made her wait, pressing kisses against her breastbone, running his tongue in circles around those dark crests. Then, when he couldn't take it any longer, he closed his mouth over one pebbled tip and sucked.

"*Eric.*" She moaned his name, one of her legs wrapping around his waist, the other pinned against the cushions beneath his.

His cock ached to be inside her, but he didn't want to stop, not when she was enjoying this as much as she was. Her breath came in pants now, her hips rising as if to dry fuck him from below.

She wanted a little friction? He had just the thing for that.

He adjusted his weight and pressed his erection right where she needed it most, grinding himself against her. Her response was immediate, her eyes drifting shut, her hands coming to rest against his biceps. The motion was so like fucking that, yeah, it was arousing in a my-dick-is-going-to-bust-through-these-jeans sort of way. It wasn't enough to make him come, but it seemed to be taking her where she needed to go. That was good enough for him.

She met the motions of his hips with little thrusts of her own, the two of them completely synched as if they'd been doing this for years. Her nails bit into his skin, every muscle in her body tense, her breathing ragged. Oh, she was close, so close.

He lowered his mouth to her breast again, flicked her nipple with his tongue, nipped it with his teeth, then drew it into his mouth once more.

"*Eric.*" Her breath caught, then she arched beneath him, coming with a soft, shuddering sigh.

He stayed with her, kissing her cheeks, her eyelids, her forehead, attuned to the tremors still running through her, some thought forming in his mind about carrying her to the bed for—

Fuck.

He didn't have a condom. He hadn't planned this and hadn't brought one with him. He'd never broken his "no sex without a condom" rule, and he wouldn't start tonight. The last thing he wanted to do was leave Victoria pregnant and facing a bunch of tough choices. Besides, there were a lot of ways they could get each other off without him being inside her.

She opened her eyes, surprise on her face, her lips swollen from kissing him, her breasts still beautifully bare. "I've never … not like that."

"There's a first time for everything." He lowered his lips to hers, kissed her nice and slow. "Please tell me there's a box of condoms in that bathroom."

"I didn't see one. I'm not on the pill either, so…" Her gaze fixed on something over his shoulder, and the blood drained from her face, her entire body going stiff. "Stop. I can't! We can't … "

In a panic, she pushed against his chest, struggling to get out from beneath him.

He levered himself up and away from her and looked over his shoulder, but saw only what he'd expected to see—his computer, paper, a pen. "Honey, what is it? What's wrong?"

She got to her feet, hurried to the table, and closed his computer, then stood there, shaking, arms wrapped protectively around herself, spaghetti straps still off her shoulders. "I'm sorry. I shouldn't have … I'm so, so sorry."

It didn't take training in trauma to know that something had triggered her.

Eric got to his feet, all the things he'd let slip from his mind rushing back at him—Austin's warning, her conversation with his mother, the fact that she was Lexi's best friend.

Hawke, you dumbshit.

He walked up behind her, wanting to reassure her but afraid to touch her. "Hey. It's okay. You have no reason to be sorry."

She turned to face him, then seemed to realize that her breasts were still exposed.

Before she could react, he fastened the clasp for her, leaving her to adjust all that lush goodness herself. "You can talk to me. You know that, right? Clothes on, hands off. I promise."

"Thanks." She tugged up her spaghetti straps, and he could see she was fighting tears. "I think we made a lot of progress tonight. We should probably both get some sleep. I'll see you in the morning."

He bit back all the things he wanted to say to her, all the things he wanted to ask, and just let it go—for now. "Okay. Yeah. Thanks for your help tonight."

"You're welcome." She walked with him to the door. "Good night."

"Get some sleep." He paused with one foot in the hallway. "Call me if you need anything, even if it's the middle of the night. I can be here in two minutes."

"Thanks, Eric." She forced a smile onto her face. "You're a good man."

As he walked down the stairs, Eric was certain that the last guy who'd gotten his hands on her hadn't been.

Vic closed the door, moved the safety latch into place, then walked to the sofa, her heart in pieces. She sank into the cushions and let the tears come.

She had messed that up—big time. It was her fault. She had started it.

She had *asked* Eric to kiss her, and, oh, God, he had. He'd kissed her like she'd never been kissed in her life, kissed her the way she'd always dreamed of being kissed. First her lips, then her throat, then her breasts...

The man certainly knew what to do with his mouth.

He'd made her feel sexually alive for the first time in so very long, driving her crazy, even making her come. And he hadn't gotten anything in return.

God, she'd been an idiot.

One moment she'd been basking in the aftermath of a surprise orgasm and thinking up ways to please him, and the next she'd found herself looking at the camera lens of his laptop. She hadn't meant to push him away. Something inside her had snapped, adrenaline turning her blood to ice in the span of a heartbeat, her mind filling with all of the memories she'd been trying so hard to forget.

A lot of guys would have gotten angry about that. But Eric had done nothing but try to comfort her. He'd even fastened her bra himself.

She owed him an explanation. But, God, what would he think of her when she told him? It shouldn't matter to her. It's not like they were a part of each other's lives. Even so, it bothered her that he might think less of her.

Damn it.

She'd come to Scarlet hoping to get away from the past year. But somehow she'd brought all of it with her.

How was she going to face Eric now?

Vic felt mortified about what she'd done last night, and she was going to be spending an entire day in his company.

She pushed the thought aside and slipped into her brand new cowboy boots. The brown leather had a worn look, and there were roses embroidered along the instep and shaft. The moment she'd seen them, she'd wanted them. She walked around the room, getting used to the feel, then took a peek at her reflection and laughed. With her new dark vintage wash jeans, she looked like a cowgirl—well, minus the hat.

Deliberately leaving her phone behind, she slipped the day pack over her shoulder and hurried down the stairs, not wanting to keep everyone waiting. She stepped out into the cool morning air, the scent of pine and the breathtaking view making her forget her worries. Then she saw him.

Eric stood near the end of the driveway near the road, talking with Austin, a cowboy hat on his head.

Seriously? A cowboy hat? Was he trying to slay her? What was next? Cuddling puppies against his shirtless chest?

He looked her way, and she caught the anger on his face the moment before he hid it behind a half smile.

He and Austin weren't talking. They were arguing about something.

"Good morning." Lexi waved to her from the driver's seat of her Lexus convertible, its top down, Britta sitting in the back. "It's just the five of us. Winona is doing intake on two orphaned bear cubs. Chaska has to work, and Jesse is helping with inventory at the Cave. Austin is driving up with Eric so we can have some girl time."

Vic glanced over at Eric and Austin and wondered why Lexi was pretending everything was fine. "Okay."

Both disappointed and relieved that she wouldn't be riding alone with Eric, she got into Lexi's car and buckled up.

"Have you ever ridden a horse before?" Britta asked.

Vic nodded. "My dad insisted I take English horseback riding lessons when I was little. I was never good enough to compete, but I did learn to love horses. I've never done trail riding, though."

Lexi waited for Eric to back out in his truck, then drove down to the roundabout and out onto the highway. "You're going to love the Cimarron."

"Is it a dude ranch or something?"

That made Britta laugh. "A *dude* ranch? Don't say that in front of Jack or Nate."

While she drove, Lexi told her how the Cimarron was a working cattle ranch owned by the West family since the days of World War I. "They also breed champion quarter horses. The ranch sits on some of the most beautiful land in the county."

Britta leaned forward to be a part of the conversation. "The land is beautiful, but wait till you see their house."

The more the two of them talked, the more certain Vic became they were exaggerating. The house was incredible, and the views were breathtaking, and Jack West and his family were the kindest people you could ever hope to meet.

Nothing could be that perfect.

About an hour later, they came to the ranch's entrance, which was marked by a log archway from which hung a wooden sign that read "Cimarron Ranch."

The land *was* beautiful—steep, snowy peaks, grassy meadows, stands of evergreen trees and aspen. "All of this belongs to the Wests?"

"Everything you can see on this side of the highway," Lexi answered.

Wow.

Then they came over a rise—and Vic's jaw dropped.

The house wasn't beautiful. It was magnificent.

Made of stones and logs like Austin and Lexi's house, it was probably ten times as large, with a half-dozen chimneys and a roof made of multiple steep gables. A dozen floor-to-ceiling windows reflected the mountains that surrounded them. Off to the west stood several corrals and large outbuildings, including what had to be a riding hall.

Vic stared. "It's amazing."

Britta laughed. "Told you so."

"I think Nate is taking us out today." Lexi drove around to the back of the house and parked in a wide driveway next to what looked like a five-car garage. "He went to high school in Scarlet a couple of years ahead of us then served in a Marine Special Operations unit in Afghanistan. He was burned in an IED explosion, and we all thought he was going to die. But he's happily married now. He and his wife Megan have a school-aged daughter and a baby boy."

Vic was glad to hear that. She liked happy endings.

They had just climbed out of the car when a tall man in a cowboy hat walked out of the garage. Half of his face was scarred from burns, while the other half was untouched and strikingly handsome. He gave them a warm smile. "Hey, Lexi. How's the bride? Hey, Britta."

"I'm doing great. Thanks. How about you?"

"Can't complain." He held a scarred hand out to Vic. "I'm Nate West. Welcome to the Cimarron."

Lexi glanced down the dirt road that served as a driveway. "What happened to the guys? They were right behind us."

*E*ric got sick of the angry silence and pulled over, idling on the shoulder of the highway. They would end this here and now. "What pisses me off is that you don't trust me. I told you I haven't slept with her, and that ought to be good enough for you."

Taylor's jaw hardened. "Rose saw your truck parked there the past two nights. Are you telling me she's lying?"

The next time Eric saw Rose, he was going to give her a piece of his mind.

"Rose didn't see what she thinks she saw." *Ah, hell.* "You want the whole story? The first night I was there, we did nothing but talk. I was toned out about ten minutes after we got there, but I guess Rose didn't see me drive away. If Victoria looked like she'd been crying, it had nothing to do with me."

Okay, that wasn't exactly true. She'd said the video footage had made her cry, and he'd filmed it. But he couldn't tell Austin about that.

"What about last night?"

"I stayed for a couple of hours. We talked. Victoria *asked* me to kiss her, and I did. We made out a little, but my dick stayed in my pants. She's an adult. Who are you—her daddy?"

Taylor took this in, the anger fading from his face. "You're right. I'm sorry."

The moment the apology left Taylor's mouth, guilt twisted in Eric's gut, the image of Victoria's pale and terrified face stuck in his mind. No, he hadn't fucked her, but it had been near enough. Something he'd done had triggered her.

"Are we good, man?"

Taylor nodded.

Eric threw his truck into gear. "Any chance you want to tell me why you're going all big brother on Victoria's behalf? What happened to her?"

"You want the truth?"

Eric nodded, waiting for a semi to pass, and then merging onto the highway.

"The truth is, I don't know. Victoria made Lexi promise not to tell anyone, and you know Lexi. Once she makes a promise ... But she did tell me that some man had hurt Vic and that what he'd done was terrible. Lexi wants to kill the bastard."

Well, shit.

Eric had figured that much out for himself. "She's not the only one."

Taylor stared at him. "You care about her."

The words made Eric's pulse take off, adrenaline rushing to his head. "She's Lexi's friend. Of course I care about her."

Taylor's face split into a knowing grin. "No, buddy. I mean you *care* about her. You've got it bad, don't you? Holy shit! I never thought I'd live to see the day."

Now Eric was pissed. "She's not my type."

"Since when is gorgeous, intelligent, and fun not your type?"

"If you don't shut up, I'm going to pull this truck over again and put my fist through that stupid shit-eating grin of yours."

"Okay, man. Have it your way." But Taylor was still smiling.

Chapter Seven

Vic listened while Nate gave everyone the rundown on the day's ride. His gaze landed on her, and he frowned. "Did you bring a hat—anything to keep the sun off your face?"

She shook her head. "There's sunscreen in my moisturizer.

"That's not going to do you any good up here. Hang on a minute." He jogged off toward the horse barn.

Everyone else mounted, ranch hands helping to adjust their stirrups.

Eric patted his gelding's neck. "At this altitude, people get sunburned faster."

"Altitude again."

Nate reappeared, a white cowboy hat in hand. "Try this. Megan won't mind if you borrow it."

Vic put the hat on, amused to think what her coworkers at Jensen West would think if they could see her now. "How do I look?"

"With those boots?" Eric's eyes were shadowed by the wide brim of his hat, but she could see his grin. "Like a rodeo queen."

"Hey, I like these boots. Besides, I wasn't asking you."

While Nate held the reins, she mounted her mare — a beautiful palomino named Baby Doe. "Isn't Baby Doe the woman who froze to death at the Matchless Mine?"

"It sure is—Baby Doe Tabor." Nate told Vic Baby Doe's story while he adjusted her stirrups—how she'd married Horace Tabor before he'd legally divorced his first wife, how they'd set Denver on its ear with scandal, how the crash in silver prices had reduced them to poverty. "Baby Doe was penniless for most of her life, far longer than she'd been wealthy, but people remember her for the scandal and glamour."

"How sad."

"Riches to rags—sometimes that's how it goes." He handed her the reins. "Are you ready?"

Vic took the reins in one hand. "Thanks."

"Hey, West, are you done with the history lesson?" Austin called.

He and Lexi were bringing up the rear.

Eric, who was right behind her, j\oined in. "There will eventually be riding on this trail ride, won't there?"

"All right, all right." Nate walked over to a ranch hand who was holding the reins of a big palomino stallion. He mounted the animal in a single motion, mastering its restless response with ease. "Come on, Chinook. These city folks are gettin' grumpy."

He rode with the grace of someone who'd been raised with horses, the cowboy hat on his head and the rifle holstered behind his right leg making Vic feel like she was on the set of a western movie.

"What's the rifle for—bears?"

He chuckled. "Generally speaking, wildlife isn't a problem. People are. We get squatters sometimes, and I'd rather be prepared than sorry. We've had a few clever entrepreneurs try to set up illegal grows on our land."

"Grows?"

"Marijuana," Eric said from behind her.

"Oh."

"Hey, Taylor, are you carrying?" Nate called to Austin.

"Does a bear shit in the woods?"

A grin on his face, Nate turned his stallion and led them out of the corral and onto a trail that cut across a sweeping meadow of tall green grass and wildflowers, pausing once to glance over his shoulder at Vic. "How are you doing?"

"Great." Baby Doe was so docile that she probably would have followed Nate up the trail even if Vic were a sack of potatoes. "I get the feeling she's done this before."

He laughed. "You're right about that."

For a time, they rode in silence, the landscape quiet apart from the chatter of birds and the plodding of horses' hooves. Vic found herself awed by the beauty that surrounded her—blue sky, rugged peaks, quaking aspens. Nature lulled her senses, the rocking motions of the animal beneath her soothing away stress, fresh air and sunshine melting the tension she'd been carrying since last night.

Soon the ranch house was far behind them, the trail passing through shady groves of aspen that eventually opened to reveal a lake.

"Oh!" Vic stared. "It's so beautiful!"

The still surface of the water was a perfect mirror for the sky and the mountains, reeds near the far shore swaying in a breeze, and—

A moose!

It grazed among the reeds, velvet on its broad antlers. It paid no attention to them, but continued to feed, walking on absurd, spindly legs.

"Oh, I wish I'd brought my phone." She'd left it behind, wanting to escape Abigail's incessant emails for a few hours.

Eric's voice came from behind her again. "Got you covered, city girl."

She looked over her shoulder and saw that he was taking a photo for her with his phone. "Thanks."

They watched the moose graze for a few minutes, then moved on, Vic now acutely aware of the man who rode behind her. In her mind's eye, she could see him straddling his gelding, strong thighs guiding the animal, cowboy hat shading his face. With that image in her head, she didn't feel stupid for asking him to kiss her last night. In fact, her request seemed sensible, even necessary.

And, God, it had been incredible—every brush of his lips, every stroke of his tongue, every caress. Not to mention what he'd done with the rock-hard torpedo in his pants. She hadn't known it was possible to come like that. Yes, it had been amazing—right up to the moment when she'd lost it and ruined everything.

How on earth was she going to explain last night to him?

Eric knew the point of this ride was to enjoy the scenery, but he couldn't take his gaze off Victoria. She constantly surprised him. She'd taken on wakeboarding, and now she was riding a horse like she'd done it all her life. She sat with perfect posture in the saddle, her dark hair hanging down her back, that white cowboy hat on her head. And those ridiculous boots—all leather and embroidered roses.

What would it be like to see her in those boots—and nothing else?

The thought came out of nowhere, ambushing him, turning his blood hot.

Get your mind out of the gutter.

It was almost one o'clock when they stopped for lunch, dismounting and turning their horses over to waiting ranch hands who had driven up via an access road. Eric would have helped Victoria dismount, but she did just fine on her own.

A short walk from the road, they found a shaded picnic area, where Jack West and the rest of the West family waited by two large picnic tables that had been covered with linen table clothes and set with real dishes.

"This is classy," Eric said to Austin. "I was expecting to sit on the ground eating baloney sandwiches."

Lexi looked just as surprised. "Yeah, me, too. This is amazing."

A pretty little girl marched over to Austin, wearing little cowboy boots, a lacy skirt, and a dinosaur T-shirt, a tiara perched on her blond head. "What the hell took you so long?"

"Miss Emily, what have I told you about cursing?" Jack West called to her, hands on his hips.

So this was Emily. Nate had adopted her when he'd married Megan.

She looked at her feet. "It's okay to think it, but don't say it out loud."

"That's right."

"But you say it out loud all the time, Grandpa Jack."

"We've talked about that, too. Why is that different?"

"Because you're an ornery old cuss."

Eric met Victoria's gaze and saw that she, too, was fighting not to laugh.

"That's right. You've got to have gray hair to cuss. Now come help your old grandpa get food on the table."

Lexi introduced Victoria to everyone—Jack and his wife, Janet, and Megan, who was busy setting condiments on the table. "The two little ones are Jackson—Megan and Nate's son—and Lily. She's Jack and Janet's daughter."

And then it was time to eat.

It wasn't just the table cloths and dishes that were classy. Lunch, as it turned out, was not your average picnic. Everything was homemade, from the fried chicken and mashed potatoes, to the salads and the blueberry pie.

Eric couldn't keep his gaze from drifting back to Victoria. She was quieter than usual, watching and listening while everyone else talked and joked, sadness unmistakable in her eyes.

That was *his* fault.

Damn it.

Jack seemed to notice, too. "How's your meal, Victoria?"

"It's amazing." Her gaze shifted to Janet and Megan, her face brightening. "I love to cook. I should get your recipes for fried chicken—and the pie."

Jack's face folded in a frown. "Those would be *my* recipes, young lady."

Janet laughed. "Jack is the cook in the house. We just do the dishes."

Color flooded Victoria's cheeks. "Oh! Sorry."

"No offense taken." Jack topped off Victoria's iced tea. "Stop by the house on your way out, and I'll give you a couple of recipe cards."

"Thanks. I would appreciate that."

Then Jack got to his feet and raised his beer. "Lexi, the ties between your family and mine go back a couple of generations. We're all happy for you and wish you and Austin the very best in your new life. To the bride and groom!"

Eric stood, as did everyone but Lexi and Austin. "To the bride and groom!"

Lexi dabbed her eyes with her napkin. "Thank you, Jack. You're making me cry."

After no one could eat another bite, the Wests got busy cleaning up the table, packing everything away, refusing to let anyone help.

"We've got hand wipes if anyone has greasy fingers, and there's a privy fifty yards south of here." Jack pointed. "Otherwise, feel free to hike around until you're ready to ride again. There's a little stream off that way."

Eric took a quick bathroom break, then washed his hands. He glanced around and saw everyone but Victoria. He hiked off in the direction of the stream and found her sitting on a big boulder, looking down at the water. "Hey."

She glanced up at him. "Hey."

He sat beside her, unsure what to say next. He wanted to let her know he was sorry about last night, but he didn't want to spoil the moment by bringing up something she wanted to forget. Fortunately, she spoke first.

"The Wests are really nice people."

"They sure are. They're the biggest land-owners in the county and damned decent people. They make a sizeable donation to the Team every year and support the fire department, too. Their family has been ranching this land for four generations."

"That's what Lexi said." Victoria smiled, but the sadness hadn't left her eyes. "The way she and Britta described everything here, I thought they must have been exaggerating. Now I think they didn't do it justice."

"You were awfully quiet during lunch. Are you okay? Headache?"

"Oh, no, I feel fine. It's just ..." She seemed to hesitate. "I kept thinking how amazing it is that all of you live here together in this beautiful place. In less than a week, I'll be back in Chicago, sitting at a desk, going to meetings, working on a new campaign. This whole incredible experience will just feel like a dream."

"We haven't closed the borders, you know. I'm sure there are PR firms in Denver and Boulder if you want to move here."

What the hell had he just said?

She gaped at him. "I can't move to Colorado. Because ... well ..."

The list of reasons she'd been about to give him seemed to die on her tongue.

"I'm listening."

She looked into his eyes. "Eric, I ..."

When she didn't go on, he stepped up. It was time to own his shit. "I'm sorry about last night. I didn't mean to push—"

She pressed her fingers to his lips. "No! No, that was my fault. It wasn't anything you did. I'm the one who's sorry. You didn't push me. You were amazing."

Her pupils went wide when she realized what she'd said, a blush stealing into her cheeks. "I mean ... I wanted ... I didn't mean to flip out like that. I just ..."

He could see the struggle on her face, in the furrow on her brow and the doubt in those eyes. "You know you can tell me anything, right?"

She opened her mouth to speak but was cut off.

"Saddle up!" Austin called to them through the trees. "Whoever falls behind gets left behind."

And for the second time today, Eric wanted to punch his best friend.

V ic tapped her foot in time to the music, describing what she'd seen to Winona, her dinner salad long since eaten. "Its antlers must have been five feet wide. It looked like it was probably as tall as my horse. I had no idea they were so big. We saw a couple of golden eagles, too, and some deer, and ... what was the name of that cute squirrel?"

"Abert's squirrel," Eric answered. "And, yes, I got a photo."

"It was adorable. It had little tufts of fur on its ears. It chattered at us like it was furious with us for trespassing."

"Squirrels are very territorial," Winona said. "It probably *was* furious."

It was then Vic noticed the little smiles on everyone's faces. "You think I'm funny, but this is all new to me."

"I'm glad you had such a good time," Lexi said. "Jack refused to let us pay for it. He said it was part of their wedding gift to us. Can you believe that?"

"He's a generous man," Austin's words were upbeat, but his expression wasn't.

Something had happened with the Team today. She'd overheard Austin and Eric talking about it in low tones when they'd gotten back to the ranch house—something about a drowning. She'd only caught a few words before they'd seen her and changed the subject. Whatever had happened, it had left them both shaken, and they were trying to protect everyone else by not talking about it.

A man with a beard and long hair pulled back in a bun walked up to their table, his gaze fixed on Vic. He held out his hand. "You're Victoria Woodley? I'm Joe Moffat, the owner of Knockers. I hear you don't like my pizza."

Vic stared up at him, mortified to think that someone had passed on to him what she'd said. "Well, I ... um... The pizza is fine. It's just not what I'm used to."

"Don't try to spare my feelings." There was no anger on his face. "Just tell me how I can make it better."

Before she could answer, Eric piped up. "She promised me she'd make me some pizza. Maybe it's time for her to keep that promise and show us all how it's done."

"I said I'd do it *if* we could find the ingredients. It's not slapping canned stuff on pre-made dough and shoving it in an oven."

"You tell me what you need, and I'll get it," Joe said. "When can you come in? You can use my kitchen, and I'll even clean up."

Vic didn't have a recipe at hand, but she'd made it often enough she was pretty sure she could remember everything. She ran through a list of ingredients for the dough, sauce, and the toppings. "When will I have time?"

"How does Wednesday morning sound?" Joe asked. "That gives me some time to round up these ingredients. We don't open till eleven, so I can make room for you during our prep. It can be our lunch."

Lexi shook her head. "We'll be on our way back from rafting Browns Canyon. How about Thursday morning?"

Joe's brows drew together. "I usually do payroll Thursday morning."

And for a moment, Vic thought she was off the hook.

"But if I come in early and get payroll out of the way, that will work. How about nine? You show me how to make better pizza, and your meals for the rest of your time here are on the house." He held out a hand.

She took it, and they shook. "It's a deal."

Rain came up behind them and spoke to Joe. "You wanted to see me?"

He turned away from the table, lowered his voice. "If the Team shows up tonight, their drinks are on the house. They've had a rough day."

Rain nodded. "I heard."

The two of them walked off together.

What had happened?

"How cool is that?" Lexi took a sip of her beer. "You're going to give cooking lessons to Caribou Joe."

The idea made Vic nervous. She'd only ever cooked for pleasure. She'd never cooked under pressure before. "I hope I don't mess something up."

The band reached the end of a song, then the lead singer spoke. "We hear we've got a bride and groom in the house tonight. Lexi and Austin, this next song's for you. From what we've been told, it fits."

They slipped into a Zydeco version of *Paradise By the Dashboard Light*, their choice of song making Vic and everyone else laugh.

Austin took Lexi's hand, kissed it, and led her onto the dance floor, where people made way for them, cheering as they started to dance.

Eric took her hand. "Let's put those fancy boots of yours to work."

She pulled back. "I don't know how to dance like that."

He didn't back down. "I'll teach you. It's not as hard as wakeboarding."

He led her to the dance floor, took her right hand with his left, and placed his other hand on her back. "You hold onto my shoulder. Yes, just like that. The steps are easy. Just follow my lead. Quick, quick, slow, slow. Quick, quick, slow, slow."

It wasn't hard, but being close to Eric like this destroyed Vic's concentration, and more than once she lost the rhythm. He smelled like sunshine and saddle leather, his movements confident, his hands strong as they guided her.

He looked down at her, his blue eyes dark. "You're doing great."

When the song ended, she applauded along with everyone else, then cheered as Austin scooped Lexi into his arms and carried her back toward their table.

And there was that damned lump in her throat again.

The band started another song, a slow song with a sensual, bluesy vibe, and Vic turned to walk back to their table.

Eric held fast to her hand and drew her against him, the heat of his body seeming to enfold her. "Don't run away."

"I wasn't running."

That was a lie. He was too much, and if she weren't careful, she'd start having feelings for him. Where would she be then?

She'd be in Chicago, that's where. He would still be here in Scarlet. Besides, wasn't she done with men? And then there was the little matter of the promise she'd made herself.

"You amaze me, Victoria. Every day you surprise me."

She looked up at him. "How?"

"Saturday, it was your willingness to try something completely new. Sunday, it was your compassion toward Bear." His voice was deep and soft, the sound rumbling in his chest as he spoke. "Today, you showed me that you're good with horses. Let's not forget your skill with computers."

She didn't know what to say. Most of the time when men said kind things to her, it had to do with her body. "I've spent more time with you than I have with Lexi."

"You don't hear me complaining." His fingers traced circles on her back through the fabric of her blouse, sending shivers down her spine.

"We should probably go work on the vid—"

"We've got time for that later. Just dance with me."

"Okay." She gave in and did what she'd really wanted to do since he'd brought her onto the dance floor. She rested her head against his chest and forgot everything else but him.

Chapter Eight

Eric watched as Vic finished adding the last photo, trying to keep his mind off her and on the video. He could still feel her in his arms—the gentle swaying of her body, her soft curves, the silk of her hair beneath his fingers. It was driving him nuts. Even so, he didn't want to leave. He liked being close to her like this, just the two of them.

She dragged the cursor back to the beginning of their timeline, images playing in reverse order on the screen. "Okay, are you ready?"

"Let's see it."

She let the video run.

Eric watched as the project he'd started six months ago came together, interviews edited expertly, photos fading in and out. "I love how you did that. I wouldn't have been able to figure it out."

Vic sniffed.

He glanced over to see tears in her eyes. "You think it's that good?"

She reached for a tissue. "Would you shut up and let me listen?"

"Yes, ma'am." He held his hands up in a gesture of surrender. "I would've thought you'd had enough of this, given the amount of time we've spent editing everything."

"Shh!"

"Geez." He chuckled.

On his computer screen, Rose was talking.

Yeah, he was going to have words with her later.

"Oh, Emily knows. Of course, she knows. Whatever journey her spirit has made, she knows more about us now than we know about ourselves. She's thrilled that Lexi and Austin are together. She used to come to me for readings. She had a lot of second chakra energy just like Lexi—very fertile, very sexual."

What the hell did that mean? They didn't go into chakras in paramedic school. Eric had almost asked, but he'd known it would send Rose off on a tangent.

When the video finished, Vic's cheeks were damp from crying, but there was a smile on her face. "You know what it needs now?"

"What?" He'd thought they were finished.

"A soundtrack."

"A soundtrack?" Okay, sure. "Do you know any musicians?"

"Oh, thousands." She typed something into Google and clicked on a link. "See? There are lots of sites that offer royalty-free music. We just have to find a composition that fits, buy it, and edit it in."

He glanced at his watch and stood. "We'll have to wait till Wednesday night. It's after eleven, and you still need to get packed for the rafting trip. We leave at five in the morning, remember?"

"Oh, God. I don't even know what to bring. I've never gone camping."

He stared at her. "You've never gone camping?"

"Not in a tent."

"What other way is there?"

"Camping in a custom RV with a TV and running water and my own bedroom. Or staying in a lodge with room service in the middle of the African bush. My father once took us to Kenya. There were giraffes outside every morning. My brother and I fed them through the windows."

"Honey, that's not camping." He didn't know what that was. "Want help packing?"

"You would do that?"

"Sure."

"Just don't look at my panties, okay?"

At the word *panties*, his pulse skipped. He couldn't resist. "What's wrong with your panties?"

"Nothing's *wrong* with them. I'd just feel embarrassed if you saw them."

He hated to break it to her, but he'd seen a lot more than her panties the other night, and she hadn't seemed embarrassed then. He couldn't say that, of course. "Okay, fine. No snooping in your underwear drawer."

She shut down the computer and walked into the bedroom, flicking on the light as she entered. She went to the closet, opened it, and took out one of her suitcases and a brand, spanking new wetsuit. "I bought this."

It was distinctly feminine with short sleeves, legs that ended mid-thigh, and cheery color blocks in yellow, pink, and green.

"You bought a wetsuit? For one rafting trip?" It was high-quality, too, something a pro might own. "Most people rent those."

She shrugged like it was no big deal. "Lexi told me the rented ones sometimes smell like mildew."

Okay, yeah. "That's true."

"Do you know if we're going out on the town while we're there?"

"Out on the town—in Buena Vista?" Eric laughed. "I doubt it."

He walked to the closet, searched through her clothes, pulled out a little black beaded dress. "I'd pay money to see you in this."

She took it from him, jammed it back into her closet. "Some help you are."

"Sorry. I got distracted." He grabbed a pair of jeans, two tank tops, and two T-shirts off their hangers, then tossed them onto the bed, together with a fleece jacket and the winter coat she'd brought. Next, he dug in the bottom of her closet where her shoes were neatly arranged and took out a pair of running shoes and a brand new pair of Teva sandals. "Add two pairs of socks and two pairs of the sweet little panties you don't want me to see, and you're mostly set. You'll need your personal items, too, along with sunscreen and mosquito repellent."

She stared at the small pile he'd made. "That's it?"

"That's more than you'll need. We're only camping for one night. The outfitter Austin and Lexi hired will supply the tents, sleeping bags, and all the other gear, so unless you want to go down the river in a fancy gown or tromp around the campground in heels, yeah, that's it."

"What about pajamas?"

"In a tent?" He laughed out loud. "Just sleep in your T-shirt and underwear. That's what I do."

"Okay." She looked away, worry lines on her face.

"Hey, you can bring pajamas if you want, but—"

"It's not that. The idea of whitewater rafting scares me. I read online that people have drowned rafting in Browns Canyon."

It was true.

"Hey, come here." He drew her against him, held her. "I'll be there. Taylor, Moretti, and Chaska will be there. That's four rescue guys, and two of us are paramedics. The rafting guide will be there, too. You're not going to drown."

"How can you be sure?"

He couldn't resist. "I'm very good at mouth-to-mouth."

She laughed, pushing him away. "Yes, I believe you probably are. Now go. Let me get some sleep."

He left her suite, still grinning, and headed down the stairs and outside. He was on his way to his truck when he remembered what he'd planned to do.

He hurried across the street and knocked on Rose's door—hard.

She poked her head out of the window above him, naked as a jaybird, her breasts visible, her long silver hair tousled. "Eric Hawke? What is it? Is someone hurt?"

"Everything's fine." He hadn't meant to scare her. "It's eleven thirty-six. I just wanted to make sure you got the time right so you can tell everyone in Scarlet exactly when I left Victoria's room tonight."

With that, he turned and walked to his truck, chuckling to himself.

V ic looked at the others. "Why am I the only one wearing a wetsuit?"
Everyone else was dressed in tank tops and shorts.

Eric's gaze slid over her. "I don't know, but I'm grateful."

"Did Lexi tell you to buy a wetsuit?" Austin asked.

Lexi shook her head. "I just said most people rent wetsuits."

They left their gear in the rafting company's dressing rooms, then walked as a group down to the riverbank, where their guide, a tall man with a tanned face and shoulder-length, sun-bleached hair was waiting for them.

Was it too late to back out?

No, she couldn't do that. Lexi and Austin had paid for this. Besides, she didn't want to look like a chicken. If they thought this was safe, it was probably safe.

Then again, most of them were rock climbers.

"The number one rule of rafting is 'stay in the boat,'" said the guide, whose name was Logan. "If you break that rule and fall in, or if the boat flips, the first thing you need to do is stay calm."

Somehow, hearing she should stay calm made Vic feel anything but, her heart beating fast and hard. Ten feet away, the Arkansas River raced by them, a swirling menace of rapids and eddies.

"I'll say that again. Stay calm. Your vest will bring you to the surface. It's important that you get out of the water quickly to prevent cold shock. The safe way to do that is to point your feet downstream. Use them to keep yourself from hitting rocks. Some of those rocks you can see. Some you can't. Use your arms like rudders to steer yourself toward the riverbank." He looked over at Austin. "I know you're all in Search and Rescue, but I have to give the speech."

Austin grinned from behind his sunglasses, zinc oxide on his nose. "We understand. Safety first."

"Any questions?"

Vic had about a dozen, but she was pretty sure she'd sound like an idiot, so she kept them to herself.

"Let's get our boat in the water."

She grabbed her handle and lifted, the raft much heavier than she'd imagined. Fortunately, six other people were carrying it, too. Jesse had backed out at the last minute, showing up this morning at five a.m. in Austin's driveway to say he couldn't make it. Vic didn't know why he'd backed out, but from the looks Austin and Eric had given each other, she'd bet it had to do with what had happened with the Team yesterday.

"All right, everyone, get in. Taylor and Hawke, why don't you sit up front? You've done this more than the others."

"I'd like to sit in front of Victoria if that's okay. I promised her she wouldn't drown, and I aim to keep that promise."

"Let's put her between the two of us."

While Logan held onto the raft, everyone got into their spots, Victoria positioning herself the way he'd shown her, oar in hand.

"Okay. It looks like we're ready to rock and roll." Logan jumped into the boat and let the water take it. "We've got calm water for a while, so let's practice rowing as a team. It's important that we work together. Oars in the water."

Vic tried to do exactly what he told her to do, rowing hard when he told them to row hard, lifting her oar out of the water when he shouted, "Oars up!"

"We're coming up on our first rapid—Whitewater Park. We're going to row hard right through it."

Eric turned to look at her over his shoulder. "It's going to be fun."

She nodded, heart in her throat.

"Row!" Logan told them.

"Bring it on!" That was Austin.

They flew through the rapid, the river seeming to drop from beneath them as if they were on a roller coaster, icy-cold water spraying up around them.

Vic let out a shriek—then found herself laughing. "Woohoo!"

"Hoka hey!"

"All right!"

"Yeah!"

They hit two more sections with rapids, then came to a calm, lazy stretch. They glided along, Logan sharing the history of the Arkansas River Valley and naming the mountains that passed in the distance. "Those are the Collegiate Peaks over there, part of the Sawatch Range."

Vic took in the sights—grassy riverbanks, rocky foothills, distant mountains, sunlight sparkling on water. On the shore to their left, something moved. "A deer! Look! There's a deer!"

"Where are you from?" Logan asked.

"Chicago," everyone else said in unison.

They stopped for a catered lunch at roughly the halfway point, paddling the boat into shallow water, then dragging it onto the sand beside a half dozen other rafts from other rafting companies.

"How are you holding up, city girl?"

Victoria smiled up at Eric, her dark hair damp, her face flushed from sunshine and excitement, the mirrored lenses of her sunglasses beaded with water. "This is a freaking blast!"

He bit back a "told you so," his arm finding its way around her shoulders as they walked toward the picnic area. Other rafters and their guides crowded around the tables, but the group found a place to sit for a quick lunch of deli sandwiches, potato chips, and fresh fruit. Then the women left en masse for a bathroom break.

Why did women do that?

Hey, I gotta take a piss. Want to come with me?

Said no man ever.

Eric didn't miss the way other men's gazes followed Victoria as she passed, checking her out from head to toe. As long as they kept their distance …

"Hey, Hawke, did you hear what the other guides told Logan?" Taylor called.

Eric's head snapped around. "What did they say?"

"Distracted?" Belcourt asked, a knowing grin on his face.

Taylor ignored them both. "I heard them say that rain in the mountains near Leadville last night has pushed the flow higher than it's been since the spring melt. Most of the boats going through Seidel's have flipped today."

Seidel's Suckhole was the only true class IV rapid on this stretch of the river and a real challenge. So many boats flipped there that people crowded the cliffs above it just to watch and cheer as rafters tumbled into the frigid water.

"Good to know."

By the time the women had returned and the men had hit the john—one at a time—Logan had rejoined them.

"We've got the best rapids of the day ahead of us," he said. "Who's ready to get back on the water?"

They carried the raft to the water's edge and climbed aboard.

Eric turned to Victoria. "Here's where it gets fun."

"I can't wait!"

The rapids came one after another now, Logan calling out the names and giving them instructions on how hard to row and when. Screaming Right Hand Turn. Canyon Doors. Pinball. Zoom Flume.

Behind him, Victoria screamed and laughed like a kid on an amusement park ride, her enjoyment putting a stupid grin on Eric's face.

Heckle Jeckle. Big Drop. Seven Stairs. Widowmaker.

A wave sprayed over his side of the raft, soaking him to the skin, and probably Victoria, too. She gave a shriek, then laughed.

Raft Ripper. Graveyard. Last Chance.

"You still with us, city girl?" he called over his shoulder.

"It's not over already, is it?"

"Okay, we're coming up on Seidel's Suckhole," Logan called out to them, shouting to be heard above the water. "When I tell you to row, give it everything you've got. Row hard, and don't stop until I tell you."

They passed the Hecla Junction Access, where people on half-day trips were going ashore. A few minutes later, Eric saw Seidel's Suckhole ahead.

"What are all those people doing up there?" Victoria asked.

Eric looked up, saw a big crowd on the cliffs. "They're watching boats flip."

The raft ahead of them gathered speed, shot through the rapid, then vanished, sucked beneath the water, only to reappear seconds later, its passengers popping up above the surface and bobbing like corks as they made their way toward the riverbank.

"Okay, row! Row hard!"

The boat flew through the water, hit the rapid, then caught air, sending them sailing to the suckhole.

"Row!"

For a moment, Eric thought they'd nailed it. Then the boat vanished from beneath them, the current sucking them all down into the river.

He managed to get a deep breath before he went under, the frigid temperature a shock to the system. He kicked for the surface, glanced around for the others. He saw Logan and Taylor. Belcourt had Winona. Lexi's head popped up close to the boat.

His heart gave a hard thud.

Where was Victoria?

He did a quick three-sixty spin in the water, the fierce current carrying him downriver. Then a head popped above the surface about five yards upriver.

Victoria.

She took a deep breath, then laughed and pointed her feet downstream.

He fought the current, kicking hard to hold his position, and let the river carry her straight into his arms. Then he rolled onto his back and steered them to the safety of the sand. And there they lay, Victoria on top of him, panting for breath, the sunshine slowly bringing heat back into their limbs. It was only then that he realized the two of them had ended up on one side of the river, while everyone else was on the other.

"You okay, city girl?"

Victoria raised herself up, looked down at him, a brilliant smile on her beautiful face. "That was the most fun I've ever had."

Then she bent down and kissed him.

Up on the cliffs, people cheered.

They showered in the rafting company's locker rooms, excitement still humming through Vic's veins as she shampooed her hair.

What an adrenaline rush this day had been.

From the moment they'd hit that first rapid, her fear had vanished. Even when the boat had disappeared from beneath her, she hadn't been afraid—stunned by the cold water, yes, but not afraid. She'd kicked her way to the surface, aided by her floatation vest, to find Eric searching for her. Her heart had melted when she'd seen the worry on his face. Then the river had pushed her into his arms, and he'd held onto her until they reached the sand.

She tilted her head back to rinse the shampoo away, smiling to herself, the memory of their kiss sending a thrill through her. She wasn't sure what had come over her. Maybe it was just the adrenaline. Maybe it had been the sight of him lying there, out of breath and sexy as hell. Or maybe it had been his concern for her.

No man had ever put himself on the line for her before.

She finished her shower, wrapped a towel around herself, and stepped out to make room for someone else. She dried off, rubbed lotion into her skin, and slipped into a white cotton tank top and a pair of hunter green hiking shorts she'd added to Eric's skimpy pile. Had he really expected her to bring so little?

Dressed like this, she felt so very Colorado. Here, women dressed like they were on their way to the gym—yoga pants or shorts, T-shirts, no makeup.

She found Lexi bent over in front of the mirrors, drying her hair. "I saw that kiss."

Vic couldn't help but smile. "I think a lot of people did."

The crowd on the cliff had actually cheered.

She pulled a comb out of her makeup bag and began to work through her tangles, Lexi's silence speaking volumes. "Let me guess. You're going to warn me that Eric is a bit of a playboy and tell me I shouldn't get my hopes up."

Lexi stood, flipping her red hair back. "Just be careful, okay? You're my best friend, and he's Austin's best friend. I don't want to see either of you get hurt."

And just like that, reality drove Vic's smile away.

Chapter Nine

V ic listened from the backseat while Austin and Eric ribbed each other, their banter helping her to drive away the sense of gloom left by Lexi's warning.

"Think they've got a gas station in St. Elmo?" Austin asked.

"Dude, it's a ghost town," came Eric's reply. "We'd better gas up now. Once I lose cell service, we'll be going off a map. We don't want to get lost and run out of fuel up there."

"Good idea," Lexi said.

"Get lost?" Austin asked. "Since when do I get lost?"

Lexi laughed, shaking her head. "Are you serious?"

"Let's see …" Eric seemed to consider the question. "There was that time you got us lost on Grand Mesa. That was fun."

"That wasn't my fault. Someone had turned the sign around."

Eric went on. "What about the first time we climbed Mount Bierstadt together? You were like, 'Follow me. This is the way.' We ended up on the summit of Mount Spaulding instead."

Chaska laughed. "Wow, buddy. Really? You climbed the wrong mountain?"

His reaction made Vic laugh. "How did you do that?"

Austin met Vic's gaze in the rearview mirror. "It's easier than you think."

But Eric wasn't finished. "How about the *second* time we went to climb Mount Bierstadt and ended up on the summit of Mount Evans? That was fun."

Lexi was into it now. "There was also the time you took me to that bridal store in Denver. We drove in circles for twenty minutes trying to find the place because you'd taken a wrong turn."

Austin chuckled. "Okay, okay! I'll get gas. But I never get lost in *my* mountains."

"Okay, that's true," Eric said. "I'll give you that much."

Austin pulled over at a gas station on the edge of town. Everyone else seemed to be leaving, too, the pumps crowded with vehicles.

Vic decided to take advantage of the chance to buy a few things—water, lip balm, more sunscreen. "Does anyone want anything?"

"I'll come with you," Lexi said.

They climbed out of the SUV and walked through the late afternoon heat toward the convenience store. Inside, they found a long line at the cash register.

Vic tossed the things she wanted into a basket and went to stand with Lexi in line.

Lexi's basket was full—graham crackers, chocolate bars, marshmallows, water, mosquito repellant. "I got stuff to make s'mores. We can't camp without s'mores."

"Camp without s'mores? No way." Vic loved s'mores. "I haven't had those since I was a kid. I feel like I'm at summer camp."

"I hope you're having a good—"

"You're that chick from the website, right?" A man's voice cut Lexi off. "Hey, I'm talking to you."

Oh, God.

Panic sent Vic's heart racing, her worst fear coming to life.

"Ignore him," Lexi said, loud enough that he heard.

"I'm not talking to you, little red, though you're fine, too. I'm talking to your friend there." The man leaned down and lowered his voice. "You've got the sweetest tits, and one fine ass. How much?"

"Back off, jerk!" Vic whirled on him, found herself facing six feet of leering asshole—plus a friend.

"Who is she?" the friend asked, his gaze moving over her.

"She's that chick from online I showed you—the call girl."

"I am *not* a call girl." She whispered the words, sure that people had overheard him and were now watching.

Lexi took Vic's arm. "Come on. We can buy this stuff somewhere else."

Vic followed Lexi toward the door, the two of them setting their shopping baskets down on the end of the counter as they passed.

"I'm so sorry, Lexi."

Lexi pushed open the door. "It's not your fault."

Vic hadn't taken two steps outside when a hand closed painfully around her arm and held her fast.

"Now, come on. Don't be like that. I know who you are. I got fifty bucks for you if you'll do both of us. Is your friend a hooker, too?"

She jerked her arm free. "Don't touch me!"

Behind her, three vehicle doors opened. Vic glanced over her shoulder and saw Eric, Austin, and Chaska heading her way, rage on their faces.

"Back off, asshole!" Eric reached her first and put himself between her and the jerk. "Go get in the car, Victoria."

"Yeah, that's your name. Victoria Wood—or something like that."

Vic's stomach dropped to the ground.

"Forget him." Lexi caught her arm through Vic's and led her to Austin's SUV, where Britta stood by the open door. But Vic couldn't get herself to climb inside, fear for her friends rooting her to the spot.

The jerk sneered. "Who are you—her pimp?"

Oh, God, no!

This could *not* be happening.

Eric took a step forward, got right in the man's face, his hands clenched into fists. "Taylor, you'd better arrest this piece of shit before I kill him."

The man's gaze shifted to Austin. "You're a cop?"

"Man, let's just get out of here," said the jerk's friend. "He's probably got a gun."

"I'm an off-duty law-enforcement officer. Your buddy obviously has more brains than you do," Austin said. "Third-degree assault for grabbing her like that. Soliciting for prostitution. You'd better listen to your friend and run."

The jerk raised his hands in surrender and took a step backward. "Hey, I got no problem with you guys. I just want—"

Eric took another step forward, crowding the man. "You talk to *any* woman like that, and you've got a problem with me."

"With all of us," Chaska said.

The man's friend stared at Chaska. "What are you? Some kind of Indian?"

"Wow, you really *did* get all the brains. Yeah, I'm some kind of Indian— the kind who's going to rip your balls off and hang them over my front door if you don't beat it."

The two men turned tail and hurried away.

*E*ric turned to find Victoria standing next to the SUV's open rear door, her gaze fixed on him, her eyes wide, her face pale. He walked over to her and drew her into his arms. She was shaking like a leaf.

Son of a bitch!

"I'm so sorry," she said.

"It's not your fault. You have no reason to be sorry."

He'd had his window down and had heard what the fucker had said to her, calling her a hooker, offering her money for sex. The asshole had said he knew her, even called her by her name—sort of.

What the hell?

He drew a breath, fought to rein in his anger. He was used to helping people, not wanting to punch the shit out of them. "Lexi, do you mind taking the front seat? I want to sit next to Victoria—if it's okay with her."

Victoria nodded.

"Yeah. Sure." Lexi climbed out and got into the front seat.

Eric watched as the two men who'd harassed Victoria jumped into a rust red pickup truck. He didn't want them doubling back with a firearm. When everyone else was settled, he climbed into the seat beside Victoria and buckled his seatbelt. "Let's get the hell out of here."

"Hold on." Taylor was writing something on a piece of paper. "I want to get their plate number and see which way they go so we know whether we've got a chance of running into them again down the road."

"Good idea." Eric reached over, took Victoria's hand. "Did he hurt you?"

She shook her head, but Eric could see the red blotches on her arm where the bastard had grabbed her. They would become bruises.

Damn it.

Victoria looked over at him. "I'm really sorry."

He massaged his hand over the red marks. "You didn't do anything."

Lexi turned to look back at Victoria. "It's okay, Vic. No one blames you. It's good you guys came along, because I was about to kick that creep in the shins."

The rust red pickup truck pulled out of the parking lot, turned onto the highway, and sped away toward the junction with Highway 24.

Hell.

That's the same direction they were headed.

As he started the engine, Taylor met Eric's gaze in the rearview mirror, his unspoken message clear.

Keep your eyes open.

They made a quick trip to a nearby grocery store. Victoria stayed in the car, while Austin and Lexi went inside to pick up the things Victoria and Lexi had wanted to buy at the gas station. Then they set out for the campground, finding their way without getting lost or running into the bastards in the pickup again.

The site sat high above St. Elmo in a grove of old aspens, giving them an amazing view of Mt. Princeton and Mt. Antero. A little creek ran down a gully to the west, while the Arkansas River Valley stretched out to the east. A cool breeze blew in from the north, carrying the scent of distant rain.

While the women shaped beef into patties and Belcourt gathered wood for a fire, Eric and Taylor pitched four two-man tents—one for Lexi and Austin, one for Britta and Victoria, one for Winona, and one for Eric.

Belcourt planned to hike off into the trees and sleep under the stars without a tent.

Eric pounded the last spike into the ground with a rubber mallet, his gaze moving to Victoria, who was slicing a tomato. "How did I end up by myself?"

"Moretti stayed home."

Oh, yeah. "Poor Moretti."

Eric didn't blame him. He couldn't imagine that he would feel much like rafting after a call like that. What a damned tragedy it had been.

"Are you going to be okay alone, or do you need a teddy bear?" Taylor grinned at his own stupid joke.

"You think you're funny, don't you?"

Soon, burgers were cooking over the fire, the scent of sizzling beef making Eric's mouth water. The job of grill master went to Winona, who had more experience cooking over a wood fire than the rest of them combined. It was a skill—one of many—she'd learned from her grandmother growing up on the reservation.

Victoria sat with the rest of them, following along with the conversation, laughing when everyone else laughed, but it didn't take a degree in psychology to see that she was deeply upset by what had happened this afternoon. He could see it in the way her smile didn't quite reach her eyes—and the way her gaze searched the periphery of their camp, as if making sure no one else was there.

Her reaction was more extreme than he'd expect from a woman who'd been randomly harassed by a stranger in a convenience store. Something that son of a bitch had said to her today had shaken her to her core.

Shit.

That fucker had believed he'd known who she was. He'd been so certain that he'd offered her money for sex on the spot. But there was no way Victoria had ever been a call girl. Yeah, she could be assertive and flirty, and she'd probably had sex with her share of guys. But a woman who didn't want him to see her panties wasn't the kind of woman who'd display and sell her body online.

They ate dinner at the picnic table and then gathered around the fire to make s'mores, the sweet scent of roasting marshmallows making the camping trip complete.

"You know," Taylor said, piercing another marshmallow with the end of his stick, "St. Elmo is supposedly haunted."

While they devoured every last marshmallow and bit of chocolate, he told them a story about poor Annabelle Stark, who was raised by her strict parents in St. Elmo during its rough and rowdy days as a mining town. They refused to let her meet men and wouldn't let her attend any of the town's social functions. Annabelle remained unmarried. Then the bust times hit, and the population dwindled. Annabelle's parents died, leaving her alone in a hotel that rarely had guests.

"They say the loneliness eventually drove her mad. She died in the hotel where she'd lived all of her life, a prisoner of her parents' fears. They say she's still there, watching over the town. More than one sheriff's deputy has reported seeing a woman looking out of the upstairs window in the ruins of that hotel, but when they go to check, they find the place empty and the stairs to the second floor gone."

For a moment, no one spoke, the night silent apart from the crackling of the fire and the whisper of wind in the pines.

Eric saw Victoria shiver, whether from the story or from the chilly night air, he couldn't be sure. He got to his feet, grabbed a blanket from his tent, then walked over to where she sat on a log and wrapped it around her shoulders.

He sat beside her. "That's not very scary. All this ghost does is look out the window? She doesn't even say 'Boo'?"

Even Taylor laughed. "You got something better?"

"Nope. But Belcourt here does." Eric had listened to him tell ghost stories from the reservation one night when they'd been camping in the backcountry, and he'd found it damned hard to fall asleep afterward.

"The difference between my sister and me and the rest of you is that we believe in spirits of all kinds—good spirits, evil spirits, trickster spirits." Belcourt said. "These are not just stories. They are true things that happened to people we know."

Here we go.

V ic listened, mesmerized, as Chaska shared his stories, barely able to breathe, his words—and the man who sat beside her—taking her mind off what had happened today.

"My grandfather is a hereditary Sun Dance chief," he said, beginning a new tale. "One day I got a tape in the mail—an old cassette tape. My grandfather sent it with a note telling me he wanted me to learn the old songs so they wouldn't be lost."

Vic slipped her hand into Eric's, his fingers threading easily with hers.

"My grandfather has lived alone since my grandmother made the journey a few years ago. He's a strong man with a good voice for singing. My grandmother had a good voice, too, and the two of them did the pow wow trail together, driving around in an old camper, drumming and singing with Native people from all over this land.

"So I put the tape in an old tape player and listened, and there was my grandfather singing with a half-dozen other people, including my grandmother. I recognized her voice, though I didn't recognize the others."

Eric pulled his hand from hers and put his arm around her. She rested her cheek against his chest, his heartbeat steady.

How long had it been since she'd felt this kind of easy intimacy with a man? She hadn't even slept with him, hadn't even seen him naked, and yet sitting here beside him, she felt comfortable, protected, safe.

Chaska went on. "When I called him to thank him for the tape, I asked when he and my grandmother had recorded it. It must have been years ago. He said to me, 'I just did that the day before I mailed it to you, and I was alone in the house at the time. Your grandmother is gone. Don't play cruel jokes on an old man.'

"I told him it wasn't a joke. His voice wasn't the only one on that tape. I played it for him over the phone. He heard it, too—his wife's spirit and those of his parents and grandparents singing the songs with him so that they wouldn't be lost."

Shivers ran down Vic's spine. "That really happened?"

Winona nodded. "I've listened to the tape myself."

"I'll play it for you one day if you like," Chaska offered.

"That's okay. I believe you." Vic wasn't sure she wanted to listen to spirits singing, even friendly ones.

"I don't know about the rest of you, but I'm beat," Lexi said.

"Same here," said Winona.

There was something Victoria had to say before everyone disappeared into his or her tents. "Thanks, guys, for what you did for me today. Standing up for me like that … I don't think my own brother would have done that."

"Hey, no worries," Austin said.

"Happy to help," said Chaska.

"Your brother must be a jerk," Eric said.

"Yeah, I guess he is." Victoria wasn't ready to give up physical closeness—his fingers enfolding hers, his arm around her shoulder, his chest beneath her cheek—but everyone else was up and getting ready to sleep.

He stood first, drawing her to her feet. "You've got chocolate on your lip."

"I do?"

He ducked down, licked it away, his lips touching hers for the briefest kiss, the contact making her want more. But this wasn't the time or the place.

She took a step back. "Thanks."

"Anytime."

She helped get the food packed away, then brushed her teeth and made a quick trip to the restroom facility with Lexi and Britta. Moths danced around the fluorescent lights, the brightness making Vic squint.

"I'm sleeping in the SUV." Britta disappeared into the one and only stall.

"My sister is the Princess on the Pea."

"I just don't like sleeping on the ground," Britta said from inside the stall.

Lexi rolled her eyes at her sister. "You're not on the ground. You're zipped in a tent, away from the bugs on a foam pad inside a sleeping bag."

But Britta wasn't persuaded. "I'm sleeping in the SUV."

Ten minutes later, Vic found herself alone in a tent, eyes wide in the darkness. It wasn't Chaska's stories that kept her awake, but the vile words of the man who'd grabbed her at the gas station.

Chapter Ten

Eric lay on his back, arm bent beneath his head, staring through the tiny square of mesh on the top of his tent at the stars. He couldn't sleep, his head filled with images of her. Victoria kissing him on the riverbank, her dark hair wet. Victoria looking terrified when that asshole grabbed her arm. Victoria making s'mores and listening wide-eyed to Taylor and Belcourt's stories.

He needed to get her out of his mind. She'd be leaving Sunday, going back to Chicago, and he'd be staying here. Sunday. That was five days from now. Five days. God only knew when he'd see her again.

Shit.

He *was* falling for her. Taylor had been right.

There was only one way to deal with that. He needed to put some distance between them, clear his head. He would finish working on the video, and that would be it, because *no way* was he getting tangled up with her.

From outside, he heard footsteps, a shadow crouching near his door.

"Eric?" Victoria whispered. "Are you awake?"

He sat up, unzipped his tent fly, found her crouching there, sleeping bag and foam pad wadded up in her arms, day pack on one shoulder. "Are you okay?"

"I can't sleep. Can I stay with you?"

But this wasn't a booty call.

Even in the darkness, he could see fear on her pretty face. "Sure."

What did you just say about creating distance, dumbshit?

Yeah, well, that would have to wait. He couldn't leave Lexi's best friend terrified and alone. Besides, the idea of spending the night beside her …

Can you hear yourself, buddy?

He shoved those thoughts aside and took her gear. "I got it."

She crawled in, kneeling by the entrance while he took her sleeping pad and bag and spread them out next to his. "Sorry to bother you. I keep thinking of that guy …"

"There you go." He sat cross-legged, still half inside his sleeping bag. "We watched for them on the way here. They didn't follow us."

"I hope not." She crawled onto her bag, and he realized she was wearing a T-shirt and flannel pajama bottoms. She'd actually brought pajamas camping.

He fought back a grin.

She lay on her belly on her sleeping bag. "What if they got Austin's license plate number? They could follow us back to Scarlet and maybe even find out that I live—"

"If they *did* follow us, the only thing they'll find is trouble." The testosterone in his bloodstream had him wanting to punch that asshole in the face, but he knew from his training that threats of violence wouldn't reassure her.

Abuse had a way of making victims view their attackers as larger than life, capable of carrying out any and every threat they made. That's why so many women stayed in abusive relationships. In their minds, the men who hurt them were invincible. It galled the *hell* out of him that some random asshole had upset her like this.

He set his anger aside, tucked a lock of hair behind her ear. "Those two yahoos probably don't know how to access motor vehicle registrations. Even if they did, it wouldn't do them any good. I'm not going to let them hurt you, and neither is Austin or Chaska or anyone else in Scarlet."

She nodded, but the worry didn't leave her face. She crawled into her sleeping bag. "It's cold up here at night."

"Come here." He lay back, drew her into his arms, pillowing her head with his chest and pulling his jacket over her shoulders like a blanket. "We can share body heat."

That was the oldest climber line in the book, but he actually meant it this time. With his lower half of his body in his sleeping bag and her entire body snugly inside hers, nothing could happen anyway.

He kissed her hair. "Get some sleep."

She lifted her head off his chest, looked into his eyes. "I'm not a call girl. I was never a call girl or a hooker or anything—"

"I'm almost insulted you felt the need to tell me that."

"I just don't want you to think—"

A quiet moan cut her off, making her eyes go wide.

Oh, sweet Jesus!

If Taylor and Lexi just had to get their freak on, couldn't they do it in silence?

Another moan, followed by Lexi's whisper. "That feels *so* good."

Eric couldn't help his body's reaction, not with the sounds of fucking happening ten feet away. His cock pitched a tent in his sleeping bag, which, of course, Victoria noticed. "Don't worry. I don't have a condom with me. Besides, *if* you and I ever have sex, it will be someplace nice and private where you can scream."

She flopped down beside him, ending body contact. "Promises, promises."

"Was that a challenge?"

"Go to sleep." She looked over at him, her expression softening. "And thanks."

Vic awoke early the next morning to find herself in Eric's arms, her head pillowed on one bicep. His hand was in her hair, his fingers doing wonderful things to her scalp. "Morning."

"Morning." His voice was deep and sleepy. "How'd you sleep?"

"Like a baby, thanks to you."

"Good."

"How about you?"

He held her a little closer, kissed the top of her head. "I'm not complaining."

It felt natural to lie here beside him, his arms around her. She closed her eyes again, savoring it, feeling more relaxed than she had in months, feeling safe.

From outside the tent, she heard the crackle of a campfire.

"Someone is already up."

"Belcourt. He's always up with the damned sun. Wakes everyone else up, too."

She snuggled deeper into his chest. "Well, I'm not getting up yet. I like it here."

Once she left his arms, she would find herself in the real world again.

Eric chuckled. "No rush."

Soon everyone was up and awake, bacon sizzling over the fire, the scent of coffee in the air, and it was evident she was going to have to leave this refuge.

Then it dawned on her. "Everyone's going to see I was in your tent and think we slept together."

He laughed. "We *did* sleep together."

She fought back a giggle. "You know what I mean."

"They already think we've been getting it on. Rose told everyone in Scarlet that my truck has been parked at the inn every night, so they put two and two together."

Vic sat bolt upright, understanding now. "That's why your mother thought you and I ... Why didn't you tell me?"

Eric sat up, cupped her cheek with one hand, and kissed her forehead. "Sorry, but I think I've ruined your reputation."

No one said anything when she crawled out of Eric's tent, though Lexi did shoot her the "ohmigod, girl, we have *got* to talk" look.

Vic glanced around at the landscape, which looked different in the morning light, golden sunlight spilling into the valley below, the mountains behind them pink, the sky an endless blue dome. "God, it's beautiful."

Had she ever felt so alive?

Winona cooked them a feast for breakfast—scrambled eggs, bacon, blueberry pancakes, and coffee boiled in a pot set directly on the embers.

Eric motioned Vic over to her spot on the log and brought her a plate, sitting beside her, refilling her coffee, and treating her as if he truly was her lover, the intimacy she'd shared with him last night lingering into the morning.

Lexi looked over at her and laughed. "I never thought I'd see the day when you drank your coffee black."

Vic took another sip. "It's amazing."

"Are you the designer coffee type?" Britta asked.

"Until today I was." As she looked around her, Vic felt that these were the friends she'd been waiting for her entire life. She hadn't realized until this moment how lonely her life had become since Lexi moved away. Her co-workers in Chicago were rarely interested in getting together outside of the office, and since the nightmare with Stewart, she'd hardly gone out anyway. Although she'd only known Britta, Winona, Chaska, and Austin for a short time, she felt almost as comfortable with them as she did with Lexi.

After breakfast, they packed up and hit the highway, arriving in Scarlet just before noon. Austin dropped her off at the inn so that she could shower and change and be ready for them to pick her up for a late lunch.

Eric got out of the SUV with her and carried her bag upstairs, giving her a slow kiss on the mouth that made her toes curl.

She slipped her arms around his neck, kissed him back, not wanting it to end. "Mmm. Are you coming to lunch?"

He shook his head. "I've got some things to do at the firehouse, but I'll see you this afternoon at the rock gym."

Now was the time to put her foot down. "I am *not* climbing."

He grinned. "Says the woman who was afraid to go rafting and then loved it."

"You just had to rub that in my face, didn't you?"

"Yep."

"Who all is going to be there?" She asked the question casually, but he seemed to understand the fear that lay behind it.

He ran a thumb over her cheek. "Hey, that bastard and his buddy are far behind us. It's just going to be Lexi and Austin and members of the Team."

She wanted to tell him that it could happen again with someone else, that if a man in a gas station in Buena Vista had recognized her, it could happen anywhere. But, of course, she couldn't, not without explaining.

He kissed her again, winked. "Admit it—you're going to miss me."

She did her best to look indifferent. "Not at all."

She watched him leave, her lips still tingling, then took a quick shower and changed into khaki climbing shorts and a black tank top. She'd just finished putting her makeup on when she remembered that she hadn't checked her phone or her email since leaving yesterday morning early. She was probably in trouble with Abigail, but, God, it had felt good to be unplugged and free.

She hurried over to the chest of drawers, where she'd left her phone charging, and found a half-dozen texts and sixteen emails. One was from Lexi.

OMG! Are you and Hawke lovers?

Smiling to herself, Vic answered.

No. I was scared. He let me sleep in his tent. But I would say yes if he asked.

The rest of the messages were far less interesting. They came from Abigail and Jeff, who was supposed to be filling in for her. And a weight she hadn't carried for a brief and glorious twenty-four hours settled on her shoulders once again.

So much for feeling alive.

She sat at the table, booted up her laptop, and went through the emails one by one.

Eric could see something was troubling Victoria the moment she and Lexi walked into the rock gym. He finished tying on his climbing shoes then walked over to meet her.

"What's wrong?"

"Her boss," Lexi answered. "She doesn't seem to care that Vic is on vacation."

Oh. That again.

"Did you find a bunch of messages waiting for you?"

"Sixteen."

"Jesus."

"I told her I was going camping and wouldn't have cell service. She reminded me I work in the fast-paced world of public relations and marketing and threatened to give my promotion to someone else."

What a bitch! "Sounds like you need a new boss."

"I wish."

"Do you want to rent a harness and shoes just in case?" Lexi asked her.

Vic shook her head. "I'm here as a spectator."

Eric grinned. "We'll see about that. You're quite the daredevil. You just don't know it yet."

While Lexi got her harness and shoes on, he took Victoria around, introducing her to the Team members she hadn't already met. "This is Harrison Conrad. He's climbed Everest a couple of times now. That's Mitch Ahearn, Megs' partner. This is Kenzie Morgan. She trains and handles search dogs for us. This is Creed Herrera. You already know Moretti. The woman talking with Sasha is Nicole Turner."

At the sound of her name, Sasha looked over and saw them, a big smile sliding over her face. She bounded over to Victoria and gave her a big hug. "How's our badass wakeboarder?"

The surprise on Victoria's face made Eric want to laugh. There were probably thousands of people who would pay to have Sasha Dillon hug them and call them a badass in public.

He went on with the introductions. "You remember Megs, right?"

"Hi, Megs."

But Megs stared past Victoria. "Well, I'll be damned."

Eric turned to look. "Holy shit."

"Who is that?" Victoria asked.

"Gabe Rossiter. He's a tenured Team member and one of the best climbers in the history of the sport. You want to talk about a badass. He let himself fall off a three-hundred-foot cliff to save the life of the woman he loved. He survived, obviously, but lost his leg. He still climbs."

Victoria's expression melted. "Oh!"

Yeah, women always loved that story.

Eric met him with a bear hug. "Hey, man. What the hell are you doing here?"

"I heard there was free climbing today," Rossiter joked. "How did Taylor convince any woman to marry him?"

"That's what I'm wondering." Austin walked up behind them. "Hey, Rossiter. Glad you could make it."

Rossiter hugged him, too, slapping him hard on the back. "Congratulations, man. I'm so happy for you. Where's the bride? I need to meet the woman who's brave enough to take you on."

Austin introduced Lexi and Rossiter—and then it was time to climb.

Eric left Victoria on a bench against the far wall and teamed up with Moretti on a 5.12 route, while Taylor belayed Lexi on a 5.10.

"I like having the gym to ourselves." Moretti tied into his harness. "We should do this more often."

"We can do it again when you get hitched," Taylor called over to them.

"Me? Right. That will be the day." Moretti stepped up to the wall. "Climbing."

"Climb on!" Eric called out.

It was clear right away that Moretti was off his game. The big man had learned to climb almost overnight, putting in long hours at the gym, heading into the canyon, tackling big routes. Hell, he climbed cracks in his spare time, coming back cut up and bruised with a big grin on his face. But today, he was having trouble.

His toe slipped off a ledge, but he held on, the fingers of one hand on a tight little crimper, two fingers of his other hand jammed in a pocket.

"Come on, buddy. You got it," Eric called up to him.

Moretti hauled himself up against the rock using the strength in his shoulders and arms and lifted his foot again, catching the ledge this time and moving upward. A few moves later, he slipped again, this time coming off the wall.

Eric arrested his fall. "Shake it off."

Moretti was suffering. No doubt about it. To his credit, he pulled himself together, got back on the wall, and finished the route.

"Way to go, man." Eric lowered him to the floor, turning to glance at Victoria.

She was watching them, longing on her face. Oh, yeah, she wanted to try it. She was going to break. It was just a matter of time.

Vic watched as Lexi climbed, amazed. She climbed the way they did, each move planned, her motions graceful and strong.

She reached the top of the wall and did a fist pump. "Woohoo!"

"Way to go, babe!" Austin shouted up to her. "Awesome!"

Down on the other side, Sasha had just started up a route, her friend Nicole holding the rope. She seemed to fly up the wall, her body moving in unbelievable ways, stretching out so that she was almost sideways on the rock then shifting to bring herself upright. Beside her, Gabe Rossiter was hanging bare-chested and almost upside down on an overhang on what was clearly the toughest route. He reached for another handhold, his fellow Team members shouting encouragement. Chaska was also climbing without a shirt. He lunged upward, caught a hold, the muscles of his arms and back straining as they bore the entire weight of his body.

"Way to dyno, Belcourt!" someone shouted.

A woman with a long, dark ponytail—Kenzie, the dog trainer—sat down beside her with the guy who'd climbed Everest—Vic thought his name was Harrison—the two of them talking about someone.

"Megs said he did everything he could to save that little girl. He jumped into the water without a harness to get to her, but the current was just too strong and washed her away. He got washed downstream, too, but managed to self-rescue. Megs said he ran down the road, trying to catch up with the girl, but just couldn't reach her. He basically watched her drown."

A lump formed in Vic's throat.

So that's what had happened to Jesse.

How unspeakably horrible.

A family had lost a child, and Jesse was torn apart.

"He's lucky to be alive," Harrison said. "Did they get the rest of the family out?"

Kenzie nodded. "Megs said he's blaming himself for not being fast enough. She's sidelined him. Until he gets counseling, she won't let him go on more calls."

"I bet this has dredged up a bunch of shit from his time in Iraq," Harrison said. "He watched a lot of men die over there."

"I hadn't thought of that."

Across the room, Gabe reached the top of his route to cheers and was slowly lowered to the ground. A moment later, Sasha did the same.

She threw her fist in the air. "Climb like a girl!"

Vic watched while Jesse untied the rope from his harness, saw that he was furious with himself for falling.

"Don't worry about it, man," Eric said. "We all have off days—everyone except Rossiter, but he's not actually human."

"I heard that." Gabe showed Eric his middle finger.

And it dawned on Vic that every Team member here had risked his or her life trying to save others, and they did it as *volunteers*. Lexi had told her no one got paid to work for the Team, not even Megs.

A sense of emptiness crept into Vic's chest.

She'd never done anything to make a difference. She spent her days coming up with witty slogans so that companies could sell goods and services. She could argue that this helped businesses succeed and that that, in turn, meant jobs, but that wasn't the same thing as saving someone's child. It wasn't even close.

Eric walked over to her. "Are you sure you want to sit this out?"

Lexi was right behind him, out of breath, her face flushed from exertion. "You've got some of the best teachers in the country right here. Sasha and Eric got me started."

"Is my girl Vic going up?" Sasha called. "Count me in!"

Eric pinned her with his gaze and held out his hand. "Do you trust me, Victoria? Climbing is about two things: skill and trust. Skill can be taught, but you've got to have trust to get anywhere. I promise I won't let you fall."

Chapter Eleven

Vic got to her feet and took Eric's hand. "If I die..."

Eric grinned. "You won't die. You're going to have fun and go home amazed at how well you did."

Eric led her over to a part of the wall where no one was climbing. "We'll start with something super easy, and I'll go up with you."

While Lexi ran to get Vic a harness and a pair of climbing shoes, Eric and the others planned it out among themselves. Lexi would belay Vic while Austin belayed Eric. Sasha wanted in on it, so she drafted Rossiter to belay her.

Vic stepped into the harness, watching while Lexi showed her how to tighten it and make sure it was safe. Then Eric tied her into one end of the rope, and the next thing Vic knew, she was standing at the base of the rock wall, looking up at a bunch of brightly colored holds. "Oh, God."

"I'm going to be on one side of you and Sasha's going to be on the other. We'll coach you the entire way up, okay?"

"Okay." She tried not to sound afraid.

"Reach up for those two handholds, and lift your right foot onto that jug."

Vic did what Eric told her to do, her heart thrumming. She was a whole six inches off the floor now. "What next?"

His hand pressed against her lower back, pushing her hips toward the wall. "Keep your pelvis tucked in. You'll create a lot more work for yourself if your center of gravity is hanging out in space."

"Try to use your legs as much as possible," Sasha told her. "Women's legs are as strong as men's when you take body mass into account. It's our upper bodies that tend to be weaker. Let your legs do the work."

Vic did what they told her to do, the two of them following her up the wall, neither of them exerting much effort, while she was sweating and out of breath, her arms and shoulders soon exhausted.

"Let's just hang out here and rest for a minute," Eric said.

"Shake it out. Like this." Sasha let go with one hand, turned that shoulder away from the wall and shook her arm out, then did the same with the other side.

Vic tried to do what Sasha had done, but dizziness rushed over her when she saw how high she was. She grabbed onto the holds again, pressing her body against the rock wall, her eyes squeezed shut.

"I didn't know you were afraid of heights," Eric said.

"Neither did I!"

"Hey, it's okay. You're safe." Eric's calm voice cut through some of her panic.

"You can do this!" Lexi shouted. "You're doing better than I did my first time."

Vic found that hard to believe.

As usual, Sasha was nothing but sunshine. "Don't look down if it scares you. Your height on the wall doesn't mean anything. You could be five feet up or five hundred feet up, because even if you fall, all you're going to do is swing."

Vic looked over just in time to see Sasha let go. Her stomach dropped, but Sasha simply sat there in her harness, swinging in mid-air.

Sasha shrugged. "See? No problem."

Vic nodded, still trying to recover from her rush of vertigo.

Pull yourself together.

Eric and Sasha knew what they were doing. Lexi wouldn't let her fall. No one would let her get hurt.

She drew a breath. "Okay. I'm fine. Keep going."

She looked up, reached for the next hold and the next, doing her best to let her fear go, Eric and Sasha coaching her each step of the way.

"That's a ledge hold. Curl your fingers like this." Eric held out his hand to show her how to position her hand. "Perfect."

She was so focused on her movements and on the sound of Eric and Sasha's voices that she didn't realize how close she was to the top until her fingers hooked onto that last hold. She drew herself up on a rush of adrenaline to the sound of cheers and shouts. "Oh, my God! I did it!"

Eric chuckled. "You sure as hell did."

She let go, swung into his arms, and kissed him.

From the floor below, she heard Gabe say, "Who's getting married again?"

"I can't even open the door. My arms are noodles."

Eric opened the door, trying not to laugh as Victoria dragged herself through the front entrance of the inn and over to the elevator.

She pushed the button. "I am *not* taking the stairs."

"I'd say you've earned a free ride."

The Team had celebrated Taylor and Lexi's upcoming wedding and Vic's successful first day of climbing with dinner and drinks at Knockers. His city girl had climbed to the top of the wall not once but *three* times, the third time successfully managing a 5.6 route without coaching. Now, she was paying for it.

He'd given her an ibuprofen from the first aid kit in his truck, but it hadn't yet taken effect. "You should take advantage of that huge tub for a hot soak tonight, maybe pour in some Epsom salts."

"Mmm. God, that sounds perfect."

As soon as they entered her suite, she walked to the sofa and flopped onto the cushions. "That's it. I'm dead."

He couldn't help but laugh. "You can't die yet."

"I can't?"

"We have to finish the video. Tomorrow night is Central City."

"Oh, yeah." She sat up, got to her feet, and shuffled over to the table, still looking beautiful. "What kind of music would you like for the soundtrack?"

"Hey, the soundtrack is *your* idea. Couldn't we just plug in some of Taylor and Lexi's favorite songs?" He thought about that for a second. "Scratch that. Taylor likes country."

No way was he putting a country soundtrack to the only video he'd ever make.

She sat, opened his browser, and went to a site she obviously knew well. "They've got lots of stuff here."

They spent the next half hour sampling musical compositions, narrowing their choices down to two.

"I think this one will be easier to work with. Plus, it's got that emotional swell there toward the end. We can loop the beginning and put that during that last part of your mother's interview that always makes me cry."

"Let's do it."

She bought the music, downloaded it, and then started editing it, a process that seemed to take a fair amount of concentration, her brow knitted, her gaze fixed on the screen. Though Eric knew he *should* be paying attention to what she was doing, perhaps even making suggestions, he couldn't take his gaze off her face.

Did she have any idea how beautiful she was, how smart, how fun? How could she still be single? What was wrong with those big city men?

He'd watched her take on new challenges every day she'd been here, doing things she'd never done before, things that were completely outside her experience. She'd succeeded every time, surprising herself and earning everyone's respect.

Then there was the way she cared about people, especially those who were vulnerable. He'd seen her slip Rain another twenty for Bear tonight when she'd thought no one was looking. If she'd been a bitch to Bear, it wouldn't have mattered to Eric how beautiful she was. He wouldn't have been able to stand her.

So, yeah, it was safe to say that his attempt to put distance between the two of them was failing big time. He was aware of this—so aware, in fact, that he'd stopped by the county clinic to get tested for STIs and bought a fresh box of condoms. There were two in the aluminum carrying case in his wallet—and ten more in his first aid kit. Not that he was planning anything, but if events headed in that direction again, he didn't want to be left holding his dick in his hand.

"Okay, I think this will—"

Over on the coffee table, her cell phone buzzed, making her jump, irritation chasing away the fear that shot across her features.

She got to her feet.

Eric was really starting to hate her boss. "Ignore it."

"I can't." She retrieved her phone, checked the message. "The guy who's supposed to be covering for me is in over his head, and Abigail told me she'd give the project to someone else if I couldn't multi-task a little while on vacation. Those were her words exactly."

Fuck that.

"You didn't ask me, I know, but life is too short to put up with that bullshit. Unless you love what you're doing—and I know you don't—you need to quit and find a job you enjoy and a boss who respects you."

She tapped out a quick reply, then walked back to the table, cell phone in hand. "That's a nice thought, but what would I do?"

He drew her into his lap. "What do you love?"

She seemed flustered, either because of his question or because he was holding her. "Well ... um ... I don't know. I guess ... I *really* love to cook, and I'm good at it, too. But I don't want to start over and go to culinary school. Owning a restaurant is a lot of hard work."

Her scent washed over him, female and sweet, making him wish they could forget the video and get naked. Then again, she was leaving in four days, going back to the big city and her shitty job. What was he thinking? "Work doesn't feel like work if you love what you're doing."

"Does your job never feel like work?"

"Sometimes it does. I hate paperwork. There are days when it feels like I'm managing an adult daycare center and drowning in bullshit, but those days are rare. Most of the time, I feel incredibly grateful to make my living the way I do. As my mother says, 'You've got to choose the life you want to live, or something will choose you.'"

"Yeah, well, I thought I'd chosen." She gave a little laugh. "I got exactly what I wanted, and it wasn't what I wanted at all. The joke's on me, I guess."

"You can change your mind, you know. That's the cool thing about still being alive. There's time to change everything."

"No, not everything." She got to her feet, sat in her chair, and went back to work.

Vic put the finishing touches on the video, thanking the long list of people who'd given interviews, her mind far from the work her fingers were doing.

She should tell him. No, it wasn't that she was morally obligated to tell Eric. Some part of her *wanted* to tell him. After the closeness they'd had last night, a kind of intimacy that hadn't had anything to do with sex, she wanted him to understand, wanted him to care.

But, God, what if he reacted the way her dad and brother had? They'd blamed her for the whole thing. Her brother had even called her an idiot—a fucking idiot, actually. She hadn't talked to him since.

Uncertainty niggled at her, weakening her concentration.

"You spelled my last name wrong." Eric pointed to the computer screen. "It's got an 'e' on the end."

"Oh, sorry." She fixed the mistake. "What do you think?"

Eric leaned in and read aloud. "'With love to Lexi and Austin on your wedding day, from Hawke and Victoria.' You don't think that's too corny?"

"It's a wedding. It's supposed to be a little corny. Besides, you love Austin. I know you do. And I love Lexi. So it's not corny. It's the truth."

"When you put it like that …"

"Do you want to watch it through one last time?"

He rubbed his eyes. "Please, God, no."

She laughed. "How are you going to show this at the reception?"

"Belcourt is bringing a laser projector and a screen. He's going to handle setting up at the reception." A worried frown settled on Eric's face. "You really think they're going to like it?"

"They're going to love it. I know they will. It was an incredibly thoughtful idea. You did a wonderful thing."

"I didn't do it alone." He tucked a strand of hair behind her ear, his touch burning her cheek. It was the second time he'd done that since she'd been here. It was a simple gesture, but it felt caring and intimate. She liked it.

Tell him.

"Eric, I …" Her pulse spiked. "I'm not going to Central City. I'm just going to stay here and relax tomorrow night."

She got to her feet and went to refill her water glass, afraid those blue eyes of his would see through her.

"Does this have anything to do with those bastards in Buena Vista?"

"Yes." She turned on the faucet, let the water run, forgetting the glass in her hand. "I know they won't be there, but ..."

Just tell him.

He came up behind her, rested his big hands on her shoulders. "You know I would never let anyone hurt you, right?"

"Yeah." She turned off the water, set the glass down, not thirsty anyway. "It's not what you think."

Eric's voice was soft, reassuring. "I know someone hurt you. I don't know what he did, but I can tell it's still with you."

How could he tell that? How could he know?

She turned, almost in his arms, then pushed past him, walking to the sofa and sinking into the cushions. "God, I can't even ..."

He came to sit beside her, angling his body so that he faced her, his arm stretching across the back of the sofa behind her. "You don't have to tell me anything you don't want to tell me, but if you think telling me will help you, I'm here."

What did it matter anyway? She was leaving on Sunday.

She steeled herself, drew a breath. "I met Stewart in a night club just before Halloween. I was there celebrating with a coworker who'd just gotten a promotion. Some guy started hitting on me and wouldn't back off. Stewart came over and dragged the guy to the security desk. They threw the jerk out. I thought Stewart was a hero.

"I saw him again a couple of weeks later at a work mixer. We started talking. I thanked him for standing up to that idiot. He asked me out. He was good-looking and funny, and he'd protected me at the night club. So I said yes."

She fought to control her emotions, not wanting Eric to see her fall apart, which she did every time she talked about this. She was surprised she wasn't already in tears. Perhaps telling his mother just a few days ago was making it easier to tell him. "Our first few dates were incredibly romantic. He said all the right things, did all the right things. On our third date, we ended up at his house. The sex was really disappointing, but I figured it was just me. I've never had it as easy as Lexi."

"As easy with what?" He looked confused.

God, was he going to make her spell it out? "You know ... climaxing."

One dark eyebrow arched, disbelief on his face. "Really?"

Heat flooded her cheeks when she realized what he must be remembering. "Well, with one exception, I guess."

"Sorry. I didn't mean to take you off on a tangent. So you had a few dates with this guy, had sex with him, and it wasn't fireworks."

Now she'd come to the hard part, the part that still hurt.

"We'd been together for a few weeks when I came home from work to find him in my bed with a tall blond woman. I hadn't given him a key, but I was so shocked by seeing him having sex with her in *my* bed that it didn't occur to me he shouldn't even be there. The two of them didn't stop. They kept going and laughed when they saw me."

"How did the bastard get in?"

"The police say he'd duplicated my key while I was sleeping."

But that wasn't the worst thing he done—far from it.

*E*ric fought to keep his temper in check. Victoria didn't need his anger. What she needed was to be heard and understood. "What a son of a bitch!"

Okay, so he'd lost that battle already.

"He and his *lover* finished and walked out of my bedroom. The woman said, 'Oh, look at her face! She thought the two of you had something real.' She called me a stupid bitch and told me I'd never meant anything to Stewart."

"Stewart turned on my television, and on the screen ..." Her words faded into silence, tears filling her eyes.

"It's okay." Eric wanted to hold her, but he wasn't sure how she'd feel about that. "You're safe here with me."

She found her voice again, seeming to fight for every word. "He'd made a video ... of the two of us having sex. He'd made it without my knowledge or consent. It showed ... *everything*."

"*Jesus!*" That was not what Eric had been expecting her to say.

Tears spilled down her cheeks. "He told me the video was already online along with some photos and my contact information advertising my services as a call girl. If I wanted him to take it down, I needed to give him fifty thousand dollars. He told me that if I called the police and got him arrested, the tape and all my information would automatically go live on other sites around the world."

And it all made sense—what that guy had said to her in Buena Vista, the conversation Eric had overheard when she was talking with his mother, how she'd responded when he'd told her she was beautiful.

A lot of good it's ever done me.

Son of a bitch!

Eric had heard of men doing things like this—putting up revenge porn to get back at women who'd divorced or broken up with them. He was glad he already knew that this story ended with Stewart's ass sitting in prison. Otherwise, he'd be making plans to hunt the bastard down.

He did his best to keep the anger out of his voice. "Did you call the police?"

She shook her head, regret written on every feature of her face. "I panicked. I wasn't thinking straight. My phone started ringing almost right away. I got text messages and emails from men who said repulsive things. I was terrified that one of them would show up at the office or my front door. I was afraid my father or my boss would find out. So I promised Stewart I'd get him the money the next day."

She cast him a furtive glance, as if afraid to look into his eyes. "You probably think I'm an idiot, don't you?"

The self-doubt in her eyes put an ache in his chest.

"That wasn't your best move, but you're not an idiot. Nothing prepares a person for a situation like that."

"I felt so … *violated*. He lied to me. Every minute I was with him was a lie. Every kiss, every word he said—all lies. He used me—for sex, for money—and I fell for it. How could I have been so stupid?"

"Hey, now." Eric gave her hand another squeeze, wanting so badly to hold her. "You didn't *let* him do any of that. He's a predator. He played into your hopes and expectations. That's what criminals like him do. You couldn't have known that."

She sniffed, shrugged. "There were little signs. His attitude toward me went from hot to cold for no reason. He was vague about his job. The way he positioned himself during sex—he had to stay out of the way of the camera, didn't he?"

The image that flashed into Eric's head sickened him.

Christ.

Victoria reached for a tissue, wiped her eyes. "The next day, I called in sick, then changed my email address, my phone numbers, and the locks on my doors. I went to the bank and took the money out of my trust fund. Stewart told me to meet him at the Wicker Park fountain and reminded me that if I had him arrested, more stuff would go up online. He said a friend of his would be there to take the money from me. When I asked him how I'd recognize his friend, he just laughed and said the guy would recognize me. I knew then that he'd shown the tape and the images to his friends. But it was worse than that.

"When I got there, the man waiting for me was the same man who'd hit on me at the nightclub."

Chapter Twelve

Eric didn't like where this was going.

Tears filled her eyes again. "He walked up to me with a mean grin on his face, took the money, then looked me up and down and said he wished he'd had Stewart's job in this little caper because he would've loved to fuck me. I threw up in the bushes."

Eric felt his teeth grind.

The entire thing had been a setup from the beginning.

"A month or so later, I got an email from Stewart again. It turns out he knew my brother from rugby and had gotten my new email address from him. I clicked on the email, and there was the video again. He said it would go live unless I gave him two million six hundred dollars by the next afternoon."

"Where did he expect you to get that kind of money?" If someone tried to blackmail Eric, they'd be so screwed.

"That was the exact amount in my trust fund—information he'd gotten from my brother, who has never apologized, by the way."

What the hell was wrong with her brother?

"Did you pay that asshole again?"

"No. I got angry."

"Good."

"I realized it would never end as long as he thought he could get more money from me. I called my father and told him what had happened. He went crazy and shouted at me over the phone."

Now Eric understood why she wasn't close with her family—a brother who gave away her private information, a father whose first reaction to a predator committing a crime against her was to yell *at her*, and a mother who had apparently abandoned her for Italian men. "Didn't he do anything to help you?"

"Oh, yes, he did—when he finished yelling. He called a friend of his in the district attorney's office. They called the Chicago police, who worked with me to set up a sting. I took the money to a deli on the Riverwalk like Stewart told me to. This time, the woman showed up, the one I'd caught him having sex with at my condo. I was wearing a wire and got her on tape telling me that Stewart's having sex with me had just been a business transaction. I told her to tell him that I wouldn't pay them another dime. She said I would do whatever they told me to do. She said I should think of it as a tax on stupid."

Eric opened his mouth to say something supportive, but his temper got the better of him—again. "What a fucking bitch!"

"Police arrested her when she walked out of the deli. She fell apart and ratted out Stewart and the other guy. They had what they needed to arrest Stewart on a bunch of felonies—extortion, breaking into my apartment, nonconsensual dissemination of sexual images and some other stuff. They confiscated a bunch of flash drives, his cameras, and his computer and took the websites down. He got four years in prison, but he'll probably be out in two."

"Did you have to face him in court?" Eric could only imagine what a nightmare that must have been.

"No, thank God. He made a plea deal. I was afraid it was going to blow up in the newspapers, and then everyone would know. In Illinois, taping someone without their consent is considered a form of sexual assault, so the newspapers respected my privacy. I had to tell my boss just in case. She was more understanding than my father."

Well, that gave Eric one reason not to hate the woman.

"Stewart had always worn condoms, but I got tested for STDs anyway—twice. Thank God I was okay. But I had nightmares for months. I still do once in a while. I didn't feel safe at home, so I sold my condo and rented a place on the other side of town. I don't like being in public because I'm afraid someone will recognize me."

And now that had finally happened.

Shit.

"Every time my phone buzzes, I get a sick feeling. Even all these months later, some part of me thinks it's him."

So that's why she jumped every time her phone made a sound. It wasn't her boss. It was a post-traumatic response. "Ah, honey. God, I'm so sorry."

"I haven't been with anyone since then—no dates, not even a kiss ..." Her gaze shot to his, a blush rising in her cheeks. "Well, until you."

He could only imagine how hard it must be for her to trust men—or to trust herself—after that nightmare. "Kissing me brought it all back for you, didn't it?"

She shook her head. "It was the lens on your computer. I opened my eyes, and it was staring straight at me. My mind knew it wasn't recording, but I just..."

He understood now. "Your body reacted."

"Now you know. Do you think I'm an idiot?"

"Come here." He reached for her.

She slipped easily into his arms, rested her head on his chest.

And for a time, all he did was hold her.

Telling Eric the whole story had left Vic feeling drained, but also strangely free. Until tonight, the only person who'd known outside her own family was Lexi. Well, and his mother and Abigail. Given the way her father and brother had reacted, she'd been afraid to tell anyone else. She didn't want to be branded as the woman in the sex tape.

But Eric hadn't blamed her or berated her. There'd been no judgment in his eyes or in anything he'd said. He'd seemed genuinely sorry that this terrible thing had happened to her. He'd even gotten angry on her behalf.

God, that had felt good.

Now his cheek rested against the top of her head, both arms around her as if she were precious to him, as if he truly cared. Lexi had warned her he didn't play for keeps, but this felt real to her.

That's what you thought about Stewart.

Yes, but Stewart had deceived her, lied to her, deliberately misled her. Eric didn't have a deceptive bone in his body.

How she wished she could go back to that moment Sunday night when he'd been kissing her right here on this sofa. He'd made her come so fast, and they hadn't really been having sex. She would keep her eyes closed this time, and they wouldn't stop.

Then again, what was keeping her from picking up where they'd left off?

He's Austin's best friend.

Every time she came back to Scarlet, she'd see him. If he *did* meet someone and settle down, she'd see that, too. How would that make her feel?

She wouldn't like it, but she would hate it if she went back to Chicago without seeing where this attraction could carry them.

You made yourself a promise.

Yes, and, God in Heaven, it was time she broke it.

She turned her face to his, slid her fingers into his hair, and kissed him.

He did a quick little intake of breath, his body tensing, his lips answering hers, the contact sending a jolt of heat through her. All too soon, he broke the kiss. "You need to get some sleep. You've got a date with a pizza tomorrow morning."

She'd almost forgotten that. "Please stay."

He looked straight into her eyes, those blue irises dark. "I don't want to push you into anything you're not ready for."

She had only one answer to that. "I want you."

His body tensed again, but still, he kept his distance. He tugged on the front of his T-shirt. "I got pretty sweaty at the rock gym and haven't had a shower since."

"I like the way you smell—but if you want to shower, the walk-in shower in my bathroom is big enough for two." Then she remembered he'd taken a shower here once before. "Oh. You already know that."

Pulse skipping at the thought of what she was about to do, she stood and began to undress, taking off her tank top, then her bra, and then her shorts until she stood in front of him almost naked.

His gaze moved over her, his expression unreadable, a muscle tensing in his jaw. "Just so you know…I can see your panties."

"It's different if they're *on* me." What didn't he understand?

Then it struck her that maybe he didn't want to be with her. Maybe hearing about Stewart and the sex tape had turned him off. "If you're not interested, I—"

"Not interested?" In a heartbeat, he was on his feet. "Is that what you think?"

He didn't wait for her answer, his hand sliding into her hair, his lips coming down hard on hers. He kissed her slow and deep, his heat enfolding her, the things he was doing with his lips and tongue making her knees go weak.

God, no man on earth kissed like this.

He slowed the kiss, drew back from her, looked into her eyes. "Once we cross this bridge, there's no going back."

She finished the speech for him. "It's just sex. I know. It doesn't mean anything."

"Oh, but it does, Victoria." He touched his forehead to hers, his lips wet from kissing her. "This won't be a business transaction. It won't be casual. There won't be any cell phones or cameras or computers. It's going to be personal and real—just you and me. We're both going to remember it for the rest of our lives. Is that what you want?"

"*God, yes.*"

One corner of his mouth quirked in a grin. "Show me that shower."

She led him to the bathroom. "Voilà."

He yanked his T-shirt over his head, took his wallet out of his pocket, and pulled out a small aluminum case. "Condoms."

Then he reached for his fly.

"Let me." She reached out, unbuttoned his jeans and …

Oh. God!

He wasn't wearing underwear.

His erection sprang free of the denim, jutting upward from a nest of dark curls, the sight of it making her belly clench.

She grew wet just looking at him.

He shucked the jeans, a grin on his face. "You're staring."

She took him into her hand, making the muscles of his belly jerk. She stroked him from base to tip, aroused and intrigued by the velvet-hard feel of him. "That's only because you're so … *small.*"

He wasn't small at all, and he knew it.

He grinned, the heat in his eyes sending a shiver through her. "You know what they say. The best things come in small packages."

He reached past her into the shower and turned on the hot water.

*E*ric used the few seconds it took to set the water temperature to slow himself down, taking deep belly breaths. He remembered what she'd said—that it wasn't easy for her to come. Well, he was going to do his part to change that for her. "Let me know if this is too hot."

He turned around just in time to see her tuck her panties behind a stack of clean towels and might have teased her about it if his gaze hadn't landed on the perfection that was her ass. Then she turned to face him, and he stood there for a moment, dumbstruck by the sight of her—those full breasts with their dark nipples, her narrow waist and gently rounded belly, her full hips, the triangle of dark curls between her thighs.

"God, Victoria, you're … *beautiful.*" He held out both hands for her, drew her under the spray with him.

She reached for the soap. "Now I don't have to be jealous."

"Jealous?" What reason could she possibly have to feel jealous?

She smiled at him from beneath those long lashes. "I had a fantasy where I was your soap."

He laughed, spread his arms wide, offering himself to her. "I'm yours to lather."

She started with his chest, soapy hands sliding slowly over his wet skin, her fingers teasing his nipples until they were hard. Next, she moved down his belly, exploring his abs, lavishing special attention on his obliques, pure female desire on her face. Then she dropped to her knees before him, her soapy fingers cupping his balls and tickling his inner thighs before closing at last around his cock.

She stroked him from base to aching tip, soap making her hand glide easily over him. He fought to hold his hips still, willed his body to relax. But,

God, she was good at this. Unless she wanted to end things before they really got going...

He caught her wrists, drew her to her feet, trading places with her, water rinsing his body clean. He pried the soap from her hand, set it in its porcelain dish. "My turn."

She stood with her back to the spray, her breathing rapid, her skin flushed with arousal, her dark hair hanging in wet tendrils over her nipples.

He lifted the wet mass of her hair out of the way and wrapped an arm around her to steady her, then lowered his mouth to an already puckered nipple and indulged himself, sucking, nipping it with his teeth, tasting it with his tongue.

She gasped, then exhaled, a long shuddering breath, arching in his arms, her fingers catching in his hair. "*Eric.*"

He switched to the other breast, tugging on her nipple with his lips before drawing it into his mouth. Her head fell back on a moan, her body pliant in his arms. He slid his free hand over the silky curve of her hip to squeeze her ass, the feel of her leaving him drunk on lust. God, he wanted to be inside her, ached to bury himself in her.

But not yet. Not yet.

He drew away from her, turned her to face the wall, and spread her feet wide apart. He reached around to cup her with one hand, stroking and teasing her clit, the other hand playing with her nipples. She sagged against him, moaning, the sweet curves of her ass pressing against his thigh, her head resting on his chest.

Then he lifted the shower head out of its cradle and adjusted it from the Gentle Rain setting to Pulse. "You're not the only one who had fantasies."

Her gaze fixed on what he held in his hand. "Are you going to ...?"

"Yeah. I'm going to give you shower head." He grinned at his own stupid joke, then aimed the spray just *there*.

"Oh!" She cried out, one hand splayed against the tile wall, the other grabbing onto his forearm, her nails biting into his skin. "Oh ... *God.*"

"Does that feel good?"

Her answer was lost somewhere amid breathy moans.

He moved in closer, supported her with his body, using his free hand to press circles against her pubic mound just above her clit, keeping his pace steady. Already, she was close, her breathing now ragged, her thighs quivering.

She was so responsive, so innately sexual that it made Eric want to flay the assholes who'd enjoyed her sweet body without paying attention to the woman inside it.

"Ohgodohgod! Oh… *Eric!*" She came with a cry, her nails digging into his skin.

He stayed with her, waited until her body relaxed, then turned off the water and tucked the shower head back in its cradle, his dick so hard it hurt.

She sagged against him, still breathing hard.

He reached for a towel, wrapped it around her, grabbed the condom case. Then, because he knew she liked it, he scooped her into his arms and carried her to the bed.

*E*ric lowered Victoria to the bed and followed her down, settling his weight beside her, the hunger in his eyes making her breath catch. "*Victoria.*"

He took her mouth in an urgent kiss, and they rolled together across the bed, legs tangled, wet skin against wet skin. One big hand moved to cup and shape her breast, his thumb running lazy circles over her nipple, his erection prodding her belly. Heat shuddered through her, his touch rekindling the fire he'd just put out.

She ran her hands over the damp skin of his back and shoulders, savoring the hard feel of his muscles and the satin of his skin. Knowing what came next and eager to please him as much as he'd already pleased her, she slipped one hand between them and took hold of his cock.

He nudged his hips forward, thrusting into her grasp, the rocking motion of his body blatantly erotic. Then he withdrew his cock from her hand, whispering against her throat. "There's time for that later."

His words sent a pulse of excitement through her. She was used to being rushed, used to men who went straight from kissing to ramming. This felt like a luxury—lying on the bed with him, arousal on slow burn inside her once more, her body still weak from one of the most incredible orgasms of her life.

He kissed her throat, her clavicle, her breastbone, her breasts. He lavished attention on each nipple in its turn until she was senseless with pleasure. But he didn't stop there, his mouth blazing a path along the undersides of her breasts and down her belly until it felt like her skin was on fire.

She was burning, burning for him.

He raised himself up, crawling backward to the edge of the bed, his gaze fixed on hers. He got to his feet, grabbed her ankles, and pulled her slowly toward him. "Come here, honey."

Her heart gave a hard knock when she realized what he was doing. "Oh, no, you don't have to—"

"I want your taste in my mouth." He kissed her ankle, his eyes looking straight into hers. "I want your scent on my skin." He kissed her calf. "I want to make you scream."

Speechless, she watched as he dropped to his knees between her thighs and rested her feet on his shoulders, his fingers parting her. She heard—and felt—him exhale, his breath cool against the wetness there. She let her knees fall open, fully exposed, vulnerable in a way she hadn't been since …

Don't think about that.

Eric seemed to like what he saw. *"Jesus."*

She watched as he lowered his mouth to her and tasted her with a single, slow stroke of his tongue.

She sucked in a breath, reached for him, her fingers curling in his hair.

He moaned. "Mmm. You taste incredible."

Then he closed his mouth over her and sucked on her clit.

She cried out, shocked by sensations almost too good to bear, her hips jerking upward on their own. Oral sex had never felt like this before.

He laughed, those blue eyes of his looking up at her as he rested an arm across her hips to hold her in place. Then he did it again. And again. And again.

"That … feels … so … *good.*"

It felt better than good. It felt crazy, sweet, excruciating.

He slid a finger inside her, then two, stroking her, fanning flames that were already burning out of control. She moaned, twisted, her fingers tightening in his hair. She was lost in sensation, her mind beyond conscious thought as he tasted her, teased her, tormented her with lips and tongue and fingers. She twisted, arched, holding on by a thread, her eyes squeezed shut, her body ablaze.

The flames grew brighter and brighter—and then exploded.

"Oh … God … *Eric!*" She heard herself cry out, white hot pleasure engulfing her, consuming her in a scorching wave of bliss.

For a time, she laid there, aware of nothing but the gentle lapping of his tongue and the cinder glow in her blood, her body floating somewhere between earth and oblivion. Never in her life had she felt so replete, so completely satisfied. She hadn't even known pleasure on that scale was possible.

She opened her eyes for a moment and discovered that she'd thrown an arm over her face, her other hand clenched so tightly in the bedcover that she consciously had to release her fingers.

She opened her eyes again and saw Eric get to his feet.

He gave her a soft smile. "Welcome back, beautiful."

She opened her eyes for the third time, saw him tearing open a condom wrapper with his teeth. He rolled the condom over the length of his cock, then stretched himself over her, settling his hips between her thighs.

"Are you sure you want this?" he asked.

Oh, God, did she ever. "*Yes.*"

He reached down to guide himself, entering her with a single, perfect thrust. Oh, but it felt good, her body ultra-sensitive from having come twice already, his cock stretching her, filling her, arousing her again.

Again?

But she'd *never* …

"You are *so* wet." His eyes drifted shut, an expression of torment on his face as he began to move inside her.

Oh, God, it was sweet, the slippery friction making her ache.

He moved slowly at first, letting the rhythm build until he was driving into her hard and fast, his cock stroking some secret place inside her, each thrust sweeter than the last. She moaned, tightening her legs around his waist, her hands reaching down to clench the shifting muscles of his lower back.

Faster, harder.

She pressed her heels into the clenching muscles of his ass, her hunger building to a third peak so quickly that all she could do was cry out. "I can't …!"

She buried her face into the strong curve of his shoulder, moaned out her pleasure against his skin, climax washing through her once more. But he was right behind her, shuddering in her arms as he came.

*E*ric tossed the condom and washed up in the bathroom, unable to keep the stupid smile off his face. He felt happy, almost giddy, and more than a little off balance. He didn't know what it was about Victoria that got to him; he was just glad it did.

He walked back to the bed and found her in a sex coma beneath the blankets, her dark hair a damp, tangled mass. He crawled under the covers beside her and drew her into his arms, contentment warm behind his breastbone.

She lifted her head, looked accusingly up at him. "You're looking smug."

He couldn't help it, a grin taking over his face again. "I'm really sorry it's so hard for you to come."

Chapter Thirteen

Soft lips brushed Vic's forehead. "Hey, city girl, it's time to wake up."

She didn't want to wake up. She was so blissfully relaxed, so warm, so comfortable right where she was, Eric's arms around her, her face pressed against his chest. She snuggled deeper into him and let herself drift.

He chuckled. "I guess Caribou Joe will never learn how to make better pizza."

Vic sat bolt upright. "Oh, my God. I forgot."

"It's okay. You've still got ten minutes to get there."

She gaped at Eric, horrified. "Ten minutes?"

The clock on the nightstand said 8:50.

"Damn." She scrambled out of bed, dashed naked into the bathroom, and stared in horror at her reflection. She'd fallen asleep with wet hair and looked like she'd survived a tornado. Or maybe she was a reincarnation of Medusa with snakes on her head.

Eric leaned against the door jamb, gloriously naked, the sight of his body like a jolt of caffeine with a side of estrogen. "Brush your hair, wash your face, get dressed, and let's go. You're in Scarlet. No one cares if your hair isn't perfect."

Why, oh, why had she agreed to make pizza for Joe when she could be spending the morning in bed with Eric?

"Okay, fine." She grabbed her brush, forced it through her hair, her sore arm muscles protesting. "I wish I could take a shower."

"You just had a shower."

"But I smell like sex."

Eric closed his eyes and inhaled, his cock growing longer, harder. "This whole room smells like sex."

Doing her best to ignore the now fully erect hunk of a man who stood nearby, she finished brushing her hair and examined the results in the mirror. The side she'd slept on was flatter than the other, giving her a lovely lopsided look. She fished through her makeup bag for a ponytail holder. Typically, she only wore her hair like this if she was going to the gym, but extreme situations called for extreme measures.

"Cute," he said. "I like it."

"Are you just going to stand there with a hard-on, watching me?" It was distracting, to say the least. After last night, she couldn't look at him without thinking of fucking him. Heat flared to life between her thighs, making her wet.

He came up behind her, grasped her hips, his gaze meeting hers in the mirror, invitation and a hint of mischief in his blue eyes. "What else should I be doing?"

Me! Do me!

She wanted to shout the words but didn't. "We don't have time for that. Do we?"

He held up an unopened condom. "Want to find out how fast you can come?"

She had to be crazy. "*Yes.*"

He tore open the condom, rolled it over his erection, then nudged himself into her, their moans mingling as he buried himself all the way. He reached around to stroke and tease her, his cock moving inside her with forceful, deep thrusts.

Victoria could see it all. The hunger on his face. His cock as it disappeared inside her up to his balls, then slid out again, the condom glistening and wet. His fingers as they teased and stroked her clit. His other hand as it cupped and shaped her breast. The pleasure on her own face.

The sight was wild, primal, erotic—and, *oh*, it turned her on.

He kissed her shoulders, nipped the side of her throat. "*Vicki.*"

She came hard and fast, pleasure as sweet and pure as a sunrise washing through her, making her moan out his name. "*Eric.*"

He grinned at her in the mirror, still inside her. "That was less than two minutes."

"Really?"

"Really." He grasped her hips and drove into her hard. "Bend down. I've wanted to fuck you from behind since that day on the boat."

She did as he asked, bending over till her breasts touched the counter, aroused to see him so turned on. He pounded himself into her, claiming his own orgasm, the intensity on his face as he came making her heart thud.

He sank forward, catching the bathroom counter with one big hand to support his weight. "Damn, woman. You blow my mind."

She felt a thrill to hear him say that. Somehow, she knew he meant it.

Then he pulled himself up and withdrew from her, giving her ass a light slap as he turned to toss the condom in the trash. "Better hurry up. We've got a minute to get there."

One minute?

"We can do this." She washed and moisturized her face, her heart so light she felt like singing. She put her mascara and lip gloss in her handbag—she could put them on in Eric's truck—then hurried to dress, throwing on a T-shirt and jeans.

A minute later, she and Eric climbed into his pickup truck.

"Joe won't care if we're a few minutes late." Eric backed out of the driveway, waving to Rose, who sat on her front porch in a white robe, drinking from a porcelain teacup. "Mornin'."

"Hey, Rose." Vic waved, too. "He really *did* spend the night last night."

Rose looked delighted. "It was just a matter of time."

Eric kicked the truck into gear and headed down the street, a grin on his face. "Well, you just gave the whole town something to talk about."

They arrived at Knockers a few minutes later. It was strange to see the place empty and quiet, no band on the stage, no one on the climbing wall or dance floor, no one playing pool.

Joe met them just inside the door. "Hey, Victoria, Hawke. Lexi's already here. Thanks for coming. I've got all your ingredients laid out in the kitchen."

Joe led them toward the back, where they found Lexi chatting with a handful of kitchen staff, who were busy with the day's prep.

Lexi smiled when she saw them and hurried over to give Vic a hug, a questioning look in her eyes, her gaze flitting to Eric and back. "I told Austin I wouldn't miss this for the world—a chance to taste Chicago-style pizza again. He'll be by later."

Vic gave Lexi the answer she wanted in a smile. "I hope it turns out well."

Then a giant of a man stepped forward. His head was bald, but he had a bushy red beard over which he wore a hairnet, its loops over his ears. "I'm Rico, Joe's kitchen manager and head cook. I hear you think our pizza sucks."

Why hadn't she kept her mouth shut about the pizza? "I didn't say it sucked."

"Let's make it better," Joe said.

Joe handed them all hairnets and aprons. "If you're going to be in my kitchen, you've got to follow my rules, and, yes, that means you, too, Hawke."

Vic slipped the hairnet over her ponytail, trying to gather her thoughts. She'd never cooked under pressure before, and she didn't want to make Joe sorry he'd come in early. "We'll need a big mixing bowl, a rolling pin, two deep-dish pizza pans, and a big pot to cook the sauce in."

Rico reached up with one hand and took down a big sauce pan from a hook. "This ought to work for the sauce."

"Perfect." She set the pot on a cold burner, only too aware that everyone was watching her.

What business did she have giving a cooking lesson to a successful restaurateur and professional cook? She wasn't a professional. She just liked to cook.

"The secret to great deep-dish pizza is in the dough." She separated the ingredients for the sauce from those she'd use in the dough. "If it's not done right, you can tell. The sauce is important, too, but you can cheat in a pinch, use sauce from a jar, and still have a good pizza. You can't cheat with the dough. The secret ingredients are cornmeal, butter, and lots of olive oil."

They started with the dough, which needed a good hour to rise, Rico joining her in measuring out flour, salt, sugar, butter, warm water, and yeast. The moment her hands were busy, her nerves vanished, cooking with friends chasing away her doubts.

This was *fun*.

*E*ric watched while Victoria showed Rico and Joe how she made pizza, he and Taylor, who had finally shown up, acting with Lexi as official taste-testers.

Hey, it was a tough job, but someone had to do it.

Victoria's enthusiasm was palpable, and Eric found it hard to take his eyes off her. Even with a hairnet on her head, she was the most beautiful woman he had ever known. There was a glow about her that hadn't been there when she'd arrived in Scarlet, the happiness on her face shooting straight to his heart. Was it self-centered of him to hope that at least some of that happiness was his doing?

Knock it off.

Yes, they'd had an incredible night together, but that wasn't reason for him to lose his head. She was leaving on Sunday. She would get on a plane and fly back to Chicago, and he wouldn't see her again for a long time. He needed to enjoy the time he had with her and just let the rest of it go.

Besides, even if Victoria lived in Scarlet, that didn't mean the two of them would end up together. In his experience, most women liked the idea of hooking up with a firefighter only when they were thinking with their hormones. The reality—six to eight days each month spent sleeping alone, trying to plan a life with someone who was almost always on call, the very real risk of injury and death on the job—was much less sexy and a lot more difficult. Hell, half the men who worked for him were divorced.

And what the *hell* was he thinking anyway? Did he genuinely want to be in a serious relationship with her, a woman he'd known for a week?

"Hey, Hawke," Taylor called from across the room, apparently not for the first time. "You deaf? Check this out."

Eric went over to see what Taylor was looking at and found a Class K fire extinguisher with no pressure. "Hey, Joe, you need to get this fire extinguisher serviced. It won't do you a damned bit of good if that fat fryer goes up. Also, it shouldn't be back here behind all these mops and buckets. I could give you a citation for that."

But he wouldn't—not today.

Joe took it in stride. "Shit. Right. Sorry."

"That's what you get for letting the fire chief into the kitchen," Rico joked.

Eric drew out his cell phone, grateful to have something to think about besides Victoria. "I'll call the firehouse and have someone pick this one up and bring you a new one. I can't have my favorite brewpub burning down."

Okay, so it was the only brewpub. So what?

"Thanks, man, I appreciate it."

After the pizzas had gone into the oven, they all pitched in to clean up so that the kitchen crew could finish their lunch prep, then sat together at a table near the bar, Eric doing his best to ignore feelings he couldn't seem to control.

His empty stomach growled. "If that pizza tastes half as good as it smells, she'll have outdone you, Rico."

Whatever else you could say about Victoria, the woman could cook. It was clear to him that she hadn't been following a recipe, but going from memory, even improvising at times, guided by taste alone.

Rico laughed. "I'm willing to concede defeat when I'm good and truly beaten. Where did you take cooking classes?"

Victoria shrugged. "I haven't taken any classes. I really love to cook, so I watch a lot of cooking shows and read a lot of cookbooks."

Rico's brows shot up toward his bald dome. "You've got natural talent."

"Talent? Ha. Right." She brushed off his compliment. "How about you?"

"I got my associate degree in culinary arts while I was doing time."

"Doing time? You mean in prison?" The question was casual, but Eric saw a flash of fear in her eyes.

She was thinking of that bastard Stewart and wondering what Rico had done.

Rico nodded. "Best thing that ever happened to me. It straightened my ass out and taught me a skill. When I got out, Joe gave me a job."

"Must've been drunk," Joe grumbled, his gaze on a printout of the restaurant's staff schedule for the upcoming week.

Eric asked the question Victoria was too polite to ask, wanting her to feel at ease again. "What were you in for, Rico? Stealing cars or some shit?"

"Yeah. Stealing cars and selling the parts."

Relief came over Victoria's face. "Why did you decide to study cooking?"

"You ever taste prison food?" Rico asked.

Victoria shook her head. "That bad, huh?"

"You don't even want to know."

The little timer Rico had brought with him dinged. He turned it off, got to his feet, a wide grin on his face. "Here we go."

He and Victoria disappeared into the kitchen, while Joe got up and walked to the bar, where he filled a pitcher with beer.

"Help me with these glasses?" he asked Eric and Taylor. "Unless you'd rather skip the beer."

That had both of them on their feet.

"Free beer, and it's not yet noon," Taylor said. "It's a good day."

By the time Victoria and Rico returned with the sliced pizzas, the beer had been poured out and the table set with plates, forks, and napkins. Rico quickly served, lifting thick, cheesy slices onto plates, making sure that everyone who wanted a piece got one.

Joe cut a bite off his slice. "Now for the moment of truth."

Everyone watched while he popped it into his mouth and chewed.

"Breathe, Victoria," Eric said.

She looked nervous as hell, both hands raised to her lips as if she might just decide to close her eyes right now and pray.

Joe's brows came together in a frown, his head nodding furiously up and down. His gaze met Victoria's. "Fantastic. Rico, man, what do you think?"

Rico had sauce on the corners of his mouth. "Best pizza I've ever had, boss."

The relief and happiness on Victoria's face made Eric smile.

She turned to him. "What do you think?"

He took a bite, the tang and spice exploding across his tongue, the thick crust both chewy and crisp. "Wow."

That's all he could manage before a second bite found its way onto his fork and into his mouth and then a third and a fourth.

Joe laughed. "I think he likes it."

Taylor turned to Lexi, spoke with his mouth full. "Now I understand why you complain so much."

A horrified look came over Lexi's face, her gaze darting to Rico and then Joe. "I do *not* complain."

"Yes, you do," Eric and Taylor said at the same time.

"It's okay, Lexi," Joe said, a smile somewhere beneath his beard. "You're getting married in a couple of days, so I'll let you off the hook. Also, you're right. This is a lot better than what we serve. I'm not sure you can even compare the two. Victoria, thanks for taking the time this morning. It's settled. Your meals and drinks are on the house for the rest of your stay in Scarlet. If you ever need a job…"

Everyone laughed.

"Hey, I'm not kidding."

The smile on Victoria's face seemed to light up the world. "Thanks, Joe."

While Joe and Rico started strategizing with Victoria about how they could add Victoria's recipe to the menu, everyone else feasted, until there was only one slice left.

"Who gets the pig slice?" Eric asked, tempted to take it himself.

Victoria's head whipped around. "Can we please save it for Bear?"

Her kindness hit Eric right in the chest. "Sure. Great idea."

Taylor leaned in and spoke for Eric's ears only. "I hear she's not going with us to Central City tonight. I don't like leaving her behind."

"She has her reasons." Eric hoped he could change her mind.

Vic sat on a bench in an aspen glade behind the inn, Lexi beside her, a nervous knot in her stomach.

"It's going to be okay. Austin is not going to blame you or think you're a slut."

"Are you sure?"

Lexi laid her hand on Vic's arm. "I know him better than anyone. Yes, I'm sure. Not everyone is as big of a jerk as James or your dad."

That much was true.

They'd been on their way out of Knockers when Eric had asked Vic to change her mind and come with them to Central City.

Austin had piled on. "If it has anything to do with that guy in Buena Vista, just know that casinos have state-of-the-art security. Nothing will happen to you there. Besides, didn't we have your back last time?"

She'd agreed to go if—and only *if*—Austin still wanted her to come along once he knew the truth. But she didn't have it in her to tell the story again, so Eric had volunteered. Now, he stood in the driveway, telling Austin about the most horrible experience of her life. She couldn't see them, which was a good thing because she'd be trying to analyze Austin's facial expressions and body language and feeling terribly self-conscious.

Lexi lowered her voice. "We're finally by ourselves. What's going on between you and Eric? I've been *dying* to hear."

Vic opened her mouth to tell Lexi that she had no idea what was going on between them apart from amazing, mind-blowing sex just as Eric and Austin walked around the side of the house headed their way. "That was fast."

Austin's gaze caught hers, and she could see he was angry.

Her pulse skipped, a little trill of fear sliding through her.

He sat down beside her. "I am so sorry about the things that bastard did to you. He's lucky he's locked up where Hawke and I can't get to him. I swear by everything holy that if anyone bothers you tonight, Hawke and I will make him eat his own balls. I'll understand if you still don't want to go, but the best revenge is to enjoy your life again while that sack of shit rots in prison."

Tears welled up in Vic's eyes. "And you won't be embarrassed if something like what happened at the gas station happens again?"

Austin shook his head. "How some asshole behaves can only embarrass him."

Vic smiled, wiped her tears away. "Lexi picked a good guy."

Eric knelt down in front of her, sunglasses hiding his eyes. "Does that mean you're coming with us, city girl?"

Vic nodded. "Yes."

And just then, a wonderful, wild, and crazy idea came to her.

Oh, this was going to be fun.

Chapter Fourteen

Eric drove from his cabin to the inn, fidgeting with his damned bow tie. He knew he hadn't gotten it right, but then he'd never worn a bow tie before. He was into jeans and T-shirts, not Ralph Lauren. But if Lexi and Austin wanted to play *Casino Royale* and blow a bunch of money on food, booze, and gaming, he would dress up and go with them—and he wouldn't complain.

He pulled into the inn's long driveway, parking in the area reserved for family and friends, double checking to make sure the condom case was in his trouser pocket. Rose and Kendra sat together at a table on the back porch, the two of them bent over Rose's tarot cards, a bottle of wine and two glasses sitting between them. They stopped talking when they saw him, smiles on their faces.

Rose wolf-whistled at him. "Victoria won't be able to resist you."

"Don't you look pretty?" Kendra teased.

Bob opened the back door, rubbing a hand over his bare, hairy chest, a beer mug in his hand. "I thought the wedding was Saturday. Should I get dressed?"

"Hey, Bob."

Bob pointed with his thumb. "They're all waiting by the guest elevator."

Eric walked through the house and out the door that led to the main entrance hall, and stared. "Damn. You lot clean up nice. Moretti, I almost don't recognize you. Lexi, Britta, Win—you look gorgeous."

Lexi was living up to her nickname—Sexy Lexi—her red hair in a fancy updo, her body sheathed in a short, silky dress of white with silver beading. Britta wore a dress of shimmering purple, her hair swept up in a twist, while

Winona looked amazing in a long spaghetti strap dress of dark green satin, her shoulder-length dark hair pulled into a stylishly messy bun. But something was wrong.

Eric looked down at himself, then at Taylor, Moretti, and Belcourt. "Why is my tuxedo jacket white and yours are black? I'm not the bride."

"Thank God." Austin shrugged. "Some kind of mix-up, I guess."

"Where's Victoria?"

"She texted to say she'll be down in a minute," Lexi said.

Eric made his way over to Taylor and gave him an update, keeping his voice low. "I called the head of security at the casino and explained our concerns. He told me that any man who accosted her would be escorted out. We're supposed to check in when we get there. I'd like to do it without Vicki knowing."

Austin arched a brow. "So it's Vicki now?"

Belcourt walked over. "Is Victoria in some kind of trouble? Does she have a stalker or something?"

Shit. He'd overheard.

"Or something," Eric answered.

But Moretti had heard Belcourt. "Vic has a stalker?"

"What about Vic?" Britta asked.

Lexi glared at Eric and Taylor. "Don't say anything, okay? Just watch out for her. After what happened in Buena Vista, she wasn't going to come tonight, but Eric and Austin changed her mind."

Moretti's gaze went hard. "Any man who tries to fuck with her is going to have to go through us."

Winona looked out the window. "The limo's here. Wow. It's huge."

Then the elevator car began to move, heading up.

For some reason, Lexi looked over at Eric, a little smile on her lips.

"Do you know something I don't?" he asked.

She got a wide-eyed, innocent look. "Me?"

The elevator was moving again, coming down this time. It reached the ground floor, the doors sliding open with a *ding*.

Victoria stepped out.

Eric's heart knocked against his breastbone, and he stared. *"Jesus."*

She was wearing it, *that* dress—the tiny black one he'd seen in her closet—and damned if she didn't look good enough to eat.

"Wow." That was Moretti.

From behind him, he heard Belcourt. "Hoka hey."

The dress wasn't low cut, and it wasn't any shorter than Lexi's or Britta's. It even had long sleeves. It just wasn't really *there.*

Made of whisper-light translucent fabric scattered with black beading, it looked as if it were painted on, a sheer, shimmering second skin. He could see her belly button, the curve of her hips, the dark line of her cleavage. The beading was dense enough over her breasts and those lovely female parts between her legs to conceal them from view, but his mind was happy to fill in the blanks.

"You are beautiful." He held out a hand to her.

"Thanks. You look pretty amazing yourself."

It was only then he noticed the loose curls in her hair, the strappy three-inch heels on her feet, and the vulnerability in her eyes.

"That looks so good on you. I love it!" Lexi motioned with her finger for Victoria to turn around. "I want to see the back."

Victoria did a slow turn, and Eric felt the ground shift beneath his feet. The back was very low cut, exposing silky skin, thick beading hiding her amazing ass.

God in heaven.

She frowned at him. "What's wrong with your tie?"

Eric had forgotten he was even wearing a tie. "I'm not very good with these."

"I emailed instructions," Lexi said.

"Obviously, I didn't read them."

While Victoria re-tied Eric's tie, the others walked out to the limo. "I thought firemen were supposed to be good with knots."

"I'm better with hoses."

"Is that supposed to be sexy?" She pretended his lame joke hadn't *almost* made her laugh, a smile tugging at her glossy lips.

He shrugged. "Those hoses are big and hard and tough to handle."

"Speaking of tough to handle, I want to show you something." She stepped out of the view of the open door, Eric helpless to do anything but follow.

Then she lifted the gown to reveal …

No panties.

"Holy shit." The breath left his lungs, blood rushing straight to his groin.

How in God's name was he supposed to survive the next few hours?

Austin raised his champagne glass as the limousine started to roll. "To good friends and good times."

Most of the time when people made toasts, the words just felt like a formality, but Vic felt these words in her heart. "Good friends and good times!"

She was so lucky to be here, to be a part of this, the darkness of months of fear and isolation fading a little more each day. Austin was right. She needed to live her life to the fullest and forget about that bastard. She couldn't let what he'd done to her steal her happiness any longer.

She sipped the champagne, the bright taste and bubbles making her smile.

"How does the champagne rate, city girl?"

"Mmm. It's wonderful." It wasn't comparable to a true champagne from Reims, France, but it was still tasty.

They sipped champagne, talking and joking with one another, Vic only too aware of the beautiful man who sat beside her, holding her hand, his thumb caressing her knuckles. He looked like a movie star, the bright white of his tuxedo jacket a delicious contrast to his tanned skin and dark hair. He even smelled good, something dark and spicy mixing with the clean scent of his skin and driving her crazy.

She squirmed in her seat, an ache between her thighs that wouldn't go away. If only they'd had ten minutes alone together before it had been time to go. The heat in his eyes when he'd seen she wasn't wearing panties had aroused her so much she'd wanted to fuck him right there.

The idea to go all out on the hair and leave off her panties had come to her the moment she'd decided to go. She'd felt almost giddy getting dressed, excited by the idea of surprising him. This was something that the old

Victoria, the pre-Stewart Victoria, might have done. The look on his face when she'd stepped out of the elevator had made it more than worth the effort, but the real payoff would come tonight.

She couldn't wait.

They followed a winding two-lane highway through the mountains, the breathtaking scenery offering some distraction from her hormones. "You never run out of beauty in this state, do you?"

He kissed her temple. "Not when you're around."

After what must have been a half-hour drive, they arrived at a little town that looked like it had escaped from the set of a Hollywood western. Historic buildings with false fronts stood along narrow, winding streets, interspersed with buildings of rough-cut, quarried stone.

"There's the Central City Opera House." Lexi pointed out the window. "And that's the Teller House, famous for the Face on the Barroom Floor."

"Face on the Barroom Floor?"

"A guy painted a woman's face on the barroom floor." Eric shrugged. "That's it."

"Oh." It sounded kind of cool, really.

A few minutes later, the limousine pulled up in front of the Grand Palace Casino. Though it was obvious the place had been built relatively recently, the architect had tried to make it blend in with the rest of the town, an old-fashioned façade sitting in front of a newish five-story brick building.

The driver opened the door, and one by one they climbed out, Eric and Vic last.

Eric whispered in her ear. "Try not to flash anyone—except me."

She took advantage of the moment alone with him to lift her dress once more, her legs slightly spread this time. "That's all you get till we're home."

His brows drew together, and he gave a pained little moan. "You are cruel."

They followed the others inside, Eric's hand resting on the small of her back.

The interior was more opulent than Vic had imagined, with wooden parquet floors, luxurious oriental carpets, a grand staircase with polished wooden balustrades, crystal chandeliers, colorful stained glass windows, brass fixtures, and antique-looking furniture upholstered in deep red velvet brocades.

They all "oooed" and "ahhhed" about the place, except for Moretti.

"Paid for by people who don't understand the laws of probability," he said.

"I'm going to run to the restroom," Eric said to Austin.

Austin gave him a nod, then walked up to the front desk, where two men in black tuxedos welcomed them. "I'm—"

Vic cut him off. "I'm Victoria Woodley. The Taylor-Jewell party is here. We've got a reservation for eight in the VIP Club."

"Yes, Ms. Woodley. Right this way."

Lexi and Austin gaped at her.

She smiled. "This is my treat. It's part of my wedding gift to you. Just enjoy yourselves tonight. I've taken care of everything."

She would have paid by phone if she hadn't come with them, but she was glad she had changed her mind. Now she could enjoy their reactions.

She started to follow their host, but Austin caught her arm and drew her aside. "The VIP Club? Are you serious? The deposit for that is *huge*."

"This is so sweet of you, Vic, but we can't let you do this."

"It's already done. Besides, it's not that much." She took Lexi's hand. "You're my best friend, the only person who has stuck by me through thick and thin. Let me do this for you. You know I can afford it."

Lexi got tears in her eyes. "You are the best friend ever."

"Stop that before you ruin your mascara. Besides, *you* are the best friend ever."

And so the matter was settled.

Eric caught up with her just as they reached a beautiful elevator with polished brass panels on the doors. He leaned down and whispered in her ear, "Are you kidding me? The VIP Club? Those two must have spent a fortune on this. Jesus!"

"It's exciting, isn't it?"

Eric held Victoria's hand as they walked with Taylor and Lexi toward the blackjack tables. Moretti was locked in a grudge match with the slot machines, while Winona and Belcourt were playing poker, Britta watching over Belcourt's shoulder.

"Every man in this room is looking at Lexi and Vic," Austin said to Eric in a quiet voice. "They've been staring all night."

"Can't say I blame them." As long as they kept a respectful distance and didn't make the women uncomfortable, Eric wouldn't have to punch anyone.

Lexi giggled. "You're just imagining it."

No, they weren't.

Taylor wrapped his arm around her shoulder. "You're tipsy."

Hell, they were all buzzed. They'd had wine with their prime rib dinner, the men topping that off with cognac. Now the champagne flowed freely.

How much had this cost Taylor and Lexi anyway? Eric was afraid to ask.

They sat down at the blackjack table.

The dealer, a young woman with short dark hair and a friendly face, greeted them. "Are you all playing, or is it just the gentlemen?"

Lexi sat and plopped the hundred dollars worth of chips they'd each been given as VIPs onto the green felt. "Deal me in."

Austin swept the chips into his hand and placed them in her palm. "Hang on, sweetheart. That's not how you play this game."

Victoria stood behind Eric's chair. "I'm just watching. Thanks."

"Don't you want to blow a hundred bucks of Taylor and Lexi's hard-earned money?" he asked her. "I know I do."

She just smiled, a hint of mischief in those brown eyes.

Damn.

All evening, desire for her had been smoldering in his belly, need for her coiled around the base of his spine, anticipation making his sexual hunger sharper. It was a sweet form of torture, a kind of merciless foreplay, walking around the posh VIP Club, the image of her in that dress without panties burned into his brain. He laughed and joked and talked, but his thoughts were wrapped entirely around the things he would do to her.

She would pay for this. Oh, yes, she would.

The dealer gave them each two cards, sliding them deftly out of the shoe. Eric got a king and a five—a hard fifteen. Austin got a pair of sixes, while Lexi got two fours.

Eric and Lexi both motioned for the dealer to hit them, while Taylor surrendered, automatically losing half his bet.

"What's the matter, Taylor? Afraid you're going to lose?"

Eric's next card was a seven. "Damn."

He'd busted, losing ten bucks.

"What's the matter, Hawke? Can't count to twenty-one?" Taylor joked.

But Lexi got an ace and beat the house for twenty bucks.

Victoria leaned in, her scent surrounding him, her voice a warm purr in his ear. "You seem a little distracted."

Hell, yeah, he was distracted. He didn't even have to touch her for his pulse to race. He could *feel* her beside him, his senses full of her—the satin glide of her hair as it slipped over her shoulder, the light in her eyes when she looked at him, the glossiness of those lips when she smiled, the maddening sweetness of her scent.

"Keep it up, honey, and see what it gets you," he whispered.

He busted on his next hand, too, and the next, while Lexi continued her winning streak, and Austin lost as often as he won. And so it went for most of an hour until they'd rotated dealers twice. In the end, Eric had lost all but one five-dollar chip, Austin had more or less broken even, and Lexi had somehow won a hundred bucks.

"Beginner's luck," Taylor teased, handing the dealer a tip.

Lexi looked affronted. "Clearly, you guys have no clue how to play blackjack. Want to try roulette? There's no skill involved."

That made Taylor laugh. "Hawke, I think we've just been insulted."

Chuckling, Eric got to his feet and took Victoria's hand. "Easy come, easy go. At least it wasn't my money."

"Sorry you lost it all," she said.

"It's your fault." He ducked down and brushed his lips against hers, breathing in her scent. "I can't quit thinking about you."

"Good."

They played roulette for a while, Eric watching Victoria lose most of her chips. Then they tried the craps table, where Taylor crashed and burned.

"Taxes on the casinos' profits go to fund state parks and wilderness preservation. So I'm paying my own salary—sort of," he said.

"Trying to make yourself feel better about *losing?*" Eric asked.

Moretti rejoined them. "Hey, I won twenty bucks. You guys out of chips yet?"

"I'm not," Lexi bragged. "I won a hundred dollars at blackjack."

Then a cheer went up at the poker table, and Belcourt and Winona got to their feet, smiles on both of their faces.

Britta applauded. "Way to go, Win!"

"I beat you! I finally beat you." Winona said. "I beat the genius."

Belcourt wasn't taking it hard, a smile on his face. "Well done, little sister, but, hey, don't forget your chips."

They had dessert and coffee back in the dining room, cashed out their chips, and then it was time to head downstairs, where the limo was waiting to take them back to Scarlet. One of the hotel staff walked over and handed Victoria a black check holder.

She opened it, signed some kind of receipt, and handed it back to him, but not before Eric caught a glimpse.

Eight thousand nine hundred dollars and change.

She had paid for this?

What a Victoria thing to do. She'd paid for it, and she hadn't made a big deal about it. She'd even let him believe Taylor and Lexi were footing the bill.

He helped her into the limo, sat beside her, kissing her cheek as he slipped his arm around her shoulders. "You are incredible. You know that?"

"You just wait."

It was going to be a long damned drive back to the inn.

Chapter Fifteen

Vic walked with Eric to the elevator, his fingers twined with hers. He pushed the button—three times—and they waited, the silence humming with sexual tension. The door opened with a *ding*, and they stepped inside.

He was on her the moment the door closed, backing her up against the elevator wall, his mouth coming down on hers in a brutal, punishing kiss.

God, yes.

She'd waited all night for this. She buried her fingers in his hair, surrendering to him, the urgency of his need for her sending a dark thrill through her blood.

He slid one hand down her hip to her thigh, lifted her leg and wrapped it around his waist, his erection straining against his trousers. And then she remembered.

"Security cameras. What if … ?" Still, she couldn't quit kissing him.

He lowered her leg, broke the kiss, and pressed his forehead to hers, breathing hard. "This elevator needs to move faster."

It seemed to take forever to reach the third floor, Vic's heart still pounding, her body jittery with unmet sexual need.

Finally, the car stopped, and the door opened.

Eric swept her out and across the hall, one clever hand sliding between her thighs to caress her while she fumbled with the key card. "You're so wet. Have you been wet like this all night, thinking of me, thinking of what I'm going to do to you?"

"*Yes.*" She finally got the door open, stepped inside, and flicked on the light, while Eric kicked the door shut behind them. And then they were in each other's arms, picking up with that kiss right where they'd left off.

They stumbled across the floor together, Vic tugging at the starched fabric of his shirt, yanking it out of his trousers, her hands hungry for the feel of his skin. He drew away from her long enough to shed his jacket, tear off the tie, and rid himself of his shirt. She reached for his fly, fought with some kind of hidden metal clasp. He took over, so she reached for her own zipper.

"No." His voice was rough, dark. "The dress stays on."

He jerked open his fly only enough to free his erection, and she caught just a glimpse of his cock before he turned her to face away from him.

Oh, God, she wanted him inside her. *Now.*

He bent her over the sofa, rucked her dress up over her hips. "Jesus."

He slid one big hand over the bare skin of her ass, making her whimper with impatience. She heard the quiet rip of a condom wrapper. Then he forced her legs wide apart, one finger sliding from her clit to the entrance of her vagina.

"You teased me all night. Is this what you want?"

"Yes, yes, *yes*. Fuck me."

He filled her with a single slow thrust that felt like salvation, an answer to hours of wanting him. "God, I love your pussy."

He gave her just a moment to get used to having him inside her before he began to move, slowly at first then faster until he was driving into her hard, a big hand grasping one hip, his fingers digging into her skin, the other reaching around to tease her clit.

God, it felt good, *so* good. He was relentless, his deep strokes making the ache inside her worse, stretching her, filling her, driving her crazy.

Faster, harder, deeper.

Wanting every inch of him, she arched her lower back and heard him groan in approval. She fought to hold on, her fingers digging into the sofa as he drove her headlong toward a shattering climax, pounding her pleasure home.

He followed her over the edge, finishing with a few powerful thrusts. He sank against her, out of breath, his hands bracketing her body on the back of the sofa. He pressed kisses along her nape. "Vicki. My Vicki."

As her heartbeat slowed, one thought cut through the post-orgasmic bliss.

How could she possibly say goodbye to him?

*E*ric soaked in the enormous bathtub, Victoria leaning back against him, her head resting on his chest, their legs mingling. Music drifted through the suite from the radio. It was classical, but Eric was too content to care. He caressed one beautiful breast, his other arm stretched out across the back of the tub, warm water lapping lazily at their skin. His mind drifted, his body replete. "You did a crazy wonderful thing tonight."

"I'm glad you liked it. I wondered how you would react."

It took him a moment to realize that she'd misunderstood him. "I'm not talking about your lack of panties, though that was crazy and wonderful, too. I'm talking about eight thousand nine hundred dollars plus change."

She craned her neck, looked up at him. "You saw? No one was supposed to see."

"Good eyes. What can I say?"

"I hope Austin and Lexi didn't see it, too."

"Even if they didn't, I'm sure they have some idea how much it cost."

"Lexi is my best friend. Besides, it's only money."

His mother had often said those words, but for different reasons. When buying antibiotics for him had left her with no money for food. When she'd had to choose between snow tires and paying her utility bill. When the school had asked parents to help cover the cost of a field trip and she'd had nothing to give.

"It's only money," she'd say, smiling down at him. "We'll make it somehow."

When he'd been old enough to work, he'd helped out, doing chores outside so his mother could rest, getting odd jobs to earn his own spending money, shoveling sidewalks and splitting wood all winter to help pay the heating bills. There'd been times when a little cash—far less than what Victoria had spent tonight—would have made a world of difference to him and his mother. Yes, there were more important things than money, but money went a long way toward making life easier.

That's why you went for the high-paying job, isn't it, buddy?

Right.

"What's it like to grow up like that?"

"With money, you mean?"

That's what he'd meant. "Sorry if that seems too personal."

She laughed. "I'm sitting naked with you in a bathtub. You've been inside me. Is there anything more personal than that?"

He chuckled. "I guess not."

"I didn't really understand that my family was any different from anyone else's until I started grade school. My father didn't want us growing up to be what he calls 'the useless rich,' so we went to a public school. Other people's parents would pick them up, but we had a bodyguard who came for us—basically a manny with a gun."

She told Eric how her mother had divorced her father when they were little and had largely vanished from their lives. "I can remember her complaining to a friend over the phone that she would never have had kids if she'd realized how much work it was to be a mother. I must have been four or five at the time. She had a full-time nanny, but even so, we were too much work."

What a bitch. "That must have hurt."

"I felt like a burden, like something she regretted. She and I are *not* close."

He could understand that.

"My father tried to be there for us, but I don't think he ever intended to raise us by himself. He worked most of the time, but every summer we went on a month-long vacation somewhere in the world. Those are my best memories."

She told him about playing on the beach at Nice; visiting the supposed home of Santa Claus in Rovaniemi, Finland, where she'd ridden in a sleigh pulled by reindeer; camping on an island in the middle of Lake George in New York; sleeping overnight in the Tower of London; staying at that inn in Kenya where she and her brother fed giraffes through the window and heard lions roaring nearby.

"We had chores like other kids. If we did our chores, we got paid an allowance. That was all the spending money we had. He demanded that we go to college and not slide by on privilege. He paid our way through college, but we had to have part-time jobs. We also had to maintain good GPAs. I didn't gain access to my trust fund until I graduated from college. I'm grateful for those lessons. The last thing in the world I would want to be is a brainless socialite."

Eric kissed her head. "You're nothing like that. You're generous with your friends and even with strangers. Everything you do comes from your heart. If you hadn't told me your family had money, I wouldn't have known."

It was true. Every word.

"Really?"

"Yes, really."

But Eric didn't know what to think about her father. It sounded like he'd done his best to be a good dad—until the moment when his daughter had needed him most. Then he'd gotten angry and blamed her.

Well, no one was perfect.

As if she'd read his mind, she went on. "I know my father cares about me. I just wish he hadn't reacted the way he did when I told him about … what had happened. He acted like I was trying to be the next heiress with a sex tape or something. I hadn't even known I was being recorded."

"I'm sorry he wasn't there for you." He kissed her hair.

In the other room, her cell phone buzzed.

Her body tensed. "At two in the morning, Abigail? Really?"

He needed to ask the obvious. "Why do you stay in a job you don't like, working for a boss who treats you like this?"

She seemed to consider it for a moment. "It's important to me to have a career, to be successful at something. I can't just quit and sit on the beach all day. I'd feel like a loser. Eventually, I'd run out of money. Besides, what would I do? I don't want to go back to college."

"Well, Joe offered you a job."

She laughed. "Can you imagine me telling my dad that I'd quit Jensen West and was moving here to be a cook at a brewpub?"

Eric didn't think it sounded nearly as crazy as she did. "Does it matter what he thinks if you're happy?"

"I suppose not, but I don't want to feel like a failure."

"You remember what my mom says about success, right?"

"The path to success is the one that enables people to feel at peace with themselves. Yes, I remember."

He changed the subject after that, afraid of coming across as pushy or giving the impression he was trying to talk her into moving to Colorado. Which he was.

The conversation moved on—to Eric's childhood, his memories of high school with Lexi and Austin, why he'd joined the Team—until the water grew cool. They climbed out of the tub and dried each other off.

Then he scooped her up and danced his way to the bed with her in his arms, waltzing in time to the music, dropping her onto the sheets, and stretching out on top of her. "How about we fuck until we break this bed?"

This time, when he made love to her, he took time for tenderness, dallying over all the sweet little details he'd skipped a couple of hours ago.

And, oh, yes, he made her scream.

Vic watched Eric sleep, the sun already up outside, the scent of freshly baked croissants and coffee drifting up from the dining room below. He was such a beautiful man. Dark lashes rested against his tanned skin, his muscular chest rising and falling with each deep, slow breath, his body relaxed in sleep. The sheets had crept down below his hips, exposing his cock to her view.

She'd never felt overly attached to the penis of any of the handful of men she'd been with in her life—except for Eric's. Maybe because of what he did for her when he was inside her. Of course, that wasn't really his penis. That was his brain and his heart—the man in control of the penis. Still...

She'd never had a night like last night with anyone before. It wasn't just that reaching orgasm was easy with him. It's that he made her feel that he truly cared about *her*. He knew his way around a woman's body. That was for sure. But nothing he did felt automatic. He wasn't like most of the men she'd been with, who'd gone down on her only to get her to go down on them and who'd complained about it when she hadn't come fast enough to suit them. He truly seemed to enjoy bringing her pleasure for *her* sake. She'd never known any man like him.

She glanced at the clock, saw that it was time to get up. Today was spa day. She needed to be ready to head to Boulder by nine-thirty, and that meant breakfast and a shower. But she didn't want to wake Eric—unless...

Smiling to herself, she crawled down to kneel between his splayed legs, then took his cock in hand, and ran her tongue along the underside from his balls to the tip.

His body's response was immediate, his cock growing harder in her hand.

She licked him again, this time taking his length into her mouth and sucking. His cock went fully erect. She teased him with her tongue, tracing the thick rim of the head, licking away the pearl of moisture that emerged from the tip, flicking her tongue across the underside.

She heard a sharp inhale, looked up to find him watching her, shock on his face.

She began to move, using her mouth and hand together, stroking him.

He moaned, his fingers sliding into her hair, holding it to the side so that he could watch. "*Vicki.*"

She kept up the rhythm, trying to follow his body's signals, going faster when his hips urged her to, increasing the pressure, cupping and rolling his balls in her free hand.

His every exhale was a quick gust of breath now, his body rigid, his balls drawing tight. "*Jesus.*"

He came with a groan, arching off the bed, one hand clenched tightly in her hair, the other fisting in the sheets. She drew her mouth off him, finishing him with her hand, his cock contracting, thick cum shooting onto his belly.

Slowly, his body began to relax.

"Good morning," she said.

He chuckled, his blue eyes warm. "Good morning to you, too."

She reached for a tissue.

He took it from her, wiped off his belly, tossed the tissue into the trash. "Come here, woman."

She crawled upward, straddling him, and taking his mouth with hers.

His arms wrapped around her, holding her tight, his head lifting off his pillow as he kissed her back.

As sweet as this was, it couldn't last forever.

She broke the kiss, glanced over at the clock. "I need to get up. It's spa day."

"Just do something for me before you go. It will only take a few minutes."

"Sure."

His lips curved in a sexy grin. "Sit on my face."

*E*ric walked through the open bay doors at the firehouse, needing
something to take his mind off Victoria. She was leaving Sunday—two
days from today. Although he'd told himself a half dozen times that it didn't
matter, that he wasn't really involved with her, that he'd gotten along fine
before she'd come to Scarlet and he'd be fine when she was gone, he no
longer believed that. It *did* matter.

Victoria was everything he hadn't known he was missing, everything he
hadn't realized he wanted. And she was leaving.

He found Bill, the department's mechanic, just inside the bay repairing
an air pack. "Hey, Bill."

"Hey, chief. How's the wedding hoopla going?"

"The rehearsal is this evening. I thought I'd catch up on paperwork."

"We're out of toilet paper," Bill called after him.

How could people who could problem-solve inside a burning building
find it so hard to deal with everyday shit? "Did anyone think about bringing a
roll from home or dipping into petty cash and buying some? Jesus!"

Welcome back to reality, buddy.

He made his way past the various apparatus—an engine, a ladder truck, a
water tender, two ambulances, an emergency rescue vehicle, and four
ATVs—to his office. First, he called Food Mart and asked Mick, the manager,
to send over a case of TP, since no one else was apparently capable of doing
so. Then he spent the next hour going through a week's worth of emails and
incident reports.

It had been a pretty quiet week. A fatal MVA involving a motorcycle in
the canyon. An EMS call involving Mrs. Beech, the old high school English
teacher, who'd collapsed in the Food Mart parking lot. An MVA with injuries,
this time involving a car and a bicycle. Hank's hash oil explosion.

How was Hank, anyway? Eric would have to give him a call.

Then he came to the report of the fatal rollover MVA involving the little
girl who'd drowned. She'd unbuckled her seatbelt, trying to help her injured
mother, and the creek's current had carried her right out of the car's broken
window. Moretti had tried to reach her, breaking with Team safety
procedures by jumping into the water with no rope or harness, but he hadn't

been able to catch her. There was nothing he could have done differently, nothing anyone could have done.

Bad fucking business.

Eric pulled a box of cards out of his bottom desk drawer—condolence cards—and filled one out, signing it on behalf of the Scarlet Springs Fire Department and addressing it to the child's parents. It wouldn't make one damned bit of difference to them, but it was the only thing he could do.

He'd just stuck a stamp on it when Taylor called to suggest they take Moretti climbing to get his mind off things. "That's a good i—

The department's tone sounded out through the hallway.

Dispatch called them over the scanner. "Scarlet FD, we have a report of a car fire on Fourth of July Road."

"Sorry, man, got to go."

Fourth of July Road sat high above Scarlet in an area that was almost entirely wilderness. It was a narrow, winding road with steep drop-offs and sharp switchbacks that made it tough to access with anything wider than a pickup. A car fire up there could easily spread to the trees and turn into a dangerous wildland blaze.

Eric replied to dispatch, feeling almost relieved to have an emergency on his hands. Unlike his feelings for Victoria, *this* was something he knew how to handle.

He shouted to Ryan, his A-shift captain, who fell in behind him as they jogged to the locker room. "I'll drive the water tender. You head up in your pickup."

"I thought you were on vacation."

"I'm taking a vacation from my vacation."

Ryan laughed. "You got it, chief."

Chapter Sixteen

Vic sat with Lexi, Britta, and Winona in the ocean-themed waiting room at the spa, trying to catch up on her emails from Abigail. The women were all wrapped in fluffy, white bathrobes, fresh from getting facials. Now it was time for the manicure and pedicure.

"I think we should match, don't you, Vic?" Lexi asked.

Vic looked up. "Yes, absolutely."

"Then let's all get French manicures and pedicures," Lexi said.

The door opened, and four manicurists walked in.

"I'm sorry, ma'am, but we don't allow cell phones in the treatment areas for security reasons. You can store your phone in your locker."

"Oh, sorry." Vic of all people could appreciate that. She got to her feet. "I need to send an important message. I'll be right back."

She stepped out of the waiting room into the locker room, quickly scrolling through Abigail's messages then answering all of the questions in a single long text message. She ended it by letting Abigail know she wouldn't be available for the rest of the day or tomorrow either.

I'm about to head into a spa for a mani/pedi, and they don't allow phones. Tonight is the rehearsal. Tomorrow is the wedding. I'll be in touch Sunday when I get home. Call Jeff if you have more questions.

Abigail's reply was almost instantaneous.

Maybe I should give Jeff your raise.

Vic stared at her phone, stunned by Abigail's threat, anger making her face burn. She typed a reply.

Jeff is hard-working and deserves a raise.

She pressed send, shut off her phone, and locked it in her locker with her handbag, so angry she could spit. She'd done her best—mostly—to keep up with Abigail's messages and emails, but she was on vacation, her first real vacation in more than a year. She couldn't help it if the spa didn't allow cell phones. Besides, she couldn't very well get her nails done and text at the same time. Tomorrow was her best friend's wedding, one of the most important days in Lexi's life, and Vic was her maid of honor. She wasn't going to spend the wedding rehearsal or the wedding on her phone.

Not wanting to cast shadows over everyone else's fun, Vic took a deep breath and followed her manicurist to the treatment room where Lexi and the others now sat in pedicure chairs, their feet soaking in warm, scented water.

She pushed a smile onto her face. "I'm back."

But Lexi knew her too well. "Trouble at work?"

"Nothing important." She sat, slipped off her little spa sandals, and put her feet in the water. "Oh, that feels good."

Winona, who'd never had a pedicure before, was busy playing with the massage controls. "You should try this, Vic. Did you see? The chair gives massages."

Vic didn't tell her that most pedicure chairs were like this. "Cool!"

"She doesn't need a massage," Britta said. "She has Eric."

Not for much longer.

Vic forced another smile onto her face. "Should we practice your vows, Lexi?"

"I'd like that. I've got them memorized, but I'm afraid I'll be so nervous that I'll screw up."

Vic read along while Lexi recited the vows she and Austin had written, Winona laughing and struggling to hold still.

"I'm sorry," she said. "It really tickles."

"Oh, my God, Lexi, look at the clock!" Britta blurted. "By this time tomorrow, you'll be a married woman."

Lexi's eyes went wide. "It's really happening, isn't it?"

Vic took her hand. "Yes, sweetie, it is."

$\mathcal{I}$t was almost one in the afternoon when they left the spa. They ate a late lunch at a trendy sushi joint, then strolled Boulder's Pearl Street Mall, checking out the boutiques, talking and laughing the way they'd done when Lexi lived in Chicago.

"I've missed this," Vic said.

Lexi threw her arm around Vic's shoulder, gave her a squeeze. "So have I."

Vic bought a little sleeveless blue dress with a poppy-red floral pattern, taking time in the dressing room to send a text message to Eric.

All of me misses all of you.

It was the truth. She could barely think of anything but him, her mind filled with images from last night. Eric looking like a movie star in his white tux. Eric tearing off his tie and shirt and yanking down his fly, eager to get inside her. Eric dancing his way to the bed, naked, with her in his arms.

How about we fuck until we break this bed?

She waited for a response, but when he didn't reply in a few minutes, she quickly finished dressing and slid her phone back into her purse.

He still hadn't responded two hours later when they left Boulder and headed back up the canyon toward Scarlet. She tried to tell herself that he was probably just busy with Austin doing guy things. They'd talked about climbing today. Still, she couldn't shake the fear that she'd gone too far by admitting she missed him.

Oh, she hated this part of romance—all the uncertainty, having feelings she was afraid to express in case he wasn't feeling the same way. It was a stupid dance, and it wasted her time, energy, and sanity. Then again, this wasn't really a romance, was it? She didn't know what it was.

"Oh, look!" Lexi pointed as they pulled into the inn's driveway. "The tent is up."

A forty-foot-long white party tent stood on the west side of the inn. Staff from the rental company were busy setting up chairs in a wide spiral around the little stand of aspens to the south. The bench that usually sat there had been moved to make room for the wedding party at the center.

Vic and the others followed Lexi to the party tent, where staff were draping cloth banners in lavender and sage from the ceiling of shirred white fabric. "This is beautiful."

Lexi gave them a tour. "There will be antique green bottles on all the tables with bouquets. That table at the end is where we'll all sit, Austin and I in the center. There will be bouquets on that table, too. The dance floor will be on the other end. I think that's the cake table there. Or maybe that's the guestbook table."

Lexi introduced herself to the person in charge and answered a few questions, giving Vic time to run up to her room, freshen up, and change into her new dress.

And still nothing from Eric.

She willed herself to put him out of her mind. Today wasn't about her and Eric. It was about Lexi marrying the man she loved.

When Vic went back outside, she found Lexi talking with Rose, who'd dressed in a white broomstick skirt, white tank top, and a white lacy shawl.

"I appreciate your suggestions, but I think we'll just do it the way we planned."

Vic walked over to offer Lexi moral support.

"If you'd like, we could do a purification ceremony tonight—smudge the grounds, the tent, and the wedding party."

Lexi shook her head. "I think we'll just go with the ceremony the way it's written on the sheet I gave you. But thanks so much, Rose. I know you care."

"I'm just trying to bring a sense of sacredness to your joining."

Vic had an idea. "What if you smudged the space right now—before the rehearsal? That way it will all be purified before they step into it as a couple."

Lexi gaped at her.

"That's a good idea, Victoria." Rose glanced at her watch. "There's not much time before we're supposed to start."

"Austin texted to say the guys are going to be late, so there's no rush," Lexi said. "They went climbing in Eldo and hit bad traffic."

That explained why Eric hadn't texted Vic back. He'd probably been dangling in the air when her message had come.

"I've got to run home, but I can be back in about five minutes." Rose took off at a fast walk, shawl flapping in the air behind her like butterfly wings.

As soon as she was out of sight, Lexi sagged against Vic. "That ought to keep her busy for a while. I think you just saved my sanity."

They joined Britta and Winona, who sat on the back porch sipping lemonade with Cheyenne, Austin's sister, and his parents, Michael and Roxanne.

Kendra walked outside with another pitcher of lemonade and a stack of plastic cups. "The bride's girls are here. I hope the groom didn't get cold feet."

"There's no chance of that," Roxanne said. "My boy is head-over-heels."

A few minutes later, the sound of tires on gravel turned everyone's heads toward the driveway. Austin pulled up, and he, Jesse, and Chaska stepped out of the vehicle, all of them looking dirty and sweaty. They moved in on the lemonade like predators, taking cups as fast as Kendra could fill them.

Vic's stomach sank.

Eric wasn't with them.

"Where did you boys go climbing?" Michael asked.

Austin held out his cup for more. "We played around on a couple of routes on Red Garden Wall. Is Hawke back yet?"

"He didn't go climbing with you?" Chey asked.

Austin set his empty cup on the table. "He got toned out for a car fire up on Fourth of July Road. I listened on the scanner for a while. It had begun to spread to the hillside by the time he and his crew arrived, so they've had a busy afternoon."

Now do you feel stupid?

Vic had been worried that she'd made him angry or that he was just ignoring her, when he'd been off saving the world again.

*E*ric stripped out of his gear, glancing at the clock on the locker room wall. The wedding rehearsal had started a half hour ago. He didn't have time for a shower. Unless he wanted to miss the entire thing, he'd have to go as he was—sweaty and smoky and high on adrenaline.

Damn, he loved his job.

He'd arrived at the scene to find an old Ford F-150 and a quarter-acre patch of the hillside on fire. The owner had already popped the hood, letting lots of nice oxygen reach the fire and enabling it to spread. They'd divided into three teams, one for the vehicle and two for the hillside. After that, it had been textbook—apart from the volunteer who'd moved in to overhaul the vehicle fire without full bunker gear or an air pack.

"What the fuck do you think this is—a barbecue?" Eric had shouted at him through his mask. "Get away from this scene, Nelson, and read your training manual again. Move it!"

Eric hadn't lost a firefighter in the two years he'd been in charge, and he wasn't about to start now. What would have happened if that vehicle had blown with the kid standing right there, exposed?

Still, it had felt good to be out there, working his body hard, strategizing to beat the flames, taking control of an emergency before it could become a catastrophe. It had helped to clear his head, get his mind off Victoria, put things back into perspective.

Yeah, his life was sane again.

He slipped into his jeans and T-shirt, then swung by his office to shut down his computer and get that condolence card in the mail. He found his cell phone sitting on a stack of papers on his desk. He grabbed it and hurried out to his truck, checking it for calls and messages. There was only one, and it was from Victoria.

All of me misses all of you.

Her words caught him right in the solar plexus, breath gusting from his lungs.

God, he missed her, too.

So much for sanity.

He set the phone aside, figuring he'd get there faster if he just drove and didn't spend ten minutes trying to come up with some kind of smart, sexy reply.

Two minutes later, he parked his truck behind the inn, which had been transformed into a wedding theme park with a giant white tent and chairs. The others stood together on the back porch, waiting.

Shit.

He climbed out of the truck and jogged over to them. "Sorry I'm late."

Taylor grinned. "Did you have a nice fire?"

Taylor knew him too well.

Eric chuckled. "An old Ford pickup overheated and ignited fuel leaking through a cracked seal. It burned about a quarter acre of the hillside, but we got it."

Then he noticed Rose, who walked across the lawn, wafting smoke into the air from one of her sage bundles with a large black feather and saying something, the words just beyond his hearing. "What the hell is she doing?"

"Purifying," everyone said at once.

Ookay.

"She wanted to change our wedding vows and work in a purification ceremony, but Vic suggested this instead. It's definitely keeping her busy."

Chaska stood with his back to Rose, looking pissed, arms crossed over his chest. "I guess I just have to pretend I didn't see that eagle feather."

It was illegal for anyone who wasn't a member of a federally recognized tribe to possess an eagle feather.

Eric allowed himself to look over at Victoria, who was wearing the hell out of a little blue dress with red flowers on it. He walked to her side of the table and poured himself a lemonade. "You look pretty."

There was uncertainty in her brown eyes. "Thanks."

He lowered his voice to a whisper. "I've missed you, too—all of you."

Sanity was overrated.

Eric glared at Taylor as they walked back toward the inn. "Dude, the bride has her vows memorized. What's with you? It's not like you didn't know the wedding is tomorrow."

"I'll have it all memorized by then."

"Damned straight you will, even if I have to stay up all night drilling you. You've got to come through for Lexi tomorrow, man."

Irritation flashed across Taylor's face. "You don't think I know that? Why are you more tense about this than I am? You're supposed to be the one reassuring me not to worry and telling me that everything will be all right."

"It *will* be all right—if you memorize your vows."

"How's your best man speech?"

Yeah, well, Eric still needed to write that. "I'll have it done."

Taylor fired his own words straight back at him. "It's not like you didn't know the wedding is tomorrow."

Okay, fine, so they were both procrastinators.

Lexi and Victoria walked arm in arm ahead of them, one with red hair, the other with dark brown hair, the two of them as close as sisters. They'd both gotten choked up at various points during the rehearsal, the two of them setting Britta off.

Victoria's laughter drifted back to him. "Thank God for waterproof mascara!"

The rehearsal dinner was a cookout. Eric helped Bob get his big gas grill going, while Austin took on the role of grilling burgers and vegetable kabobs for everyone. They ate together around two large rented tables loaded down with salads, condiments, and, best of all, cold beer.

Eric had just finished his first burger and his first brew when his pager went off. Austin's went off, too.

BREECE ARRESTED. MEET @ CAVE 20:00 HRS

Eric stared at his pager, then looked over at Taylor, who stared right back at him. "Holy shit."

"They caught him," Taylor said.

"Caught who?" Lexi asked.

"Ted Breece."

Lexi's face lit up. "Oh, my God! Seriously? That is fantastic!"

"Who's he?" Victoria asked. "Wait. Isn't he the jerk who stole from the Team?"

"That's him." Eric was impressed that she remembered.

The bastard had stolen more than seventy thousand dollars from the Team, which was a fortune for a nonprofit run entirely by volunteers. Lexi had done the forensic accounting work that had helped them build a case against him, but the bastard had gone on the run the moment he'd realized Megs was onto him.

"I didn't think they were ever going to find him," Taylor said. "I wonder where he's been holing up for the past year."

"I guess we'll find out."

An hour later, they sat with the rest of the Team in the ops room at The Cave, the Team's headquarters, while Megs ran through roll call of the principle Team members. Victoria had come with them as Eric's guest. Lexi was a supporting Team member in her own right and had a special interest in this, so she'd come, too.

Megs stood at the far end of the conference table, Ahearn, her partner, sitting next to her. "...Chaska Belcourt. Harrison Conrad. Sasha Dillon..."

Sasha waved to Victoria, mouthing the words, "I love your dress!"

Eric couldn't remember ever seeing Sasha in a dress, but okay.

Megs droned on. "Dave Hatfield. Eric Hawke. Creed Herrera. Jesse Moretti. Malachi O'Brien. Isaac Rogers. Gabe Rossiter. Nicole Turner. Austin Taylor. How's the weeklong fertility rite going, Taylor?"

Everyone laughed.

Taylor took Lexi's hand, a look passing between them. "It's going well. Thanks for asking. Tomorrow's the climax."

More laughter.

There was an evil glint in Megs' eyes. "Ahearn and I are coming."

And it was downhill from there.

When the dirty puns subsided, Megs got down to business. "Ted Breece, who relieved us of seventy-two thousand six hundred dollars, has been apprehended in Miami. He was pulled over when an officer ran his plates and discovered they were stolen. Apparently, he'd been hiding out with an ex-girlfriend. He is now enjoying the fine hospitality of the Miami-Dade Pre-Trial Detention Center."

The room exploded in cheers.

Eric had just one question. "Is it going to be difficult to extradite him to Colorado? If he's facing charges in Florida ..."

"My understanding is that once our governor issues an extradition request, Breece will go before a judge in Florida. The court will decide whether there are enough facts to support extradition. After that, Breece will fly the friendly skies back to Denver. He's facing two felony warrants here, and, thanks to Lexi, we've got lots of documentation."

Lexi beamed. "This is almost like a wedding present."

"Any chance we'll get that money back?" Conrad asked.

Megs shrugged. "I seriously doubt it. Breece had a bad gambling habit. He probably blew it all before he skipped town."

Megs went through what the DA had told them they could expect once Breece reached the state and the kind of prison sentence that might await him. Then she asked them all to write an impact statement—a description of how his crime had affected them as an individual volunteer with the Team.

"Can't they just turn him over to us?" Moretti asked through a dark scowl.

Eric thought that scowl probably had less to do with Breece and more to do with what had happened earlier this week. Moretti seemed sharper edged than usual. Or maybe it was Eric's imagination.

"I appreciate the sentiment, Moretti, but vigilante justice hasn't been legal here for a while now," Megs answered. "I don't want any of you writing to him to give him a piece of your mind. Let the justice system handle it, and keep the Team's reputation clean. Got it?"

After the meeting, Eric offered to give Victoria a tour.

"I got a tour last time, but you can show me around again."

So he did, answering her questions, going into a bit more detail than he otherwise might, doing all he could to make the moment last. He didn't want to say goodnight. They only had tonight and tomorrow, and then ...

She finally ended the tour when she saw that Lexi was leaving. "I need to go help Lexi get her things. She's staying at the inn tonight. You probably know that, don't you?"

"I'll make sure the groom memorizes his vows. I also need to write the best man speech. Do you have your speech ready?"

She rolled her pretty eyes. "As if ... I had it ready before I flew out here."

"Overachiever."

"Do you want help?"

He considered it for a moment, but this was between him and his best friend. It was something he needed to do himself. "I've got it."

Her expression crumpled. "I want to see you tonight—just for a while. I can call when I'm alone in my room ... unless you'd rather be alone or ..."

It was on the tip of his tongue to say that it was probably best if the two of them got some sleep, but that's not what came out.

His hands found their way to her waist. "It's almost a tradition for the maid of honor to sleep with the best man on the night before the wedding."

The light returned to her face. "Is that so? Well, I'm all for tradition."

Chapter Seventeen

Vic dried off from her bath and had just put on her silk bathrobe when Eric texted.

I'm outside your door.

She hurried to her door, opened it.

Eric stood there in a black T-shirt and jeans, his jaw dark with stubble, one arm propped on the door jamb, phone in his other hand. He'd had a shower since she'd last seen him, his hair still damp.

"I missed you all day."

"I'm here now." He stepped through the door, locked it behind him. "God, you smell good."

"I just took a bath. I never like the products they use in spas, so I—"

He cut off her words with a deep kiss, backing her up against the wall. His mouth ravaged hers, one hand sliding inside her robe to caress first one breast and then the other. But she was more than ready for him.

She'd been aching for him all day. "I want you."

He drew away from her just far enough to open his jeans and put on a condom, then reached beneath her robe, grasped her bare ass, and lifted her off her feet, pinning her against the wall with his weight.

"Oh!" She gave a startled gasp, wrapping her legs around his waist and throwing her arms around his neck to hold on.

"I've got you." He nuzzled her throat, the head of his cock nudging against her, trying to find its way inside her.

Oh, God, was he really going to do this?

He broke the kiss, his dark eyes looking into hers, his cock now right where it needed to be. "God, Vicki, what have you done to me?"

She let go of his neck, cupped his face in her hands, and kissed him. "*Fuck me.*"

Slowly, he buried himself inside her, inch by excruciating inch.

"You are so ... *tight.*" He moved slowly at first, his rhythm picking up thrust by thrust until his hips were a piston, driving his cock into her hard and deep and fast.

She'd always wanted to have sex like this, but none of the men she'd been with had even tried, perhaps because they knew they weren't strong enough to handle it. Oh, she loved how feminine and desired it made her feel.

"*Oh, yes.*" She fought to keep her eyes open, turned on by the intensity on his face as he drove into her, but it just felt ... too ... damned ... good.

She moaned with every thrust now, her self-control shattered. God, she wanted this, wanted more, wanted him. The slick glide of his cock. The sweet stretch deep inside her. That wonderful, precious ache.

She cried out his name, climax crashing over her in a perfect wave of bliss, drenching her with pleasure. But he was right behind her.

His breath caught, his body shuddering as orgasm carried him away.

For a time, they remained as they were—out of breath, hearts pounding, him deep inside her. Then he reached down, took hold of the condom, and withdrew from her.

She moaned in protest. "No."

Chuckling, he lowered her to her feet, walked off to the bathroom, and washed up.

Drunk on sex, she walked to the bedroom, drew down the covers, and fell across on the sheets. He found her there, undressed, then crawled into bed and took her into his arms, his warmth enfolding her.

"I wish I could fall asleep inside you."

"I wish that, too."

It was after midnight when they got out of bed, threw on clothes, and raided the guest kitchen downstairs. Victoria, who knew the inn now better than Eric did, led the operation. They found leftover fruit from breakfast in the refrigerator, along with a few leftover croissants, which they warmed in the microwave. Grabbing a jar of Nutella and a butter knife, they crept up the stairs, Victoria fighting giggles.

Then they got naked again, crawled back into bed, and began to feast.

"Did Austin get his vows memorized?" Victoria popped a grape into her mouth.

Eric nodded, his mouth full of pineapple.

"Is it strange that this person you've known your entire life is getting married?"

Eric swallowed. "Nah, he's always done everything first. First to hit his growth spurt. First to have his voice change. First to hit puberty. He was working on biceps when I was still singing soprano."

She laughed, scooped Nutella onto a spoon and ate it. "Were you jealous?"

"Yeah, I think I was. My mom told me the sperm donor had been tall, so I'd catch up to Austin one day. But it seemed to take a long damned time."

"Everything feels like forever when you're a teenager."

That was a fact. "He was the first to get laid, too. He hooked up with the girl the rest of us wanted, the girl we all talked about at lunch and after school."

"Sexy Lexi. I know that's the nickname *you* gave her."

There was no denying it, so he didn't try. "Guilty as charged."

"I bet that *really* made you jealous."

"I felt pretty inferior. Here he was having actual sex with a real, live girl, and I was stuck fucking my fist. But I was happy for him. It was hard not to be happy for them—the It Couple—until it all went sideways."

She nodded. "I know all about that. It was hard for me to like Austin at first because all I'd ever heard about him was what a jerk he was."

"I bet." He'd gotten the same thing, only in reverse.

Victoria looked up at him from beneath her lashes. "When she came back, you hit on her. I know you did. She told me."

"I don't know if I'd go that far. I asked her out once." He grinned. "I guess I thought I had a shot at her with Taylor out of the way. I figured she and I would hook up and then she'd go back to Chicago."

He realized the moment the words were out that he'd said the wrong thing.

Victoria looked up at him, another spoonful of Nutella hanging in midair. "Is that what we're doing—hooking up until I go back to Chicago?"

He felt ambushed by her question, and so he said the first regrettable, stupid thing that popped into his head. "We both knew you were only going to be here for a week. We've done our best to make the most of that."

She stiffened, the softness disappearing from her face. "Right. So I *am* just a hookup—like all the others."

"You really want to have this conversation now—at one in the morning?"

She dropped the spoon into the jar. "It's late. You should probably go."

Wait. She was kicking him out?

Shit.

He could see he'd hurt her. He just didn't know what to do about it.

Say something, stupid, but not something stupid!

He wanted her to understand that she meant more to him than any woman ever had, but he couldn't put the words together fast enough. So he got out of bed, grabbed his clothes, and dressed. When he looked over at her again, she was wearing her bathrobe, her arms crossed over her chest as if to protect herself.

His stomach knotted.

Goddamn it. This wasn't how it was supposed to go. She didn't need to protect herself from *him*.

Say something, man.

"The answer is no." He turned to go.

"What?"

"You asked if I think of you as just a hookup. The answer is no."

Not knowing what else he could say, he did what he didn't want to do. He left her alone and drove home.

W hen Vic's alarm went off at five, it felt like a slap in the face. *No freaking way.*

She fumbled in the dark for her phone to turn off the awful sound, hoping she'd set it wrong. But it really *was* time to get up.

She dragged herself to the bathroom, flicked on the light, and studied her reflection in the mirror. She looked like she'd stayed up too late and had cried herself to sleep, which is exactly what she'd done. Perfect. Because what Lexi needed today was a maid of honor who looked like hell.

"It's your own fault," she said to the woman in the mirror.

The woman said nothing, but walked toward the shower.

Vic turned the water on as hot as she could stand, stepped into the spray, and reached for her shampoo, a memory of sharing this shower with Eric nudging its way into her mind, making the space feel empty.

He hadn't said anything out of line last night. He'd told it the way it was. They'd both known from the beginning that she would be leaving tomorrow. They'd both known nothing could come of this, and they'd made the most of the time they had together—until she'd gone all emo on him last night.

What had she expected him to say? Had she imagined he'd profess his undying love? Maybe beg her to stay in Scarlet?

Okay, maybe some part of her had wanted that.

Now, she had only one night left in Colorado, one night left with him, and he probably wouldn't want to spend it with her for fear that she'd get emotional and ruin things just like she'd done last night.

She rinsed her hair, slathered on conditioner, then scrubbed her skin and shaved her legs, last night replaying in her mind again and again. Feeling him pound into her up against the wall. Stealing food from the kitchen. Asking him to leave.

Eric was the most amazing man she'd ever known. He was caring and courageous. He loved his mother and his friends, and it showed. No, he wasn't romantic in a hearts and flowers way, but when he looked at her, when he kissed her, when he was inside her, he made her feel like she was the only woman on earth. And she'd sent him away for being honest with her.

Apologize to him.

Yes, she would apologize. She would find time, maybe before the ceremony, to tell him she was sorry. Hopefully, he would forgive her, and they could enjoy one last night together.

And if he doesn't want to spend tonight with you?

The thought put a pang in her chest.

She needed to set all of this aside and focus on Lexi. Today was Lexi's big day, one of the most important days of her life, and Vic would not spend it feeling sorry for herself or pouting over a man—not even Eric.

She finished her shower, slathered moisturizer on her face and skin, and blew her hair dry—a process that seemed to go about ten times faster in Colorado than in Illinois. Then she put on panties and a strapless bra, slipped into her bathrobe, and dashed around the suite, straightening it to make room for the others.

By the time she heard Lexi and Britta giggling on the stairs, Vic felt awake and in control of her emotions. She ran to the door, threw it open.

"Good morning!" Lexi's face glowed.

Vic hugged her tight. "My God, Lexi, you're getting married today."

Britta breezed past them. "The stylist just texted to say she's on the way, and Kendra is on her way up with breakfast and coffee. She says someone ate the fruit she had Sandrine set aside for this morning. I told her it was probably Vic and Eric."

Lexi and Britta laughed, as if this suggestion were funny.

Vic shut the door behind them, grateful they couldn't see her face.

*E*ric stood at the floor-to-ceiling windows in Austin and Lexi's living room, looking out over Scarlet, tension a knot in his chest. He hadn't meant to hurt Victoria, hadn't meant to make her believe that she was just some woman he'd fucked for fun and would soon forget. Well, he had fucked her for fun, but not *just* for fun.

Upstairs, the bedroom door opened, and Taylor stepped out, all tuxed out apart from the jacket itself—trousers, white shirt, gray vest, sage-colored silk tie. He walked down the stairs, fighting with his cufflinks. "Can you figure these out?"

"Sure." Eric took the cufflinks from him and put them on one at a time, then took Taylor's jacket from him and held it up while he slipped it on. "Hey, you look great, man. You're going to make Lexi proud."

"You, on the other hand, look like a man with a lot on his mind."

Eric shook his head, irritated with himself. "Sorry."

Taylor laughed. "Hey, we've known each other for too long to fool each other about anything."

That was true.

Taylor went on. "I'm betting that your problem is about five-foot-four and has a sweet face and gorgeous brown eyes. Am I right?"

Yep, he'd nailed it.

So Eric explained, knowing they had only a few minutes before Moretti and Belcourt came back inside from cleaning the trash out of Taylor's SUV. "She more or less asked me whether I thought of her as just another hookup."

"And you said something really stupid."

"I tried to fix it before I left, but, yeah, I did. Her question took me by surprise, and I just couldn't think straight. She asked me to leave. She wasn't angry about it. She didn't throw a fit. She just asked me to go." He almost wished she'd shouted at him. Maybe then he'd be pissed off and wouldn't feel so desolate.

"You're in love with her, aren't you?"

"What? No!" Eric turned toward the windows again. "Yes. Hell, I don't know. I've never really been in love before. Besides, how can two people fall in love in a week? That's ridiculous, man. It just doesn't happen that way."

"Well, you've spent more time together this week than some people who've been dating for a couple of months."

Eric supposed that was true. "That doesn't change the fact that it's only been seven days."

"When I asked Lexi out the first time, it was after school. I walked her home, carried her backpack. We spent maybe fifteen minutes together, but my life changed in those fifteen minutes. I fell in love with her then and there. We were only teenagers, but that was it for me."

"Sure it was—if you don't count the twelve years that the two of you spent apart and the other people you were with in between."

"That was my fault. I was young and stupid. If I had trusted in our relationship, if I had trusted that things would work out in the end, I would have saved us both a lot of time and heartache."

Eric had been there. He knew it hadn't been quite that simple, but he wouldn't argue with Taylor on his wedding day. "So what are you saying? Trust Victoria?"

"Yeah. Trust her with your feelings."

"What do you mean?"

"After what she's been through, it must be really hard for her to trust men."

"That's obvious."

"From what Lexi tells me, she doesn't trust herself either."

Eric hadn't thought of that, but it ought to have been obvious, too. Some part of her blamed herself for what had happened, so, of course, she'd have trouble trusting herself with men and relationships.

Taylor went on. "If the two of you are going to have a chance, one of you is going to have to give up everything and move across the country, right? We both know you'd dry up and die if you moved away from the mountains, so it has to be Vic. That's a lot to ask of her, especially when she believes she can't tell a good guy from a bad one. If you want her to trust you, you need to trust her. You need to be the first one to say it."

"To say what?"

"I love you."

"Whoa. Wait." Moretti's voice came from behind them. "Are we interrupting something, man?"

Britta, still in her bathrobe, squealed from her post at the window. "The guys are here! Oh, wow, Lexi. Austin looks sharp. They all do."

Winona hurried over to see, already looking lovely in her dress. "Before this week, I'd never seen my brother in a tux. This is the second time now."

"Your brother is hot, if you don't mind my saying so," Britta said.

Winona laughed. "I don't mind. It's true. He's also a geek."

Lexi sat at the table, getting doused with hairspray and looking remarkably calm for a woman who was about to walk down the aisle. The stylist, whose name was Shawna, had put her hair in a low chignon, weaving thick plaits in and out to make a beautiful, elegant knot.

"There you go. What do you think?" Shawna stepped back.

"It's beautiful." Vic handed Lexi a small mirror.

Lexi stared at her reflection. "I love it. I want to see the back."

She got up and ran to the bathroom, her voice calling back to them after a moment. "Oh, wow! It's perfect."

Shawna basked in the praise, her own hair in a messy bun, her makeup flawless, her nails long and red. "Now, should we do the dress first or the flowers?"

"The dress," Vic answered. "We don't want to damage the flowers."

She crossed the room and took down the garment bag that held Lexi's wedding gown, tugging down the zipper and carefully removing it from the hanger. "Are you ready for your gown, Lexi?"

"Is it time?" Lexi walked out of the bathroom, handing Shawna the mirror.

"We've got twenty minutes till you need to be downstairs."

"Then I'm ready." Lexi walked over to her and held up her arms as Vic carefully lowered the dress over her, Shawna helping to make sure the layers of white fabric didn't snag in her hair or brush against her makeup.

Vic zipped it, straightened out the skirts, then stepped back. A lump lodged itself in her throat, and her hands found their way to her face. "Oh, Lexi, you're so beautiful."

The off-the-shoulder bodice had a twisted sweetheart neckline that fit snuggly around her breasts, the midriff accented with beading, the skirts made of the lightest silk chiffon, which would catch the breeze and flow around her as she walked.

The others gathered around.

"Don't you start!" Britta jabbed a finger at Vic. "She's right, Lex. You look amazing. Austin won't be able to take his eyes off you."

"Beautiful," Winona said simply.

Shawna motioned to Lexi to sit down again. "Okay, let's get these flowers in your hair."

Vic retrieved the box that Kendra had brought upstairs and set it on the table, then hurried off to put on her own dress. "Winona, can you help me with the zipper?"

The bridesmaids' dresses were identical to Lexi's, except that they were all a deep shade of lavender and didn't have the beading.

Winona hurried to help zip the gown, then stood back. "Wow. You look pretty amazing, too."

"I think I've gained ten pounds while I've been here." Vic adjusted the bodice, then fidgeted with the skirts.

Winona shook her head. "I don't think so—unless it all went to your boobs."

It *did* look pretty tight up there.

Unable to do anything about it, she walked back into the main room to find Shawna pinning sprigs of lavender, eucalyptus, white rose buds, and deep purple lisianthus along the top edge of Lexi's chignon.

"Britta, do you want help getting your gown on?" Vic asked.

"I supposed I'd better get dressed, huh?" Britta hurried over to where her dress lay draped over the back of the sofa.

Vic had just zipped her in when someone knocked on the door. She answered to find Bob and Kendra. "She's getting flowers put in her hair. Come in."

"Don't you all look pretty?" Kendra's smile was colored around the edges with envy. She'd always been jealous of Lexi and Britta—and their mother.

"Let me see you, Lexi girl." Bob walked over to his daughter, then stared in blank amazement as she got to her feet, a bright sheen coming into his eyes. He nodded, clearly at a loss for words. He reached into his pocket and took out a small box. "These were your mother's. She'd want you to have them."

Eyes wide with surprise, Lexi opened the box. There on black velvet sat two perfect white pearls with diamond accents. "They're lovely."

"They were my gift to her after you were born," Bob told Lexi.

Vic looked down at them. "Those are going to look even better with your hair and dress than what you're wearing."

Lexi took off the dangly earrings she was wearing and put on the pearls, a sheen in her eyes. "What do you think?"

Her father cleared his throat again. "Beautiful—just like your mother. She'd be so proud of you if she could see you now."

"Oh, great," Britta said. "Thanks, Dad. Way to make everyone cry."

The photographer entered and got a few photos of the last-minute preparations. Then Vic walked to the box of flowers and retrieved Lexi's bouquet. She carried it over to Lexi and held it out for her. "Now you're a bride."

Lexi took the flowers. "Thanks."

Her father glanced at his watch. "We'd best head down. If you want to back out, kid, you need to do it now."

Lexi laughed. "Nice try, Dad. Not a chance."

Chapter Eighteen

Eric walked with Austin, Moretti, and Belcourt down the wide, spiral aisle toward the space in front of the aspens, where Rose stood in a long purple gown, a silver headband bound around her brow, her long silver-gray hair tied back with purple ribbons. It looked like the whole town had turned out. People with invitations sat in the chairs, while those who hadn't been invited sat on blankets on the grass. Attire ranged from long gowns and suits to shorts and T-shirts.

Yeah, this was Scarlet.

Some folks said hello as they passed. Jack and Nate West stood, shook Austin's hand and then Eric's.

"Don't you boys clean up nice," Megs said.

Austin chuckled. "Why, Megs, is that an actual skirt you're wearing?"

"I figured why not go all out, given it's a special occasion and all."

Joe was wearing a suit with a bolo tie, Rain sitting beside him in a pretty black dress. Rico had worn his best pair of overalls and a clean T-shirt. Gabe Rossiter wore jeans, a white shirt, and a sports jacket. His lovely Navajo wife, Kat, sat beside him.

"Is that you, Rossiter?" Austin joked.

Gabe got to his feet, shook Austin's hand. "I can't remember seeing so many Team members washed and pressed at the same time."

He had a point.

And there was Sasha in a bright pink *dress*. Wow.

She jumped to her feet as they drew near and planted a kiss on Austin's cheek. "I'm so happy for you."

Eric glanced at his watch. "If you stop to kiss everyone, we won't make it to Rose before the ceremony starts."

Laughter.

"Okay, okay." Austin chuckled. "Save it for the reception, folks."

They made their way to Rose, who was very much in high priestess mode. "Namaste, gentlemen. What a beautiful day for this joining."

"Hey, Rose." Austin kissed her cheek. "Don't you look pretty?"

"Feng shui teaches us that purple and silver are especially auspicious colors for a wedding. I tried telling Lexi that but ..." Rose's gaze dropped to Austin's lavender boutonniere. "Lavender and sage are auspicious, too."

Austin looked up at the boom mic that dangled from a tree branch above them. "You guys tested the sound system, right?"

"Yep."

"The rings. Did you remember—"

"They're here in my pocket. We've got this. You focus on those vows."

"Right. Thanks."

Austin's mother and father appeared, entering the space through a rose arbor at the southwest corner of the house. They made their way through the spiral, his father shaking Austin's hand, while Roxanne kissed her son's cheek. Then came Chey on the arm of her date—a med student she'd met in Denver. She also gave Austin a kiss.

"How about a kiss for your brother by another mother?" Eric teased.

She laughed, kissed him, too, then sat.

A moment later, Kendra appeared, looking elegant in a long gray dress, a corsage pinned to her chest, a camera swinging from her hand.

"Never wear gray to a wedding," Rose whispered in a sing-song voice.

"It will be okay," Eric reassured her. "How are you holding up, buddy?"

Taylor blew out a breath, his brow creased with emotion. "I can't wait to see her."

"It won't be long now."

When Kendra had made her way through the spiral and taken her seat, the music started—Coldplay's "Yellow" performed by the Vitamin String Quartet—and all eyes turned toward the rose arbor.

"They're playing your song, brother," Moretti whispered.

But Eric wasn't sure Taylor even heard him. Every fiber of the man's being was focused on that archway, those wedding nerves finally kicking in. Eric was feeling it, too, truth be told.

This was it. Austin and Lexi were tying the knot.

Winona was the first to appear, looking amazing in a pretty lavender gown, a bouquet of purple and white flowers in her hands. When she stepped into the spiral, Britta appeared. She wore the same gown and carried the same bouquet, her strawberry blond hair hanging in long waves down her back. And then Victoria came into view.

Eric's brain went blank, his heart thudding against his breastbone. He could only manage details at first—her delicate shoulders, the wave in her dark hair, the swells of her breasts, the tuck of her waist, the flowers in her small hands, the way her skirt seemed to flow around her as she walked, the smile on her lips.

God in heaven, she was beautiful.

He couldn't take his gaze off her as she crossed the lawn and entered the spiral, working her way toward him, Austin's words coming back to him.

Trust her with your feelings.

Then everyone stood.

Oh, yeah. The bride.

Eric jerked his gaze from Victoria, and there she was—Lexi. She crossed the lawn on her father's arm looking like a million bucks in bridal white, flowers in her red hair, a big bouquet in her hands, a serene smile on her face.

Eric glanced over at Austin and saw a sheen of tears in his eyes.

Victoria took her place across from Eric, almost afraid to look at him, worried she'd look into his eyes and see the damage she'd done. She fixed her gaze on Austin instead, her happiness for him chasing away her gloom. He looked so handsome in his tux, lavender boutonniere pinned to his chest.

And—*oh, God*—there were tears in his eyes.

Eric leaned in and whispered something to him, a grin on his face, and Austin blinked, nodding, a faint smile playing on his lips, his gaze fixed on Lexi as she made her way through the spiral.

Vic looked away, still unwilling to risk eye contact with Eric. Instead, she focused on Lexi, who made her way around the aspens for the final time, stopping with her father at the single vacant chair, kissing him on the cheek, and leaving him there to walk the last few feet by herself. Her pretty face was a picture of joy, her eyes bright.

She reached Austin's side.

He took her hand, raised it to his lips, kissed it, the love he felt for her there on his face for the world to see. "You are so beautiful."

Together, they turned to face Rose, who beamed at both of them as the music came to an end. She reached behind her for a cord that hung down the white trunk of an aspen tree and turned on the mic.

"Beloved friends and family, we are gathered together today in this place to witness and celebrate the marriage of Austin Taylor and Lexi Jewell. Some of you watched them grow up. Some of you went to school with them, while others are co-workers or friends from college. Today is a day of joy, so it's okay to laugh, to applaud, to smile, or to cry.

"Lexi and Austin chose to get married here in this spot because it was here, sitting among these aspens, that they first fell in love. It was here they had their first kiss. It was here they sat to plot ways of spending more time together. And it was here where Lexi's parents were married back when these trees were saplings."

Vic hadn't known that last part.

The lump in her throat grew harder.

Rose went on to share the story of Austin and Lexi's romance—the G-rated version. Judging from the laughter when she mentioned Austin's old pickup truck, it was a story most people in attendance had heard before in its NC-17 form. Vic laughed with them, the lump in her throat easing, a soft breeze carrying the scent of lavender and roses, tickling her skin, catching her skirts.

And then it was time for Lexi to say her vows.

Vic sent her a burst of good vibes.

You can do this!

Lexi looked up into the eyes of the man she loved, her voice strong and clear as she spoke. "I, Lexi Rose Jewell, take you, Austin Michael Taylor, to be my husband in a marriage of equals. I commit to you all that I own and all that I am—body, heart, and soul."

As Lexi said her vows, Vic's gaze drifted of its own accord to Eric.

Her heart gave a hard knock.

Oh, God.

He was watching her, his eyes looking right into hers, their blue depths a mirror for the torrent inside her. In a heartbeat, the world seemed to shrink until it was just the two of them, the vows Lexi spoke filling the space between them.

"I promise that you will be the source of my pleasure—and my solace in times of pain. I promise to share your dreams and your fears, to comfort you and shield you from harm, and to show you respect, love, and devotion through all the joys and struggles of our lives together. Most of all, I promise to be your faithful and true friend, honoring you above all others, from this moment until my dying breath.

"I make this promise in love, keep it in faith, nourish it with hope, and will renew it in my heart every day."

There was a murmur of approval from the crowd, and the spell broke, the real world returning. Pulse still racing, Vic glanced over at Lexi and realized she'd finished her vows.

Now it was Austin's turn.

*W*hat the hell had just happened?

Eric didn't know. Something had passed between him and Victoria, and now his heart was pounding like he'd just run a mile in full bunker gear.

Snap out of it!

He wouldn't be any good for Taylor if he couldn't focus.

"Most of all, I promise to be your faithful and true friend, honoring you above all others, from this moment until my dying breath. I make this promise in love, keep it in faith, nourish it with hope, and will renew it in my heart every day."

Cheers.

Relief surged through Eric. Taylor hadn't screwed up his vows once—as far as he could remember.

Rose looked straight at Eric. "May I please have the rings?"

The rings.

"Oh! Yeah." *Shit.*

Laughter.

Eric reached into his vest pocket, took out the two platinum wedding bands, and put them into Rose's upturned palm.

Rose held the rings out at chest level, placed her free hand above them as if casting a spell on them. Eric wouldn't be surprised if that's what she was actually doing.

"Your wedding rings are the outward sign of the love that unites you. They are made of platinum, a precious and rare metal that endures forever. Lexi's has diamonds, the toughest substance known to us. Like all circles, your rings have no beginning and no end. Wear these as a symbol of your love, which is precious, rare, and endures forever."

Lexi turned to give her bouquet to Vic.

Rose handed Austin's ring to Lexi. "Lexi, place this ring on Austin's finger and repeat after me. With this ring, I become your wife. Wear it as a symbol of our love."

Lexi took the ring, repeated the words, and slid the ring onto Austin's hand, the two of them sharing a private smile, and damned if they didn't look happier than Eric had ever seen them.

Rose repeated the words for Austin.

"With this ring, I become your husband. Wear it as a symbol of our love."

Rose was clearly enjoying every second of this. She held up her hands like a priest who'd just said mass. "Lexi and Austin, you have taken vows before witnesses, declaring your love and committing yourselves to each other. By the power vested in me by the State of Colorado, it is my great joy to pronounce you husband and wife. Please, seal your vows with a kiss!"

They were in each other's arms in a heartbeat, and this wasn't just a peck on the lips, Austin holding her close, Lexi going pliant in his arms.

People began to laugh.

And still they kissed, deep and slow and hard.

"Get a room!" someone shouted.

That finally brought them back to reality.

"Friends and family members, I present to you Austin and Lexi Taylor."

Eric cheered and applauded along with everyone else, his gaze drawn again to Victoria, who handed Lexi her bouquet and kissed her on the cheek.

Then the recessional began—Joe Cocker's "You Can Leave Your Hat On."

More cheers and laughter.

Austin and Lexi linked arms and danced together back through the spiral. They'd gone maybe twenty feet when Austin scooped Lexi into his arms and spun her off toward the rose arbor.

Now, finally, *finally*, Eric got to touch Victoria. He stepped forward, offered her his arm, and the two of them walked back down the aisle together.

"You look beautiful," he whispered to her. "I could barely take my eyes off you."

"Thanks. You, too." She gave a furtive smile. "Can we talk?"

"I think we have to sign the marriage certificate and then pose for a bunch of silly photos. There might not be time until after lunch and all the speeches. But, yeah, we definitely need to talk."

They passed Megs and Ahearn.

"What's the matter, Megs?" Eric teased. "Got something in your eye?"

"It's these new contact lenses." Megs dabbed her cheeks with a tissue.

"Right."

When Victoria laughed, it felt like the rising of the sun.

They signed the marriage certificate, then posed for photos for the better part of an hour. Vic hadn't managed to get a single private moment with Eric. Guests now took their seats in the party tent, the sides of which had been tied back, while the catering staff hurried to set up a buffet.

It was then Vic finally saw Eric alone, strolling across the grass.

She lifted her skirts and hurried over to him. "Do you have a second? I really want to talk with you."

He glanced toward the tent. "They're about to open the buffet, so we don't have much time."

"I wanted to apologize for how I reacted last night."

"You have no reason to be sorry."

"You're not angry with me?"

His brows drew together, and he pulled her with him behind the rose arbor. "I'm not angry at all. I'm sorry for what I said last night. I didn't mean it the way it sounded. But, hey, we've got all night to talk this through."

Somehow she didn't think they'd spend much of the night talking.

He ducked down and kissed the swells of her breasts.

"Bobbing for apples?" a man's voice asked.

Lexi's dad.

Eric drew back, tried to look casual. "Hey, Bob."

Vic's face burned.

"Come on." Eric took her hand in his, and they walked together toward the tent.

Then Vic saw him—Bear.

He stood on the sidewalk in front of the inn, watching, hat and Bible in his hands.

"Hang on." She ran over to Bear. "Hey, Bear, would you like some lunch and wedding cake? Come join us."

He stared at her. "Gosh, you look pretty."

"Thank you. That's sweet of you. Come have lunch with us."

"Are you sure it's okay?"

"I'm sure."

He followed her like a child to the tent, where Eric was already getting a place set for him at the end of one of the tables.

"See?" She pointed. "There's your spot."

Eric gestured toward a chair. "Hey, Bear, come eat."

She wasn't sure Bear knew what to do at a buffet, so she fixed a plate for him and sat it down before him, together with a glass of lemonade. "I've got to go sit with Lexi and Austin now, but if you need anything, let me know, okay?"

Bear nodded. "Truly I tell you, whatever you did for one of the least of these brothers and sisters of mine, you did for me."

She gave him a smile. "You're welcome."

Eric walked with her to the buffet and handed her a plate, using the opportunity to lean in close. "God, I adore you. Your heart is pure gold."

His words put a glow behind her breastbone.

The meal was delicious—a choice of herb-roasted chicken breast with rhubarb compote or salmon with lemon and herbs, and roasted new potatoes with parsley, salad, roasted asparagus, and green beans with mint. Wine was available, but she stuck with lemonade—until Eric brought her a glass of champagne.

"For the toasts," he said.

"Is everything under control with Chaska and the projector?"

He nodded. "Belcourt and Moretti are going to bring in the screen and projector as soon as you finish your toast."

That was perfect.

She took a sip of champagne. "Are you nervous?"

Dark brows drew together. "Taylor is my best friend. I don't want to fail him."

She squeezed his hand. "You won't."

And then it was time.

Butterflies did a quick dance in Vic's belly, more for Eric than for herself. She did lots of public speaking as part of her job. But this was new for him.

Eric tapped the side of his champagne glass with his knife, the *ding-ding-ding* bringing an expectant silence. "When I sat down to write this, I didn't know whether it was supposed to be short and sweet or longer. But since rangers complain that firefighters talk too much, I figured Taylor knew what he was getting himself into."

This statement brought guffaws from people scattered throughout the tent—presumably other firefighters and park rangers, who got the in-joke.

"Austin Taylor is my best friend. I don't remember not knowing him. My mother, Robin, babysat him so she could stay home with me. I'm certain the two of us were a handful."

"You were," Robin called out, making everyone laugh.

Eric went on to describe some of their most memorable antics. Skipping school so they could fish and being caught in the lie by Austin's father. Trying to construct a real, operational lightsaber at age ten, only to catch his mother's Tuff Shed on fire—the event that led Eric to want to be a firefighter. Thinking they were buying weed their first year of high school, only to be busted in possession of dried oregano by their PE teacher.

"We were both grounded for a month—for buying *oregano*."

Laughter.

"But about that time, we began to notice her. Lexi Jewell. We'd known her all our lives, but in middle school, she went through some changes. By the time we got to high school…" Eric paused. "Well, she'd become the prettiest girl in the school, maybe all of Scarlet Springs. We talked about her at lunch. We talked about her after school. If one of us actually talked *with* her, we felt like we'd won the damned lottery. 'Lexi Jewell said hi to me in the hallway.'"

More laughter.

Then he shared how Austin, who'd gone through some changes too, had gotten up the courage to ask her out—and she'd said yes.

"Man, I hated him. I was so jealous. Not only had he hit puberty first, but he'd gotten the girl the rest of us wanted."

He told them about Lexi and Austin's breakup and how Austin claimed to despise her for years after that. "Then one day twelve years later, she shows up in town. Austin acts like he couldn't care less. But in less than a week …"

Eric's gaze shot to Vic's, and he seemed to forget what he was going to say.

He swallowed. "In less than a week, they'd fallen in love. Again."

He turned to Austin and raised his glass. "Taylor, you are like a brother to me. You brought your father into my life, shared your little sister, gave me an extra mom. You helped me set that shed on fire and discover my true calling. You're my climbing soul mate, my wingman and co-conspirator, and the best buddy a guy could have. I've watched you and Lexi from the beginning and know better than anyone else that the two of you were always meant to be. To Lexi and Austin!"

Vic stood and raised her glass along with everyone else. "To Lexi and Austin!"

She remained standing, taking a moment to organize her notes, ignoring the stirring of butterflies in her stomach. Okay, so she was a little nervous.

"I didn't meet Lexi until our first year of college at the University of Illinois. She was studying to be a certified public accountant, while I was focused on marketing and public relations. Somehow the computer system decided we would get along, and so we were put together as roommates.

"That computer must have been a genius machine because who could have predicted that a girl who'd grown up near Central Park in Manhattan and a girl who'd grown up in Scarlet Springs would have so much in common.

"I think it was probably our first day as roommates when Lexi told me about this jerk back home who'd just broken her heart, some guy named Austin Taylor. Oh, I hated him for her."

She glanced over at Austin, saw that he was laughing with everyone else.

She shared a few stories of their college years together, ending with Lexi's return to Scarlet. "When Lexi told me she was going back to Scarlet Springs for a while, I was against it. Not only was I going to miss my best friend, but I was afraid that Austin, that big jerk, would somehow dig his talons into her again. I warned her.

"I would like to state for the record that I was right."

Cheers and applause.

Vic raised her glass. "Lexi, you're the sister I never had, and, Austin, you turned out to be Lexi's knight in shining armor after all. You make Lexi so very happy, and that's all that matters to me. To Lexi and Austin—and happy endings."

As she spoke the words, Vic felt a trickle of sadness. Her own story was turning out to be quite different from Lexi's. By this time tomorrow, she'd be on her way back to Chicago and far from the man she ... *loved.*

The word came so naturally to her mind that it took a moment for the whole thing to sink in. When it did...

Oh, my God.

Adrenaline zinged through her.

She didn't just care about him. She was in love with him.

She was in love with Eric.

Chapter Nineteen

*E*ric watched as Belcourt finished hooking up the laser projector and inserted the flash drive with the video. When he got the thumbs-up, he tapped on his champagne glass again, waiting till the tent fell quiet. "As soon as Taylor and Lexi got engaged, I started a special project. I had no clue how to finish it. Luckily, Victoria, our lovely maid of honor, had the skills needed to step in and turn my idea into a reality. Can we get the side flaps lowered to make it dark?"

Event staff hurried to comply with his request, a handful of guests stepping up to help, too, until the party tent was dim.

"Belcourt?"

Belcourt started the video.

Music played, Eric's mother's face appearing on the screen.

"Emily Jewell was my best friend."

At those words, Eric heard Lexi and Britta give a quick little gasp.

On the screen, his mother was still talking. "I remember the day Lexi was born and how proud Emily and Bob were of their little bundle. She was cute as a newborn, too, that girl. Lots of red hair, those big green eyes."

A photo of Emily showing off her rounded belly appeared then faded into one of her holding newborn Lexi, all bundled in blankets, in front of the inn. That image faded, cutting to video of Frank, who owned the Pump 'N' Go gas station.

He repeated Eric's question. "What would Emily Jewell say if she knew Lexi was marrying Austin? She'd say, 'Did that boy ever get out of diapers?'"

Laughter.

Eric looked over at Lexi and Taylor and saw they were laughing, too, tears running down Lexi's cheeks, Britta wiping tears away with her fingers. He nudged Victoria, who followed the direction of his gaze, then looked up at him, tears in her eyes too. She moved closer, slid her arm around his waist.

Oh, yeah. He liked that.

Then Mrs. Beech, who'd been everyone's English teacher in Scarlet Springs for the past century or so, appeared on the screen. "Why Emily would be pleased as punch to hear her daughter was marrying that Taylor boy. He was always such a nice boy. He was a good skier, too. He grew up to be a park ranger. Did you know that?"

"Yes, ma'am," Eric's own voice answered. "We work together sometimes."

More laughter.

The video cut to Rose. "Oh, Emily knows. Of course, she knows. Whatever journey her spirit has made, she knows more about us now than we know about ourselves. She's thrilled that Lexi and Austin are together. She used to come to me for readings. She had a lot of second chakra energy just like Lexi—very fertile, very sexual."

And so it went, the stories of so many intertwined lives being told on the screen in personal anecdotes and faded photos, Lexi and Austin growing up before everyone's eyes. Then music began to swell, and Eric's mother appeared on the screen again as the video came to its end.

"Emily was my dearest friend. This town lost something precious the day she was killed. I believe in my heart that she'll be with us on Lexi and Austin's wedding day, watching. She'd be so proud of the woman Lexi has become, and she'd be happy that her baby girl found love with a good man.

"Congratulations, Austin and Lexi. We're all so happy for you."

The image faded, and credits scrawled across the screen. "With love to Lexi and Austin on your wedding day, from Hawke and Victoria."

The tent erupted in cheers and applause, event staff hurrying to tie back the tent's flaps again to let in light.

Lexi stood, dabbing her eyes with a tissue, a bittersweet smile on her face. "Leave it to you two to make me ugly cry at my own wedding reception."

More cheers.

She hurried over to them, planted a kiss on Eric's cheek, giving them each a hug. "Thank you both so much. That meant the world to me. Can I have a copy?"

"Of course," Eric said. "That's why I made it."

Taylor stepped up, drew Eric into a crushing hug. "Thanks, man."

As they walked off to cut the cake, Victoria wrapped her arms around Eric's neck. "That was a beautiful thing you did."

"I didn't do it alone, you know."

Then he kissed her, not giving a damn who saw.

Vic ran her fingertips over the bride's bouquet—tiny lavender buds, soft rose petals, fragrant eucalyptus. She hadn't tried to catch it. She'd stood in the back, figuring one of Lexi's other unmarried friends deserved some excitement. She'd been maid of honor, after all. But the darned bouquet had hit her right in the boobs.

Lexi ran over to her. "I can't believe you caught it."

Vic narrowed her eyes. "Did you do that on purpose?"

Lexi shook her head. "No! I swear I didn't."

"Okay, then." Vic didn't believe it signified anything. She wasn't superstitious. "Are you and Austin leaving soon? You've got a plane to catch."

The dancing had died down, and guests were now leaving at a trickle.

"We'll probably leave in the next half hour. I want to stop at the mine shaft and toss in a piece of cake for the knockers. You can come with us if you'd like."

"Sure." Vic didn't have to ask which mine shaft, and she didn't have to ask why. Lexi truly believed that a tommyknocker who'd called himself Cousin Jack had helped save her life a year ago, and it was an old Cornish tradition to share food with them. "It was a beautiful wedding. Truly, it was."

"Thank you. And thanks for all you did to—"

"You'd better watch the cake, Ms. Taylor." Austin walked up to them. "It's disappearing fast. Bear asked us to wrap an extra piece for him so he can get to his afternoon preaching session at the roundabout. You want a piece to throw in for Cousin Jack. Kendra wants to know if we're saving the top layer for our anniversary."

"Of course we are." Lexi hurried away with her husband.

For the first time since early this morning, Vic was alone. She strolled across the wide lawn past the rose garden, looking west toward the mountains, their breathtaking beauty helping her to hold a growing sense of melancholy at bay. She closed her eyes, inhaled, savoring the scent of the air—so unique to the Colorado mountains.

You're in love with him.

The thought sent ripples through her.

Yes, she loved him, but it didn't matter. He wouldn't leave Scarlet. He *couldn't* leave Scarlet. Just like the mountains and rivers, he belonged here.

Although she would love to relocate here, she needed some means to support herself. Her trust fund was for emergencies and retirement, not to enable her to sit on her butt. She'd considered what Eric had said about working for a big Denver PR firm. But the thought of moving across the country just to be near a man who might never feel for her the way she felt for him seemed like a spectacularly foolish thing to do. Given her track record when it came to men, it probably spelled disaster. She couldn't afford to make another big mistake.

Yes, she'd be closer to Lexi, too, but how would it feel to be a part of that group of friends if Eric found someone else and moved on?

Back in the party tent, she heard Bear's preaching voice as he offered Lexi and Austin his blessing. "What God has joined together, let no one put asunder."

The sweetness of it brought a smile to her lips.

She watched as he made his way across the yard toward the street, one precious piece of wrapped wedding cake cradled in one big hand, his Bible in the other. "Goodbye, Bear."

She didn't say it loud enough to be heard.

When would she see him again? When would she see this place?

If only she could inhale and hold it all inside her, right there close to her heart. There was something peaceful here, something she'd never felt anywhere else. She would visit, of course. She would come back for Christmas. She'd never seen the mountains in the wintertime. Maybe she would even ask Eric to teach her to ski.

He stood with Austin and the other groomsmen as Austin gave them each a gift bag. Lexi had given her bridesmaids engraved Kate Spade gold bangles. Vic's said, "Best friends forever," and had today's date. She watched to see what Austin had given them, but when Eric took his gift out, she had no idea what it was.

He laughed, held it up. "Excellent!"

Obviously, he was pleased with it—whatever it was. Probably climbing gear.

From the front of the inn came the sound of shouting.

She hurried toward the front yard to see what was happening—and stared.

Two young men followed Bear down the sidewalk shoving him, teasing him, trying to grab the cake from his hand, a beat-up SUV with California plates moving slowly along the street beside them.

She ran as fast as she could in heels, rage making her face hot. "Stop it!"

"Come on, man! Give it to me!"

"Just take it from him."

Bear turned his body away from them, cradling the cake against his chest. "He who oppresses the poor taunts his Maker."

"What are you—some kind of retard?"

"Leave him alone!" she shouted.

The men heard her this time and turned to look at her, their gazes raking over her, smiles taking over their faces.

"Well, hello, there," said one with bleached white hair and tattoos on his neck and arms. "What's your name, sugar?"

She tried to reach Bear, but they wouldn't let her pass. "Let him be. He hasn't done anything to you. Go on your way. Bear, find Eric or Austin, okay?"

The SUV had stopped in the street, two more young men watching, big smiles on their faces as if this were merely entertainment. She knew now that she ought to have gone for help rather than trying to deal with this alone. She didn't even have her phone.

Bear stared at her, fear in his eyes, cake still held protectively against his chest.

"What if we don't want to go?" said the one with the white hair. "What if I'd rather have you suck my cock?"

She ignored the taunt. "There are a hundred people at this wedding who care about the man you're bullying, including law enforcement."

"Ooooh! I'm scared."

The other one—the man who hadn't spoken to her—grabbed Bear's cake away from him and smashed it on the front of his jacket. "Eat that, retard."

"Don't touch him!" She started toward Bear, but the one with the white hair shoved her.

"Back off, bitch."

Victoria stumbled backward, one heel catching on the hem of her dress. She fell back into the street.

Squealing breaks. An approaching bumper.

Pain exploded against her skull.

And then ... *nothing.*

*E*ric saw the bastard shove Victoria, saw her fall backward into the path of an approaching car. His heart gave a sickening thud, fear like ice in his blood. "Vicki!"

He shouted back to Taylor. "Call EMS! Call Scarlet PD! *Now!*"

Please let her be okay!

His brain couldn't form any other coherent thought as he ran toward her, his mind taking in only fragments of what was happening on the street.

A woman jumping out of the car to stare down at the street in front of her vehicle. The bastard who'd pushed her jumping into the SUV. The SUV's tires squealing as it sped away. Bear standing as if frozen.

Eric reached the front of the car—and he saw her.

Victoria lay unconscious on her back, her head mere inches from the car's tire, the bouquet smashed beneath it, its petals crushed.

"Jesus, Vicki." He dropped to a knee beside her, bent over her, pressed his fingers against her carotid, searching for a pulse. "Can you hear me, baby?"

Years of training kicked in, forcing his panic aside.

Her airway was clear. She was breathing. Her pulse was rapid and weak.

She was going into shock.

"I didn't hit her," babbled the woman from the car, clearly terrified. "I'm sure I didn't hit her. I was already slowing down because those boys were in the way. It's their fault! One of them pushed her into the street."

"I saw, ma'am," he said. "It wasn't your fault. Why don't you come over here and sit on the curb?"

He didn't want her having a coronary or going into shock, too.

In the distance, he heard the wail of sirens.

He stripped off his tux jacket, laid it over Victoria, then shifted position and opened her eyes, relief surging through him to find her pupils equal, round, and reactive.

Then Taylor was there. "EMS and the PD are on their way. What the hell happened? Was she hit?"

"I don't think so. Some son of a bitch shoved her into the street. She fell backward. I think she hit her head. Did anyone get the plate number?"

"I ... I didn't even think about that," said the woman.

Bear finally spoke. "They tried to take my cake. Let the thief no longer steal, but rather let him labor, doing honest work."

So they'd tried to take Bear's cake, and she'd stood up for him.

"Come here, buddy," Taylor said to Bear. "Why don't you sit down?"

"Is she ... *dead?*" Bear asked in a tiny voice.

Eric left it to Taylor to help Bear and the woman from the car, their words fading into the background as he focused on assessing Victoria.

He rubbed a pressure point on her breastbone hard with his knuckles, deliberately trying to cause her pain. "Victoria, can you hear me?"

She didn't move, didn't even moan.

Damn it.

Come on, honey.

"That young man just shoved her, and she fell right in front of me."

"Thanks for the information, ma'am," Taylor's voice was calm. "The police will want to hear what you saw."

"Oh, my God! Did she get hit? What happened?" That was Lexi.

Eric let Taylor answer her questions.

There wasn't even a mile between the firehouse and the inn, but it seemed to take fucking forever for the ambulance to arrive. When it did, Silver was driving, Ryan riding shotgun. They jumped out, grabbed gear out of the back.

Eric brought them up to date. "I think she hit her head. She's breathing. Pupils are normal. Pulse is rapid and weak. Ryan, grab a C-collar. Let's get some fluids going and give her some O2. Then we can—"

A hand came down on his shoulder, gave him a squeeze.

He looked up.

Taylor.

"Leave this to them, okay? You've done your part. Just let them work. You've trained them well. They know what they're doing."

"Right." Eric made room for them, took Victoria's hand in his, watching while Silver started an IV in each arm. "Victoria, can you hear me? We're right here. We're taking good care of you."

And then it hit him.

His hands started to shake.

Jesus.

She'd almost been killed.

Victoria had almost been killed.

Victoria heard Eric's voice. She could hear him talking to her. He sounded worried. But no matter how she tried, she couldn't answer him.

Eric walked the length of the ER waiting room. They'd taken Victoria back for a CT scan more than an hour ago. What the hell was taking so long?

She'd started to come around on the ambulance ride to Boulder, opening her eyes and squeezing his hand when he asked her to. Her pupils had remained normal, and fluids had helped stabilize her blood pressure. But she'd been unconscious for so long. Things like "skull fracture" and "brain bleed" had started running through his mind.

She's going to be okay.

"Hey, Hawke," Taylor called. "You're pacing again. Come and sit down."

Lexi and Austin sat near the window together, talking quietly, their flight to Hawaii canceled, their honeymoon on hold for the moment. They were still dressed as bride and groom and drew a lot of stares from the people walking in and out.

Eric walked over to them, sat beside Taylor. "What is taking so long?"

"I don't know. Maybe she's waiting in line for the CT machine or something. Or maybe the radiologist—"

An ambulance pulled into the bay—a Boulder EMS company's rig—and EMTs pulled out a stretcher. The man with the bleached white hair lay on it.

"That son of a bitch." Eric was on his feet.

Taylor stopped him with a hand to the chest, leaning in close. "The chief of Scarlet FD cannot beat the shit out of a patient in the ER, not even one who deserves it. Besides, it looks like he's in bad shape."

"Fuck. Yeah. Right. Sorry."

They had a C-collar on the bastard and had intubated him. His face was pretty banged up, large-bore IVs in his arms, fluids wide open.

A Forest County sheriff's car pulled in behind the ambulance, and Julia Marcs climbed out.

"You stay here with Lexi. I'll find out what the hell happened." Taylor turned and walked out the sliding doors.

He and Julia talked for a moment, then walked inside together.

"Hey, chief. Hey, Lexi." Julia glanced at her watch. "You look awfully pretty in that gown, Lexi. Sorry this happened today."

"Thanks. We're sorry, too."

"As I was telling Taylor, a description of the SUV the assailants were driving went out over the county channel. About an hour later, I saw them pulling out of the parking lot at the Mine Shaft and turned on my lights. They didn't stop. The driver drove down the canyon like a maniac and lost control at the intersection of Ninth and Canyon. Rollover MVA. The other three had their seatbelts on and are on their way to the Boulder Hilton, but this guy didn't and was ejected."

"Shit. I'm sorry." Eric knew cops hated car chases that ended with injuries. "It looks like he's in bad shape."

"Yeah. Now I need to hang around past the end of my watch so I can finish my report. How's your friend?"

Eric shrugged. "That's what we'd like to know. She was only semi-conscious when we got here, but she—"

A man in green scrubs walked over to him. "Eric Hawke?"

Eric's pulse jumped. "That's me. How is she?"

The doctor gestured to one of the private rooms. "Why don't we talk over here where we can have a little more privacy."

Shit. Damn it.

That's what doctors said when they had bad news.

He, Taylor, and Lexi followed the doctor into a room with a table and a few chairs. The doctor closed the door behind them.

"We're both advanced life-support paramedics," Eric told him, hoping that would encourage the doctor to get to the point and not talk to them like they were two-year-olds.

"The good news is that she's conscious with no neurological deficits that we can see. She knows who she is. She knows where she is. She knows that she was maid of honor at your wedding. She doesn't remember what happened, which isn't surprising. That's very common with concussion."

"Oh, thank God!" Lexi looked like she might cry from sheer relief.

Eric took this in. "So what's the bad news?"

"She's got a skull fracture. It's a simple linear fracture, and scans show no sign of subdural hematoma or swelling. She's having some nausea and dizziness, but that's to be expected. Mostly, she's got a very bad headache. Because she was out for so long, I'd like to keep her here overnight, keep her under observation, try to get her comfortable."

"Thanks so much." Taylor shook the doctor's hand.

But Eric couldn't stand it any longer. "I want to see her."

Chapter Twenty

Victoria felt someone stroke her cheek and opened her eyes to find Eric looking down at her. "Eric."

"Hey." The smile on his lips did nothing to hide the crease of worry between his brows. "How do you feel?"

"My head … hurts a lot."

"You'll be getting another dose of morphine in about twenty minutes."

She reached out for his hand. "I'm so glad to see you."

He gave her fingers a warm squeeze. "Lexi and Taylor are here, too, remember?"

"They are?"

"Hey, Vic." Lexi appeared beside Eric, still wearing her wedding gown, Austin beside her. "We're still here."

Vic didn't understand. "Weren't you supposed to be on a plane?"

"We canceled our flight," Austin told her. "We're going to stick around until we know you're okay."

"But why … how?" It was all so confusing.

Eric stroked her forehead. "Do you remember why you're here?"

Of course, she did. Except that when she tried to recall what had happened, her mind went blank. "No."

Eric exchanged a glance with Lexi and Austin. "You got a bad bump on the head and have a concussion and a skull fracture. You're having some problems with short-term memory, but that's not unusual."

She looked from Eric to Austin and Lexi. "I ruined your wedding, didn't I? I ruined your honeymoon."

"No!" they said together.

"No, sweetie, you didn't ruin anything. Don't think that for a minute." Lexi reached out to touch her knee.

"You're a hero to everyone in Scarlet now," Austin told her.

"I ... I am?"

Then Eric told her how she'd run out to the street in front of the inn to protect Bear from some meth-head bullies who were trying to steal his cake and how one of them had shoved her, sending her toppling backward into the street.

"You hit your head hard, and you were out for at least ten full minutes."

It was like hearing a story about someone else. She truly couldn't remember any of it—defending Bear, arguing with meth-heads, falling into the street.

"Is Bear okay?"

"He was pretty shaken up about what happened to you, but he's going to be all right. Winona got him settled down. Megs helped him clean his jacket. Kendra brought him another piece of cake."

"What about the meth-heads? Did anyone catch them?"

The three exchanged a glance again.

"Yeah," Eric said. "They caught them. They're in jail."

"Good." Then it occurred to her. "How many times have you told me this?"

"Four. Or five now, I think."

"Wow." She closed her eyes, her head throbbing.

"Are you in a lot of pain?"

"Yes." It was like the worst migraine ever.

She heard a beep, and then Eric spoke. "Victoria is still in a lot of pain. Can you please call the doctor to ask him to boost the dosage and do something to help her now?"

"I'll be right in," said a woman's voice through the speaker.

"I called your father to let him know what had happened," Lexi said. "I told him you're going to be okay."

Eyes still closed—the light hurt—Vic thanked her. "What did he say?"

"He wants you to call when you're up to it."

So he wasn't coming out here. She supposed she shouldn't be surprised.

"Your boss called. Eric spoke with her." There was a note of amusement in Lexi's voice that brought Vic's eyes open.

"Oh, no. What did you tell her?"

"I told her that I couldn't tell her anything due to patient privacy laws. Then I whispered that I was the first paramedic on the scene and that you were in the hospital with a skull fracture, and we weren't yet sure how badly injured you were."

"Oh, my God." Vic laughed, then winced at the explosion this caused inside her head, pressing her fingers to her temple. "What did she say?"

"She wanted to know your hospital room, so I told her. Then she asked when I thought you'd be discharged. I told her I didn't know because I was just the paramedic and not a doctor. But I told her you probably wouldn't be able to travel for a week."

Vic couldn't help but laugh again, despite the pain. "You're terrible."

"I just want her to leave you alone so you can rest."

She squeezed his hand. "Thanks."

The door opened, and a nurse in maroon scrubs breezed in, something in her hand. "Are you in a lot of pain?"

Vic nodded.

The nurse injected medication into her IV.

Vic's eyes drifted shut, and she floated away.

Eric helped Victoria into his truck to make certain she didn't get dizzy and fall. When she was buckled in, he walked around to the back of the vehicle and made a quick call to Megs. He would never ask her to do anything like this under normal circumstances, but he was desperate.

"Megs here."

"Hey, I need your help. Can you and whoever else is around head to my house, climb in through the bathroom window, and clean the place? I haven't been there much for the past week, and it's a pit. I'm headed that way with Victoria—"

"Oh, my gentle Jesus." She moved the phone away from her mouth, but not far enough that Eric couldn't hear her. "Hawke wants me to tone out the Team to clean his house for Victoria. He must be in love."

He hadn't asked her to tone out anyone. "There's a six-pack in it for those who volunteer. I don't want her to see the place when it's a wreck."

Megs laughed. "You mean you don't want her to see how you really live. You've got it bad for her, don't you?"

"You have no idea. Please, will you do it?"

"Sure. I'll see who else is willing to help me."

"Thanks, Megs. I owe you big time."

"I probably owe you a few, too, but who's counting?"

"Thanks so much. We're leaving Boulder now."

"How is she?"

"She's still having bad headaches and short-term memory problems. Light hurts her eyes. But her scans have all been normal. She's going to be okay."

"I'm relieved to hear it. She's got guts."

"Yes, she does." Eric thanked Megs again and ended the call, then walked around to the driver's side door and climbed in.

"An important call?" Victoria asked him.

"Just Megs. Team stuff." He shoved his key into the ignition, and then his pager went off. He slipped it off his belt, scrolled through the message.

MEET AT HAWKE'S HOUSE. HE'S BRINGING VICTORIA HOME AND ASKED US TO CLEAN HIS PIGSTY. MUST BE SPOTLESS IN NEXT 30 MIN. BRING YOUR OWN HAZMAT GEAR.

Jesus!

The Team would never let him live this one down.

They talked of little things on the way up the canyon. Victoria was unusually quiet, a slight frown on her face. Was she in pain?

"Hey, are you okay?"

"I'm so happy that I'm here with you, but I feel bad about missing work. I feel like I'm playing hooky or something."

She had rescheduled her flight for next Saturday. Eric had managed to trade for more days off, but he would be on call. Still, that gave them the better part of six more days together—unless someone set the town on fire.

He reached over, took her hand. "You have a skull fracture and a concussion, for God's sake. You heard the doc. He said you need lots of rest."

"He also said I could travel."

"He said you could travel *if* you felt up to it—which you and I both know you don't. Cut yourself some slack, okay?"

She nodded, tried to smile. "I'm not very good at that."

"I've noticed."

Eric drove to the inn first to get Victoria's bags. Bob and Kendra had moved her things downstairs into Lexi's old bedroom to make room for the suite's new occupants.

"The inn looks like itself again," Victoria said.

The party tent was gone. The chairs were gone. Britta was gone, too, having caught a flight to California.

Victoria went inside with him to say hello. "Did Lexi and Austin make it to the airport this morning?"

It was the third or fourth time she'd asked someone about them.

Bob didn't know that. He got to his feet. "They sure did. They should be getting *leid* real soon."

Kendra shook her head. "You really think you're funny, don't you?"

Victoria gave Bob a smile. "It was a beautiful wedding. Thanks for having me as your guest. The Matchless is one of the most comfortable suites I've ever stayed in."

"You're welcome, honey. We're just glad you're going to be okay." Bob gave her a hug, then turned to Eric. "What did you think? Is the bed comfortable?"

"Yeah, Bob, that bed is comfortable. I suppose I should thank you, too."

"Nah, we'll just send you a bill."

Kendra gave Victoria a hug, too. "Don't listen to him. He's kidding."

Eric loaded Victoria's bags in his truck, then they headed off to his place, making light conversation. The closer they got to his cabin, the more nervous he felt. He wasn't ashamed of how he lived. But somewhere in the past twenty-four hours, it had dawned on him that the woman he loved might as well be from a different planet. She had traveled the world, while he'd spent most of his life in Scarlet. She had a college degree, while he had a high school diploma. And then there was the bit about her being a millionaire.

What could a woman as sophisticated as Victoria possibly see in him? She would probably take one look at his cabin and realize she'd made a mistake.

Knock it off, dumbshit.

"Tell me about your house," she said.

"It's a cabin."

"Cool."

"I rent it from this couple that lives up the mountain. It sits on their property. It's small, but I don't need much space. Most of what I own is climbing gear. I spend a lot of time at the firehouse anyway."

"I bet it's cozy."

He felt an irrational urge to laugh. "That it is."

A familiar green Subaru came around the curve headed their way, Megs at the wheel, Sasha in the passenger seat, Ahearn following them in his white Jeep Cherokee. As they passed, Sasha stuck her entire upper body out the window and gave him a thumbs-up.

"Oh, hey, there's Sasha." Victoria waved.

Eric coughed. "I wonder what they were doing out this way."

Five minutes later, he turned off onto the dirt road that led to his cabin, feeling terribly self-conscious. He could stand in front of her naked and feel completely at ease, but taking her to his home… He'd never brought any woman here.

"Oh, God! Is that it? It's like a gingerbread cottage. I love it."

"Yeah?" He let out a relieved breath and pulled into his driveway.

Vic waited until Eric reached her door to climb out, protective hands helping to steady her as she stepped to the ground. "I'm okay, really—just a slight headache."

"I'm not taking any chances." He took her hand in his. "Let's get you settled inside. Then I'll come back for your bags."

"Can't I see the outside?"

"Okay. Sure."

It was the most adorable cabin Victoria had ever seen, like something from a postcard. The bottom half was built of large rounded river stones, a wide stone chimney rising past the steeply gabled roof. Four broad steps led to a covered porch beneath which firewood stood neatly stacked. The front door was painted a cheery color of red, the window casings bright blue.

He led her around to the right. "Taylor and I built this deck a few years back. The owners bought the materials, and I got a discount on my rent for doing the work."

A few simple Adirondack chairs sat on the deck, and Victoria could imagine the two of them kicking back with a few beers here on a summer evening.

Then she saw it. "Look! You have your own creek."

It ran down from the hillside about thirty feet from the cabin, babbling its way over rocks and through groves of aspen before heading off down the mountain.

"It's not really mine, but, yeah, it's nice. Sometimes deer and elk come down at night to drink."

"It must be wonderful to live that close to nature."

He grinned. "It is—until there's a forest fire or the creek floods."

"What a beautiful place." She crossed the lawn to the creek's edge and just stood there, breathing in the stillness, a bittersweet ache in her heart. She didn't want to leave Scarlet. She didn't want to leave *him*.

He led her to the back of the cabin, where a big electric log splitter sat beneath a tarp, firewood stacked in big, circular piles. "I've started getting in my wood for the winter. It gets pretty cold up here, so I've usually got a fire going in the woodstove."

She liked the sound of that. "I bet it's beautiful when it snows."

He gave her hand a little squeeze. "Why don't you come back and find out?"

Oh, she planned on it.

Inside, the cabin was clean and simple—and very Eric. A blocky leather sofa sat in the living room across from a flat screen TV. Magazines with titles like *Outside*, *Rock and Ice*, *Climbing*, and *Fire and Rescue* sat in neat stacks on a coffee table of polished pine around a glass vase of flowers that looked like they'd come from the wedding—sprigs of lavender, eucalyptus, purple lisianthus, and white roses.

She bent down, sniffed. "Did Lexi give you these?"

Eric looked at the flowers as if he'd never seen them. "Oh. Yeah. Nice, huh?"

There was a single bookshelf that was stacked two deep with books, DVDs, and CDs, a Bose iPod dock on the top shelf charging an old iPod classic. Photos of mountains hung in simple frames on the wall. A small wooden table sat on the far end of the room across from a small galley kitchen, its white Formica countertops sparkling clean.

"The bathroom is right there. There's a tub and shower—the usual. The bedroom is through there. Like I said, the place is small."

"It's not much smaller than my condo."

He looked surprised at this. "Really?"

The bedroom had a single four-poster bed, its handmade quilt pieced together in shades of green and brown with applique moose across the bottom.

Vic ran her hands over it. "Did your mom make this?"

"It was a Christmas present a few years back."

"It's amazing."

A photo of his mother sat on a chest of drawers made of unfinished pine, the bright smile on her face and the affection in her eyes telling Vic that Eric had taken the photo himself.

"Where do you keep all your climbing gear?" She had half expected to find herself stepping over coils of rope, but so far she hadn't seen anything.

He pushed back the sliding door of his closet. "It's all here."

The closet was full from floor to ceiling with neatly arranged boots, ropes, helmets, harnesses, axes, and a bunch of stuff Victoria didn't have names for. "Wow. Okay, let me rephrase this. Where do you keep your clothes?"

He chuckled and pointed to the chest of drawers. "But, hey, no peeking at my underwear."

"Very funny."

"Why don't you rest, and I'll go get your bags."

She put a pout on her face. "The tour is over?"

"Well, there's nothing else to see unless you want me to show you the toilet."

She gave him her best innocent look—and sat on his bed. "I was hoping you could show me how your bed works."

The breath left his lungs, his brows drawing together. "Are you sure? The doctor said you need to rest."

"What if I promise to lie on my back? I read somewhere that sex is good for headaches."

The crease between those dark brows got deeper, but still he didn't move. "Probably not your kind of headache."

"Oh, come on. I haven't had you inside me for thirty-six hours, and I'm *dying*. Isn't it your job to save people?"

"Well, if it's a matter of life and death ..." He pulled his T-shirt over his head, revealing that amazing torso of his. "You just lie back. I'm a professional. I'll take care of everything."

Eric held Victoria in his arms, his fingers tracing lines over the silken skin of her back, her scent filling his head. A breeze blew through his bedroom window, the heat of sex cooling into a kind of blissed-out languor, the afterglow stretching into a long, intimate silence.

Then it hit him as it hadn't before.

He'd almost lost her. She'd come so close—*so* close—to being killed. Another couple of inches and the car's tires would have crushed her.

He drew her closer, kissed her hair. "You scared me to death."

She cocked her head to look up at him. "I did?"

"I saw that bastard shove you. I saw you fall in front of that car. From where I stood, it looked like it hit you. My heart just seemed to stop. I ran. I couldn't even think. I just ran to get to you. I think I shouted to Taylor to call for help." Eric couldn't remember, the details blurred by adrenaline. "I was so afraid I'd lost you. I don't think I've ever been more scared in my life."

She raised herself up to look at him, her breasts pressing against his ribcage, her gaze warm. "I'm so sorry."

"Hey, you have no reason to apologize. It's not your fault. I'm the one who's sorry. If I'd seen what was going on, if I'd gotten there sooner ..."

"I'm just glad they caught the guys."

"So am I." He hadn't told her that the one who'd shoved her into the street had died. He wasn't sure what that would do to her.

"It's so strange to hear you and Austin and Lexi talk about what happened when I don't remember any of it. It's almost like it happened to someone else."

He brushed a strand of dark hair from her cheek. "I bet it is strange."

"The doctor said I probably won't ever remember what happened."

Eric knew this. He'd been standing right there when the neurologist had told her, but he didn't say so. She was worried about the short-term memory loss, and he didn't want to upset her. "That's common with concussion."

"You helped save my life."

"I didn't do much. You would've survived even if no one had been there. And if you'd been hit ..." There probably wouldn't have been anything he could have done. "I don't want to think about that."

She smiled. "I kind of like this."

"Like what?"

"Knowing that you got all shaken up over me."

He tickled her side. "Oh, you do, do you? You like knowing that I almost went out of my mind?"

"No one has ever freaked out for me before."

Trust her with your feelings.

If he was going to tell her, now was the time.

He stroked her cheek. "That's because no one has ever loved you the way I do."

She gaped at him, tears coming into her eyes. "Y-you mean that?"

Now that the words were out, it felt as if a weight had been lifted off his chest. "God, yes, I mean it. I'm crazy in love with you, Vicki."

Her lips curved in a trembling smile, one tear sliding down her cheek. Then a look of worry pushed her smile aside. "How many times have you told me this?"

He laughed. "Just this once."

"Good." Relief brought her smile back. "That's definitely something I would want to remember, because I love you, too."

Then she kissed him.

Chapter Twenty-One

The next few days felt like a dream to Victoria. It was like being wrapped in a blanket of happiness. Life was so easy with Eric. She went to sleep each night in his arms and woke up beside him each morning, feeling a kind of contentment she'd never known. It wasn't just the sex, though sex with him was freaking amazing. Eric was there for her the way no man ever had been.

"This is the closest I've come to paradise," she told him one evening as she snuggled with him in one of his Adirondack chairs on the deck, watching the sunset.

"Me, too." He kissed her hair, held her closer.

They made a trip to Food Mart each afternoon to buy ingredients for suppers that she made. It was wonderful to have so much time to play in the kitchen, and she was thrilled to see how much he enjoyed her cooking.

"If I keep eating like this, I'm going to become the fat firefighter," he said after finishing off a meal of pot roast, garlic mashed potatoes, and arugula salad. "Will you still love me when my gut is hanging over my bunker pants?"

She still had bad headaches. She couldn't spend more than fifteen minutes on her laptop, the light from the screen triggering dizziness and pain. When the headaches got to be too much, she rested. But even then she felt cherished. Eric came to check on her, brought her water and pain pills, sat beside her, rubbed her back.

They went on short walks when she felt up to it. He told her the names of the flowers and trees and shared stories of growing up in the mountains. She got to know the property around his cabin pretty well and saw the landlord's house. A big two-story home with multiple decks and lots of floor-to-ceiling windows, it sat higher up the mountain in a meadow. It reminded Vic of the house at the Cimarron, though it was much smaller.

"The house, the property, the cabin—it's all up for sale," Eric told her. "I'm not sure the new property owner will want to rent out the cabin. Next time you come to Scarlet, I might be living somewhere else."

"Oh, I hope not. I love this place."

Eric left her alone only twice—once Sunday evening when he'd been toned out with the Team to rescue a hiker with a broken leg and once Tuesday afternoon when he'd responded to a planned burn on private property that had gotten out of control thanks to unexpected wind.

"This is what it's like, you know—getting called out all the time, never being certain when I'll be home, not being able to plan."

She remembered what his mother had shared with her—that Eric was afraid no woman would want to put up with his schedule. She wrapped her arms around his neck, stood on her tiptoes, and kissed him. "That's your job, and I love you for it."

"Are you certain?" Doubt put a crease between his brows.

"Yes." She kissed him.

V ic awoke early Thursday to a soft kiss.

Eric stood beside the bed, wearing jeans and a yellow Team T-shirt. "The Team got toned out for a rescue. It sounds pretty technical. I'll be back as soon as I can."

She caught his hand. "Be careful."

"Always." He gave her fingers a squeeze and was gone.

She dozed for a while, then got up and made breakfast and coffee. She ate her yogurt and fruit out on the deck, the fresh morning breeze carrying the songs of birds and the gurgling of the creek—okay, and the distant growl of a semi on the highway.

After breakfast, she tidied up the kitchen, took a shower, then went for a short walk, the land that surrounded the cabin now so familiar to her. The big boulder covered with lichens in different shades of green. The columbines that grew in the shade. The little pools in the creek. The rocky outcropping where a pine tree grew in seemingly nothing but rock. The field of golden banner down by the road.

A bittersweet ache gnawed at her breastbone. God, she was going to miss this place. She was going to miss *him*.

She'd never felt so close to anyone in her life, never felt the relaxed kind of intimacy she shared with him. The two of them fit together so well. Being away from him was going to hurt.

But she couldn't just quit her job, tear up her roots, and move to Colorado next week. She'd be acting on emotion, setting herself up for more heartbreak, more mistakes. Before she could move here, she would have to know what came next in her life. More than that, she would have to be sure about Eric—and about herself. They'd known each other for less than two weeks, after all—not counting last summer.

It's not that she doubted her feelings for him. She just didn't trust herself to see the situation clearly. She needed to think things through with the logical part of her mind, and that meant going back to Chicago and facing her life there.

As much as she knew this was true, she hated it.

She made her way back to the cabin to find the driveway empty. When she got inside, she checked her cell phone. No messages. She hoped he was okay. She hoped everyone on the Team—and the person they were trying to rescue—was safe.

Worry niggled at her, sliding into her thoughts like storm clouds creeping across a sunny sky. Was Eric okay? Would anyone think to let her know if something happened to him? Whom could she call to find out what was going on?

Stop being silly.

He'd told her it was a technical rescue. He was probably just working hard, hanging upside down on a rock somewhere.

If she lived with him, this is what her life would be like all the time—spending days by herself, waiting for him to come home, wondering every time he left the house whether he'd get injured or even killed on the job.

Could she handle that?

The answer came to her without a moment's hesitation.

Yes, she could.

If he could handle the danger and the emotional fallout that came from being a first responder, she could damn well handle loving him. Besides, he knew what he was doing. He hadn't become fire chief or a primary Team member by shirking on safety. He knew what he was doing. He wouldn't take unnecessary risks.

To keep her mind busy, she took out her laptop, checked her email, then looked at public-relations firms in Denver, Boulder, Fort Collins, and Colorado Springs. There were fewer than ten large companies in the entire state, and none of them had anything other than entry-level positions available at the moment. She would have kept searching, but looking at the screen made her head ache.

She'd just started making egg salad for lunch when Eric pulled into the driveway. Relieved, she met him at the front door. Immediately, she could see on his face that something was wrong. "What is it?"

He let the screen door shut behind him, took her into his arms, and held her, raw emotion surging through him. "God, it's good to have you to come home to."

She held him tight. "What happened?"

"It turned out to be a body recovery. A young climber fell, hit his head. There was nothing we could do."

She could hear the strain in his voice. "I'm so sorry."

He held her for a moment longer, his body communicating a need he couldn't. Then he shut all the emotion away.

He stepped back, kissed her. "Joe called. He wants you to come to Knockers tonight. He hasn't had a chance to treat you yet for the pizza lesson, and he and some of the others also want to say goodbye."

At the word "goodbye," her stomach sank.

Her stolen week in Scarlet Springs was almost over.

Eric drove down the mountain toward town, warmed by what his fellow Scarlet Springers had done to honor Victoria. She hadn't noticed—not yet. He slowed down, wondering how long it would take her.

"Please promise me no one is going to make a big deal out of anything."

"Like what—your protecting a defenseless person from men who outnumbered you and were bigger than you are?"

"I didn't do anything the rest of you wouldn't have done."

When it became obvious that she would never notice, he slowed to a near stop and pointed. "Look."

A square piece of plywood sat propped against the O'Connor's mailbox, words painted on it in bright orange spray paint.

THANK YOU, VICTORIA.

She stared. "Is that for me?"

"You know any other Victorias in Scarlet?" He sped up again.

"But why?"

She really didn't seem to understand why people felt so grateful toward her. But then, he'd never seen her do anything for accolades or attention.

He tried to explain. "You're not from here, but you defended one of ours. You protected a vulnerable man who can't protect himself and were almost killed. Is it so strange that people want to thank you?"

They passed two more road signs before reaching the highway and heading into town. Another stood facing outward at Frank's gas station.

"Gosh." She looked over at Eric, wide-eyed. "I didn't really *do* anything."

"I don't know what to tell you. I guess these folks think you did."

He passed through the roundabout, heading toward Knockers. Almost every business they passed had a homemade sign propped out front or stuck in the window. Some had smiley faces. Others had hearts. The one at the new dispensary had a marijuana leaf. But most just had words, all saying, "Thank you, Victoria."

The parking lot at Knockers was pretty full for a Thursday night. He parked, then went around to spot Victoria, still unwilling to let her risk falling. They walked hand in hand toward the entrance.

He could *feel* her tension. "Try not to look like you're walking to your execution."

That made her laugh. "I just feel silly."

He opened the door, stepped into the brewpub to find the Timberline Mudbugs on the stage, the tables full, people sitting around, waiting to be seated. He walked up to Marcia, the hostess, to get them added to the waitlist. "Two."

Marcia smiled. "Hey, Hawke. We've got your table ready. Right this way."

He followed her toward a table for four near the center of the place. "We're getting the royal treatment tonight."

Most of the Team was here, sitting in their spot near the climbing wall. Rose was here, too, with her latest beau—the guy with the bushy beard who ran the marijuana dispensary next door to her shop. What was that guy's name again?

Eric and Victoria were seated for less than a minute when Rain appeared at their table, carrying glasses of ice water. "Your money's no good in this place, Victoria. Whatever you want, it's on us. If it were me, I'd go for the shrimp and prime rib, the whiskey—the expensive stuff."

Victoria laughed. "Thank you, Rain. Please thank Joe for me."

"Sure thing."

Eric reached over, took her hands, looked into her big brown eyes. "Do you have any idea how good it feels to be the man who gets to walk in here with you?"

Her gaze went soft and warm in a way that just about killed him. "If it's anything like the feeling I get being the woman you're with, then it must be pretty special."

God, he was going to miss her.

Don't think about that.

When Rain returned, Victoria ordered the grilled chicken salad and an Italian soda. He ordered the prime rib and a beer.

He caught sight of Joe and excused himself from the table. "I'll be right back."

He walked over to the bar. "Hey, Joe. Victoria's feeling pretty self-conscious about all the attention. She doesn't think she did anything special. She doesn't want anyone making a fuss over her."

Joe glanced over Eric's shoulder in her direction. "Okay. We can keep it low-key, but someone here wants to thank her."

He pointed to a table near the kitchen.

Bear sat there, finishing his dinner, a big glass of milk next to his plate.

"Think she'll object to that?" Joe asked.

"Nah. I think we're good there."

"Also, I might or might not have asked the Mudbugs to do a special cover in her honor tonight."

"Thanks for understanding." Eric walked back to the table.

"What was that about?" Victoria asked.

"Just trying to make sure Joe doesn't embarrass you."

The food arrived a few minutes later, a frown coming over Victoria's features when she took her first bite of the chicken.

"Don't tell me you don't like this either."

"No, it's fantastic. I wonder what they use as a marinade. It tastes like …"

"Margarita mix." Joe stood there, a bottle of champagne and three glasses in his hands. "I'm glad you like it. Mind if I join you?"

Joe rarely stepped out from behind the bar during business hours, and he almost never sat with patrons. So when he pulled out the chair and sat, people gawked.

He set a champagne glass before each of them, opened the bottle, and poured. They made small talk while Eric and Victoria ate, discussing the wedding, the weather, and Rico's ongoing effort to get Chicago-style deep-dish pizza on the menu.

"I'm going to miss this place," Victoria said, looking around her. "There's no place like Knockers in Chicago."

"I was serious about that job offer," Joe said.

That seemed to fluster her. "My degree is in public relations, not cooking."

Joe shrugged. "I have a master's of science in mining engineering."

Eric could have tongue-kissed the man. Not that he really expected Victoria to leave her life behind to work in a restaurant, but he could hope…

When they finished their meals, Joe got to the point. "I understand from Hawke that you don't want us making a fuss about what you did. I get that. I really do. But Bear is important to us. It goes against the grain in this town not to honor our heroes."

"I'm not a hero." There was a dark frustration in her eyes. "You all keep saying I did something really brave, but I can't even remember it."

So *that* was the problem.

"I know someone who remembers it all—every bit of it." Joe motioned to Rain, who walked over to Bear's table.

Some of the tension left Victoria's face when she saw him. He shuffled over, hat in his hand, his head bowed, his long hair in tangles.

Joe got to his feet, pulled out the fourth chair. "Have a seat, Bear. You've got something you want to say to Victoria, don't you?"

"Yes, sir." Bear sat, lifting his gaze to Victoria at last. "Hello, Victoria."

"Hi, Bear. How are you?"

The question seemed to confuse him, or maybe he was just nervous. "Thank you," he said after a moment.

She gave him a soft smile that made Eric's heart ache. "You're welcome."

"Are you okay?"

She reached over, touched her hand to his arm. "I'm fine."

His face crumpled. "I thought ... I thought you were *dead*. That man shoved you into the street. You fell hard, and the car ..."

Eric tried to reassure him. "She was knocked out, but she's fine, buddy."

"Truly, I'm okay."

Some of the distress left Bear's face.

"How did it make you feel when Victoria came to help you?" Joe asked Bear.

Bear looked into Victoria's eyes. "Greater love has no one than this: to lay down one's life for one's friends."

Joe looked over to Victoria. "Do you still think you did nothing?"

Victoria blinked back tears. "I guess not."

Joe picked up his champagne. "Are you sure you don't want any, Bear?"

Bear frowned, shook his head. "Demon's drink."

The band was just finishing a song, so Joe waited till the applause faded, then stood. "Can I have everyone's attention?"

Silence fell over the place.

"Last week, a visitor to our town came close to being killed while trying to defend one of our own—Bear—from a group of bullies. That visitor, Victoria Woodley, doesn't want us to make a big deal out of what she did. That's just the kind of person she is. She doesn't even remember what happened. Let's all raise our glasses in thanks. Victoria, you'll always have a place here in Scarlet. To Victoria!"

Shouts rang out through the pub.

"To Victoria!"

Eric raised his glass. "To you, my angel."

Tears ran down Victoria's cheeks now. "Thanks. You're all so sweet."

Joe turned toward the band. "Hit it!"

The Mudbugs' lead singer spoke into his mic. "This is for you, Victoria."

Then the band broke into a Cajun rendition of Sam & Dave's "I Thank You." Those who knew the song laughed and began to sing along.

"Dance with me?" Eric asked.

"I would love to." She stood, gave Bear a hug, then followed him onto the dance floor, her hand in his.

As he took her into his arms and started leading, Eric would have given anything to freeze time and make the night last forever.

Vic ran her hands over Eric's bare chest, his arms bracketing her on the bed, his body raised up above hers. "I like it this way the best."

"Really?" He thrust into her again, slow and deep. "Why?"

She tried to find the words, distracted by the hard feel of him inside her. "I like to see your body move. I like to feel your strength. I like to feel overpowered by you."

She wasn't sure she was making sense. She could barely talk.

"Yeah?" He took hold of her wrists one at a time and stretched her arms over her head, pinning her to the bed, using just enough strength to make it feel real. "Does my sweet Vicki like a little domination?"

A dark thrill ran through her to feel herself restrained by him. "*Yes.*"

There was no need for words after that, as he drove into her hard, pleasure carrying both of them away.

*E*ric held her afterward. "We have to talk about it sooner or later."

For a moment, she said nothing, her fingers tracing lines across his chest.

"I don't want to leave you, but I have to go back. I need to think it all through. I love you, Eric, and I'm happier with you than I've ever been. But we've only really known each other for a couple of weeks, and moving here would be a huge change. If I'm going to do this, I have to do it the right way. I can't just uproot my life and my career based on emotions. I have to make sure it's what we both really want."

He understood why she was saying this, but part of him wanted to object. Of course it was what he wanted, but that wasn't really the issue. She was having trouble trusting herself to make a decision, and that was a problem she had to resolve.

He kissed her temple. "You have to do what's right for you. I understand that. When you're ready, I'll be here."

All he could do now was wait and hope.

Chapter Twenty-Two

Eight weeks later

Vic walked back to her office, set her files on her desk, and sank into her chair, relieved that the presentation was over. She'd worked tirelessly on this campaign since getting home two months ago. It was wonderful to have it behind her.

The executives from Merced Capital had been impressed and pleased with her work, particularly her situational analysis, which had dared to challenge their view of their niche as a company. Vic had suggested nothing less than an audacious rebranding. Abigail had been nervous about that, afraid they would reject the idea. But she'd left the conference room beaming and was now on her way to lunch with Merced's CEO.

Vic didn't care that she hadn't been invited. She didn't feel much like schmoozing. She booted up her computer and typed in her password, hoping to catch up on work emails before lunch, her fingers drawn to the diamond pendant Eric had given her on their last morning together. A half-carat princess cut diamond set in white gold, it was the most precious thing she owned because it had come from him.

"It's nothing fancy, but I hope you'll like it."

"Oh, Eric! It's beautiful. I love it."

There'd been such vulnerability in his eyes when he'd handed her the small wrapped box. She'd had to fight not to cry.

It had been only two months, but it felt like a hundred years since they'd stood there together in DIA and said goodbye.

She willed herself to focus on answering her email, setting aside for the moment the persistent unanswered question of what to do with her life. She had almost finished when her cell phone buzzed, making her pulse skip. She drew it out of her purse.

A text from Eric.

She opened it, smiled to herself, warmth blossoming in her chest. It was a selfie of him with a sexy smile on his face and a blue Post-It note stuck to his forehead that read, "I love you."

The Post-It was one of about a hundred Vic had scribbled on and hidden all around his cabin that last Friday when he'd been toned out on an EMS call. It had been her way of leaving a bit of herself with him. Every time he found one, he let her know, and she could see that it made him happy.

He sent another message, this one just text.

FOUND THIS ONE IN MY UNDERWEAR DRAWER. YOU SAW MY UNDERWEAR! LOVE YOU TOO.

That made her laugh.

She studied the photo, saw that his hair was sweaty and he was wearing his Scarlet Springs Fire Department T-shirt. He must have just finished a shift. She could almost smell him—the salt of his skin, the spice of his shaving cream.

How was she possibly going to make it to December?

She planned to spend the holidays with him and had already bought her plane tickets. But Christmas was four whole months away.

It felt like an eternity.

She saved the photo to her phone. She would download it to her laptop later and put it with the others he'd sent—photos of the aspens at his cabin starting to change, of Austin and Lexi on their deck, of a black bear that had wandered into his yard. Every photo was precious to her, a link to a place— and a man—she loved.

There came a knock at her door, and Jeff poked his head in. "Word is Merced is over the moon. Congratulations. I thought you'd want to know that I heard Abigail talking in the elevator. It looks like you've got that promotion on lockdown. I hope it comes with a hefty raise."

Jeff had done so much to help her through her first weeks back, when headaches and short-term memory problems had made it hard for her to work.

"Thanks for your help. I couldn't have done it without you, and I'm going to make sure Abigail knows that."

"Hey, we're a team, right?"

As he disappeared down the hallway, Vic wondered why this news about the promotion had left her feeling … nothing.

Two weeks later

*E*ric walked back to Rescue One, first-aid kit in hand, the ambulance heading down the canyon. Two guys had gone hiking off-trail, had gotten lost, and had spent the night out in the open in temps that had dropped almost to freezing. They'd been too embarrassed to call for help until it was clear they were in trouble. They were both suffering from exposure and dehydration, but they'd be fine.

Taylor walked up behind him. "Hey, got a minute?"

"For you?" Eric opened the rear doors of the vehicle, put the first-aid kit back in its place, and shut the doors. "Let me check my schedule."

Taylor stood there for a moment with a big grin on his face, then lowered his voice so the rest of the Team wouldn't hear. "Lexi's pregnant."

The words hit Eric in the face. "What?"

"Pregnant. You know—knocked up, with child, in the family way, bun in the—"

"I know what it means, but … Wow." He hadn't known they were trying for kids. They'd only been married for two and a half months. "That was fast."

"We're both thirty-three. We figured we'd better start soon if we wanted kids. I thought it would take longer than it did."

"It must be all that second-chakra energy Rose talked about at your wedding. Do I detect a hint of disappointment?"

Taylor shrugged. "I liked being in demand for my sperm. My days as a stud ended too quickly."

"Don't ask me to feel sorry for you. You've apparently been going at it like bunnies while I've been doing my best imitation of a monk." Apart from fucking his own fist, that is. He doubted monks did that. Then again, what did he know?

Taylor laughed. "Someone's grumpy. Heard from Vic lately?"

"She's finally got a free night, so we're supposed to talk on Skype."

"Good."

"If it were up to me, she'd be here right now, and we'd be starting a life together. But she's still working it out."

"Lexi says she's crazy about you. Give her time."

Give her time.

Isn't that what he was doing? It shouldn't take this long. It shouldn't be this hard. If she loved him, she should want to be here with him.

Shit.

Eric set his own frustrations aside. They had no place in this moment. He clapped Taylor on the shoulder. "Jesus, man, you're going to be a father. Congratulations. I'm so happy for you both. Is this a big secret?"

"Not really. Rose knows so—"

"Hey, everyone, guess what?" Eric called out, determined to beat Rose to the punch for once. "Lexi's pregnant. Taylor's going to be a father."

Cheers went up, and the Team members who were still on site moved toward them, dusty and dirty and grinning ear to ear.

Taylor narrowed his eyes, glaring at Eric. "Gee, thanks."

Megs gave Taylor a hug. "Apparently there's something you're good at besides climbing. Congratulations."

Sasha high-fived him. "How far along is she? When's the baby due?"

"She's about eight weeks right now, so she's due at the end of March."

Ahearn shook Taylor's hand. "We all expected this news when you were teenagers. I'm proud of you for making it this far, son."

That made everyone laugh.

"Drinks at Knockers?" Eric asked. "Yours is on me, buddy."

Taylor shook his head. "I need to get home. Lexi has been queasy more or less all day today. I don't want to leave her alone with that."

Megs nodded. "You're a good man."

As Eric drove Rescue One down the mountain and back to the Cave, he realized that his life had just changed. Taylor was going to be a dad. He had obligations to a pregnant wife now. He wouldn't have as much time for climbing or hanging out with friends. Well, that was as it should be.

But damn...

What would Eric be doing in March when their baby came? Would he still be alone? Would he and Victoria still be living this long-distance life?

God, he hoped not.

He'd just pulled into the bay at the Cave when his cell phone buzzed. He slid it out of the pocket on his belt.

A text message from Vicki.

CAN'T SKYPE TONIGHT. BOSS HAD OTHER PLANS. SO SORRY. I MISS YOU AND LOVE YOU. SKYPE TOMORROW?

Well, *fuck.*

He'd been looking forward to this all week. What the hell did her boss want with her now? Why couldn't Vic just say no?

Damn it.

He'd told Victoria he would wait for her, that he'd be here when she was ready, and he would keep that promise. But loving someone who lived far away was proving to be tougher than he'd ever imagined.

Vic stood with her back to the party looking out at the glittering city below, a glass of pinot noir in her hand, conversation mingling with the strains of jazz behind her. A few months ago, she would have found this view breathtaking, but tonight Chicago seemed cold and lonely.

She was supposed to be on Skype with Eric right now, not milling around making small talk with coworkers. It was her and Eric's first shared night off in weeks. But Abigail had called and invited Vic to dinner at her penthouse to celebrate the success of the Merced campaign. It was an invitation Vic had no choice but to accept.

Eric had been disappointed. He hadn't said it, but she'd been able to tell just the same. She couldn't blame him. She would never *choose* to have dinner with her boss over spending time with Eric, but she wasn't sure he believed that.

Ten minutes after she'd gotten that news, Lexi had called to tell Vic that she was pregnant. Vic was overjoyed for her and Austin, but their happy news had made her painfully aware of how very far away she was—and how alone.

Vic took a sip of wine, turned to glance around Abigail's apartment. She'd always wondered what the penthouse of the Aqua looked like inside, and now she knew. Abigail had, of course, had her home professionally decorated. Each piece of furniture was intended to make a statement, as was the art on the walls. Taken together, it looked more like the lobby of an ultra-modern office building than someone's living room. Vic would take the simple comfort of Eric's cabin to this any day.

"There she is!" Abigail walked over to Vic, wearing a dark blue cocktail dress with long sleeves and three strands of pearls, two young women following her.

Vic pasted a smile on her face. "I was just enjoying the view. This is amazing! Thanks for the invitation. It's a wonderful party."

That was Vic's policy for dealing with Abigail at events—thank her once and praise her twice.

"I wanted to introduce you to two of our promising interns." Abigail turned to the young women. "This is Victoria Woodley. She's one of our best and brightest, and she's about to be promoted to supervisor. The two of you will be working for her. Victoria, this is Kayla Adams and Ashley Harris."

Vic shook their hands. She'd been an intern once, too, and had felt so out of place trying to mingle with people who had real jobs. She gave them a warm smile, hoping to put them at ease. "Welcome to Jensen West. We're happy to have you with us."

She asked them a few questions—where they went to school, why they were going into public relations, where they hoped to end up one day. Their answers were as bland as their facial expressions. After a few minutes of this, she excused herself and started off toward the hors d'oeuvres.

"What a stuck-up bitch," said Kayla. "I don't want to work for her."

"Her boobs are probably fake," Ashley said.

Stunned, Vic turned back to face them. "Excuse me?"

She was used to a little backstabbing. That was just part of corporate life. But what had she done to provoke this?

They stared at her wide-eyed, their faces going white.

She opened her mouth to tell them off but was interrupted by a single thought.

You don't belong here anymore.

The words blazed across her mind, bright and crystal clear.

And suddenly it all seemed so obvious.

How could she have been so stupid?

She should be in Scarlet Springs with her best friend and the man she loved. She shouldn't be here, where no one truly cared about her. She'd rather risk everything for a chance at happiness with him than waste another moment of her life here. If that was a mistake, so be it.

She realized the two interns were now babbling excuses and apologies. She cut across them. "You're not going to get anywhere in the business world with that kind of attitude. And, by the way, my boobs are real."

People were staring now.

Vic didn't care.

She made her way over to Abigail, cutting her off mid-conversation. "I'm sorry to interrupt, Abigail, but I needed to let you know that I'm resigning, effective right now. I'll email a letter of resignation as soon as I get home. Jeff worked as hard as I did on the Merced campaign. He deserves the promotion."

Abigail gaped at her. "What? Has something happened?"

"Yes." Vic couldn't keep the smile off her face. "I just realized I don't want to be here any longer. I want to *live* my life, not work it away. I don't care if it's a big mistake; I'm moving to Colorado to be with the man who loves me."

Ignoring Abigail's stunned expression, she turned and hurried away. She had some calls to make—and, hopefully, a plane to catch.

Eric sat at the bar in Knockers working on his second whiskey. The place was almost empty apart from Joe and his staff—and, well, Hank, who'd just gotten out of jail a few days ago.

"You're in a fix." Hank looked over at Eric, sipped his soda. He was on probation, so Joe refused to sell him anything harder. "I never seen you drink like this, Hawke—sitting at the bar by yourself."

"Yeah?" Well, he'd never been in love before either.

Being in love sucked.

"You got woman troubles. I can tell. That's the worst kind of trouble for man—not counting being arrested, of course."

"I suppose it is."

Hank sipped his Coke. "You want to talk about it? You sure helped me out. If you need a shoulder, I'm here."

Eric looked over at Hank, then down at the whiskey in his hand. Here he was at almost midnight on a Friday night drinking and looking pathetic enough that Hank, of all people, was on the brink of offering him advice.

Jesus.

He was a rock-and-roll man, but his life had turned into a country song. This wasn't how it was supposed to go.

"Hey, Joe, hit me again." Hank pushed his soda glass across the bar as if it were a shot glass.

"The bar's closed, Hank. We'll see you tomorrow."

Hank got down from his bar stool, pointing to Eric with a sideways jab of his thumb. "Why doesn't he have to leave?"

Joe cleared Hank's glass. "He's not done with his drink, is he?"

"I guess not." Hank shuffled off, clearly pissed at being told to go.

Eric tossed back the rest of his drink, set the glass down on the bar. "Since you haven't kicked me out, can I have another?"

"Nope." Joe took his glass, then pulled his cell phone from his pocket to read a message. "You've had enough."

"Oh, come on. Two shots won't even put me over the legal limit."

"Exactly." Joe leveled his gaze at Eric. "That's why we'll stop at two. We need a sober fire chief."

Eric knew Joe was right. He needed to be able to respond in case the Team got called out tonight—or something crazy happened at the firehouse. In his profession, he just didn't have the luxury of getting shitfaced.

He got to his feet. "Well, goodnight."

"Sit down." Joe's tone was so stern that Eric's ass hit his seat immediately. "I know what's eating you, but I don't think you have to worry. Victoria loves you."

Perhaps Eric had had too much to drink after all. That would explain why he started babbling. "I'm trying to give her the time she needs, but this is harder than I thought it would be. I love her and want to be with her. I don't understand why she's not here if she loves me."

Joe looked over Eric's shoulder and smiled.

"I *am* here."

Eric got to his feet so fast that he knocked his chair over. "Vicki?"

"Hi." She stood there, looking like a dream in a short black dress, purple fleece jacket, and heels. Then she was in his arms.

He held her tight, some part of him wondering if he was drunk or dreaming or just out of his damned mind. "Vicki. Jesus. I can't believe you're here."

"God, Eric, I missed you so much."

"I missed you, too." He ended the hug without letting go of her, his mind racing with questions. "I thought you had to go to some kind of dinner with your boss."

"I quit."

"You … *what?*"

Words spilled out of her. "I went to the dinner because I really had no choice, but I felt so out of place. The view from the penthouse didn't even matter to me, and these two interns started talking behind my back. One said I was a bitch, and the other said my boobs were fake, and then it just hit me. I don't belong there anymore. I belong here in Scarlet with you. So I quit my job and bought a plane ticket and called Joe. I wanted to surprise you, but he couldn't pick me up, so he called the Team, and Sasha and Nicole came to get me."

Her words came out so fast that most of what she'd said went over his head—except for the most important part. She'd come back to him. "You've decided you belong here now?"

"If you still want m—"

He cut the question short, answering it with a long, hard kiss, blown away by the goodness of just being near her, the weight of missing her and worrying that she might not come back lifted off his shoulders so suddenly that he was floating. He only stopped kissing her when he heard laughter.

He and Victoria looked toward the bar and saw Joe, Rico, and Rain standing there, together with Sasha and Nicole, who waved at him.

"Hi."

He fixed an accusing gaze on Joe. "You all knew she was on her way here and didn't tell me?"

Joe shrugged. "Victoria wanted to surprise you, and since she's going to be my business partner …"

Eric's gaze snapped to Victoria. "His business partner?"

"I'm starting a deep-dish pizza business. I'll work out of Knockers, serving pizza to Joe's customers, but the home delivery part of the business will be mine alone. We haven't worked out the details yet, but I'm really excited about it. I think I'll call it 'Victoria's Chicago-style Deep-Dish Pizza.' What do you think?"

"Wow. Yeah. Good." He couldn't seem to manage more than single syllables.

"You okay, Hawke?" Joe asked. "You look a little stunned."

Everyone laughed.

But, hey, could you blame him? His entire world had righted itself in the past five minutes, and it was taking a moment to sink in.

He looked into Victoria's beautiful brown eyes. "I've never been better."

The ten-minute drive to Eric's cabin seemed to take an eternity. The kiss at Knockers had ignited a spark in Vic, and she wanted him.

"Hurry," she said. "It's been so long."

"Tell me about it."

Then she remembered. "I'm on the pill, so no more condoms."

He moaned. "Don't tell me that while I'm driving. We'll end up in a ditch."

She pressed her thighs together to ease the ache and tried to think of other topics besides how horny she was. She ended up telling him again, more slowly this time, how she'd walked out of Abigail's dinner party. "You should have seen the look on her face. I almost feel sorry for her."

"I don't." He pulled into the driveway, handed her his keys. "I'll get your bags."

She walked up the porch steps, slipped the key into the lock, and stepped inside on a rush of happiness, her gaze moving over the familiar space.

He walked in behind her, set her bags on the floor, and locked the door, shutting out the night. "Welcome home."

She turned to face him. "I like the sound of that."

And then they were on each other, kissing deep and hard. Eric's strong body surrounded her, his erection pressing against her belly. "*Vicki.*"

He grasped her buttocks, lifted her off her feet, and carried her to the kitchen table, not once breaking the kiss. "I need to be inside you."

"Yes. *Now.*"

He rucked up her dress to her hips, yanked off her panties, then pulled down his zipper, freeing himself. The breath left his lungs in a long exhale as he entered her, the two of them moaning together at the pleasure of it.

His eyes drifted shut, a look like pain on his face. "*Jesus.* God. Vicki. You feel too good. I don't think this is going to last very long."

She wanted to ask him what the difference was between sex with and without condoms, but the thought disappeared entirely when he began to move, his silky, sweet strokes filling her, answering that deep ache. "*Eric.*"

He reached down with one hand to tease her clit, stroking her inside and out now, sensation building thrust upon thrust, until orgasm carried them both away.

They lay together in bed afterward, Vic's head resting on his chest, his arms around her, the sound of his heartbeat strong in her ear.

"What happened tonight to make up your mind? One minute, I hear you've got to go to some damned dinner, and the next, you're here."

Victoria wasn't sure she could explain. "I was about to say something to those two interns, when it all became clear to me that I was in the wrong place. All my self-doubt just vanished. I realized I'd rather risk everything for a chance at happiness with you than waste another moment of my life there. I deserve to be happy, to live the life that I want. That life is here in Scarlet with you. I am a daredevil, after all."

He chuckled, kissed her hair. "Yes, you are. So you just left everything?"

"Yeah. I figured we could work that out. I'll need to break my lease and get movers to bring all my stuff here."

"Does that mean my climbing gear has to move out of the closet?"

"I'm afraid so, babe."

"I suppose you'll want some kind of secret drawer for your panties." His tone of voice—so serious—made her laugh.

"Absolutely." God, she loved him. "I also need to hire someone to drive my car out here."

He gave a low whistle. "That will be expensive."

"You forgot something." She lifted her head and looked up at him, unable to keep the smile off her face. "I'm rich."

He laughed, flipped her onto her back. "That was my goal the whole time, you know—to marry a woman with money."

"You're such a liar." Wait. "Did you just ask me to marry you?"

"What do you say we pick up Lexi and Taylor tomorrow morning early and drive to Vegas to get hitched?"

The vows Lexi and Austin had said to each other came back to her. "I, Victoria Christine Woodley, take you, Eric whatever-your-middle-name-is Hawke—"

He gave a little laugh. "Matthew."

"—Eric Matthew Hawke, to be my husband in a marriage of equals."

Eric joined her now, the two of them saying the words together.

"I commit to you all that I own and all that I am—body, heart, and soul. I promise that you will be the source of my pleasure—and my solace in times of pain. I promise to share your dreams and your fears, to comfort you and shield you from harm, and to show you respect, love, and devotion through all the joys and struggles of our lives together. Most of all, I promise to be your faithful and true friend, honoring you above all others, from this moment until my dying breath."

His gaze went soft. "Is that a 'yes'?"

"Yes! Yes! Yes!"

He kissed her, pulling back when she broke into giggles. "What's so funny?"

"Won't Lexi and Austin be surprised?"

Epilogue

Eric parked their new SUV and the two of them climbed out, Vic feeling more than a little nervous. They walked hand-in-hand toward the terminal, a cold November wind blowing in from the northwest.

"If he says another word about you signing a postnuptial agreement, I'm going to ask him to leave. He and James can spend Thanksgiving somewhere else."

Her father hadn't reacted well to the news of their marriage. First, he'd asked her if she was pregnant, then he'd immediately suggested an annulment. He'd even consulted an attorney on her behalf about drawing up a postnup to make sure that Eric couldn't get his hands on her money.

And now her father and brother were coming to stay in Scarlet—for a week.

"Cut him some slack. He's your dad. He's just trying to look out for you."

"He all but accused you of marrying me for money." She'd been furious and had almost hung up on him.

Eric gave her the look he saved for moments when he thought she was being too emotional. "If I had a beautiful daughter who was independently wealthy and stood to inherit a fortune—and one day I just might—I'd probably have those same worries, particularly if she married some small-town guy out of the blue."

She supposed he had a point. "You're about to meet my father and brother for the first time, and *I'm* the nervous one."

Eric chuckled. "Relax. Either they'll accept me or they won't. The good thing is that I didn't marry them. I married you."

The automatic doors slid open, and she saw them. They stood near the baggage carousel waiting for their luggage. Both were wearing plaid shirts and blue jeans. Is that how they thought everyone in Colorado dressed?

She bit back a laugh and waved.

James saw her, waved back, tugged on their father's sleeve.

Her father turned, his face lighting up when he saw her.

She hurried over to him, surprised by the rush of emotion she felt. "Hey, Dad."

He swept her up in a hug. "It's so good to see you, kiddo."

"It's good to see you, too. Eric, this is my father, Charles Woodley. Dad, this—"

Nearby, someone cried out.

Vic turned to find a woman kneeling next to an older man, who lay on the floor, mouth open, eyes staring at the ceiling.

In a heartbeat, Eric was there. He knelt beside the man, pointing first to one bystander and then another. "You call nine-one-one, tell them we need an ambulance. You call airport security and see whether they have an AED."

"Are you a doctor?" the woman asked, clearly terrified.

"No, ma'am. I'm a firefighter and paramedic. I'm going to do everything I can to help him, okay?" He checked the man's breathing, felt for a pulse, then started chest compressions.

Vic watched, pulse racing, feeling completely helpless, one of dozens of people standing around while Eric fought to save the man's life, alternating between rescue breaths and compressions.

Two uniformed airport staff pushed their way through the crowd, one of them carrying a large white plastic box. Wide-eyed, she set the box down beside him. "I don't know how to use this."

"I'll handle it." Eric's voice was unbelievably calm. "I'll keep doing CPR until you have it set up. Open it up, and turn it on."

Once the machine was ready to go, Eric tore open the man's shirt and stuck electrode pads to his chest. Then he took off the man's wedding ring. "Let go of his hand, ma'am. Here's his wedding ring. Move back a bit. Is everyone clear?"

He pushed a button, and the machine delivered a shock that made the man jerk.

For a moment, no one made a sound.

The man coughed, moaned.

Eric let out a relieved breath, turned the man onto his left side, took the man's pulse again. "Sir, can you hear me? An ambulance is on its way."

"He saved that man's life," someone said behind Vic.

Her throat tight, Vic looked up at her father and brother. "Whatever else you think of him, my husband is a hero."

Her father nodded. "So I see."

*E*ric and Victoria got their guests checked into their rooms at the inn, said a quick hello to Bob and Kendra, then went for supper at Knockers so that Charles and James could taste Victoria's pizza. While they waited for their order, she explained the business model, told them about the advertising campaign she'd worked up and how she'd had to double her staff in the first week of operation. "We just started home deliveries this month, and so far the response has been amazing."

James seemed impressed. "I think it's a great idea. You might be able to franchise this, open up stores in Denver and ..."

Sasha and Nicole walked in, both of them dressed like they'd just come from the rock gym. They waved, then took a seat near the climbing wall.

James stared at Sasha. "Is she a friend of yours?"

"Yes. That's Sasha Dillon. She—"

Eric cut Victoria off with a subtle shake of his head.

She smiled, understanding. "She's a real sweetheart."

"Call her over," James said. "Introduce me."

Victoria walked over to their table, and the two of them came back with her to say hello. "Sasha, Nicole, this is my brother, James, and my father, Charles."

"Hey."

"Nice to meet you," Charles said.

"How was the rock gym?" Eric asked.

Nicole answered. "We got a good workout."

"Are you two learning to climb?" James asked.

Oh, this was going to be good.

"I'm always trying to get better," Sasha answered.

"Let me know if you'd like some tips. I've done a fair amount of climbing."

"Really?" Sasha looked at him through innocent eyes, pointing to the rock wall. "I'd love to see what you can do."

"I'm not really dressed for it, but okay." James got to his feet.

Victoria walked away with them, smiling over her shoulder at Eric.

Charles watched as they reached the rock wall and James started giving Sasha pointers. "My son is about to get his ass handed to him, isn't he?"

Eric nodded. "Sasha Dillon is one of the best rock climbers in the world."

Eric sipped his beer, watched as James struggled up what looked like a 5.9 route, demonstrating holds for Sasha. He felt a stab of satisfaction when Sasha roped in and bolted past James, making big moves just to show off. Eric could hear Victoria's laughter from here.

Charles frowned. "I guess James had that coming, though it was unkind of Victoria to let her brother make a fool of himself. I hope she'll apologize."

"Yeah—after he apologizes to her for giving her private info to a predator."

"What are you talking about?" Charles' gaze went cold.

"You don't know?"

"Know what?"

Eric told him what Victoria had said about James giving her info—her photo, the amount in her trust fund, her contact info—to that bastard. "He's the reason that son of a bitch set his sights on her in the first place."

A muscle flexed in Charles' jaw. "I hadn't heard this."

"Well, now you know."

Charles was quiet for the rest of the evening, keeping to himself except to praise the pizza and his daughter's culinary skills. "If I'd realized how much you loved to cook, I would have sent you to school in Paris."

He stepped outside once to make a phone call. When he returned, it was clear he was furious with James.

*E*ric played climbing videos for Charles and James, doing his part to help with Thanksgiving dinner by keeping them out of the way, the scent of roasting turkey making his mouth water. Victoria and his mother buzzed about the tiny kitchen together, stirring, basting, tasting, talking—and sipping chardonnay.

"Dinner will be ready in about fifteen minutes," Victoria said. "Robin, do you want to set the table while I mash the potatoes?"

Her brother got to his feet, a smile on his face. "I could probably fit this entire cabin into my living room—no offense intended."

Victoria rolled her eyes at her brother. "I'd take this over a pricey Manhattan condo any day—no offense intended."

Eric chuckled at his wife's response. He didn't give a damn what her brother thought. "I'm going to carry in some wood to build up the fire."

To his surprise, Charles followed. "I'll help."

They put on their coats and stepped out into the twilight. A cold wind blew from the north, the sky overcast, the scent of snow in the air. Already, flakes had begun to fall.

Eric walked to the woodpile and began to fill his arms.

Charles did the same. "I wanted to have a private word with you."

Why was Eric not surprised?

He knew what the man was going to say next. He bit his tongue and prepared himself mentally for a speech about postnups. "I want you to know that Victoria and I have agreed that her trust fund is to be used only for emergencies. We plan to live off the money we earn so that we can pass that gift on to our kids."

Charles gave a nod. "Thanks for sharing that with me. I think you should spend some of it, don't you? Have a little fun. Travel. That's what money's for, right? But that's not what I wanted to talk about."

Oh? This ought to be interesting.

"First, I want to apologize for how I reacted to news of your marriage."

Okay, well, that's not at all what Eric had been expecting.

"Victoria is my pride and joy. God knows I have my shortcomings as a father, but I love my children. James is a lot like his mother, but Victoria is special. I've been setting money aside since the day she was born for a big society wedding. I always imagined a few hundred people at Trinity Church and a big reception. I've been looking forward to walking her down the aisle. Because you went to Las Vegas, I didn't get that chance."

Eric hadn't thought of that. "I'm sorry."

Charles picked up another piece of firewood. "I have myself to blame. I didn't support Victoria the way I should have during her recent hard times. Naturally, she pulled away from me."

"It would mean the world to her to hear you say that."

"I plan to talk to her before I go and make sure her brother apologizes as well."

Eric was happy to hear it. So far, this conversation was going a lot better than he'd imagined.

Charles went on. "I hope I can persuade the two of you to come back to Manhattan when your duties allow. I'd like to host an informal reception—a chance for our friends and relatives to congratulate you both."

"We can probably work something out."

"And now I'll get to the point."

Here we go. Postnups.

"I've taken the money I saved for her wedding and made it part of my wedding gift to the two of you. I don't want to offend you or intrude in your lives, but she is my only daughter, and you are my son-in-law."

Eric wondered what this gift might be and how much money Charles was talking about, but didn't ask. "I'm sure we'll be grateful."

Charles picked up one last piece of wood. "For what it's worth, I think you're exactly what my daughter needs—a man with his feet on the ground, someone who can encourage her and keep her safe, someone who isn't impressed with money. I know what she sees in you, and I'm proud of her for choosing a man based on his character and not his bank account or social standing."

Eric was stunned into silence for a moment. "Thank you, sir."

"I know you and your mother have had a hard time of it. Yes, Victoria shared that with me. The world isn't a fair place, that's for sure. I hope that over time I can become a father for you in some small way, just like Robin has become a mother for Victoria." With that, Charles turned and walked up the stairs.

Eric stared after him, a strange lump in his throat.

Vic reached over, took Eric's hand. "I am grateful for my husband. I'm grateful for my home. I'm grateful for my new life. I'm grateful for good friends. I'm grateful that my father and brother came all the way out here to spend our first Thanksgiving together with us. I'm grateful that I don't forget things all the time now."

It was her father's tradition each Thanksgiving to share reasons for feeling gratitude, and it was a tradition she was happy to keep.

"I guess it's my turn." Robin looked over at her son. "I am grateful for my son and his wonderful, beautiful wife. I have a new daughter, and I love her. She's brought so much joy to our lives. Everyone in Scarlet loves her. I'm grateful for my continued health and the health of my loved ones."

Eric gave his mother's hand a squeeze. "Well, this is easy. I am grateful to be alive and to share my life with you, Victoria. You are the greatest thing that ever happened to me. I will be grateful for every single day we have together. I'm grateful for the mother who loves me, for the food on our table, for the roof over our heads, and for the new family I'm just getting to know."

She saw his gaze meet her father's, an understanding passing between them. What had they talked about when they'd been getting wood? They'd been out there for a while.

James put down his wine. "Let's see... I'm grateful third-quarter sales figures were higher than we thought they'd be. I'm grateful that the old bag upstairs from me is moving out and taking her two yappy dogs with her. I'm grateful that my sister met a good guy and that they got married in Vegas so that I didn't have to go to a wedding. I'm just kidding. I'm grateful that you're happy, Vic."

Then it was her father's turn. "I'm grateful that my daughter is safe and alive and whole. I'm grateful for the good man she married. I'm grateful for the time we've been able to spend together. I'm grateful that I'm able to give them this wedding gift."

He placed a small brown envelope in the center of the table. "Go ahead. Open it."

Vic reached out, picked up the envelope, and opened it to find two keys inside. "What are these for?"

Her father smiled. "Look at the tags."

There was an address written on them.

"That's our address. Wait. No, it's not." Blood rushed to Vic's head. "It's … Oh, my God! You bought the house! You bought the property!"

She jumped out of her chair, ran around to the side of the table, and hugged him. "Thank you!"

"What?" Eric took the keys from her, stared at the address, then looked up at her father. "Holy fucking shit!"

For a moment, she thought he might faint.

He gaped at her father. "Pardon my French, but the property was listed for…"

More than two million dollars.

Vic had looked. She'd decided not to buy it because it would have come close to emptying her trust fund. Besides, she'd been happy in the cabin.

"It's yours now—the house, the property, this cabin. You can live here and rent the big house out. You can live there and keep this as a man cave. Robin, you could live here, closer to your son."

Robin blinked back tears. She reached out, took his hand, and gave it a squeeze. "That's quite a wedding present. Forgive my son. I'm sure he'll remember his manners when the shock wears off."

Eric seemed to have recovered—mostly. "Thank you, sir. We're both grateful."

James reached for the potatoes. "Now that that's out of the way, let's eat."

As soon as they were alone, Eric and Victoria climbed into his pickup and drove through the falling snow to see their new house.

"How much do you think your dad had socked away for your wedding?"

"I think I remember him saying it was close to a million."

A laugh burst from Eric's throat. "A million dollars? For a *wedding*?"

He'd thought Lexi and Austin had been nuts when they'd spent ten grand.

Clearly, it didn't faze Victoria.

Eric was so blown away, he almost missed the deer standing in the middle of the road. He slammed on his brakes, saving the deer and his truck.

She laughed at his surprise. "A posh Manhattan wedding can be outrageously expensive, especially if you feed everyone."

"Yeah, well, I believe that." That's what he said, but he was still trying to wrap his mind around it. "A *million* dollars?"

Victoria reached over, put her hand on his arm as if to comfort him, a note of amusement in her voice. "Are you okay?"

"Yeah. Hell, yeah. I'm fine."

"And you're okay with the gift? It made my father really happy to be able to surprise the two of us like that."

Eric had to think about it. How did he feel about his gazillionaire father-in-law gifting him and his wife with a two-million-dollar mountain home? "Sure. Shit. I mean, it's a house, right? It probably has toilets just like any other house, sinks, a place for my climbing gear."

She laughed again. "I sure hope so. Otherwise, my father paid too much."

"We'll probably have to use my salary to cover the property taxes and insurance."

She shook her head. "We can use the interest on my trust fund for that."

"Oh, okay." He shrugged, not sure what to say.

It was going to take him a while to get used to this new reality. The first two months of their marriage had been quiet, with her father playing an adversarial role. But he had apparently come around—Vicki said that seeing him save that old man's life at the airport had had a big impact on him—and now Eric was co-owner of a freaking gigantic house and a dozen prime acres of mountain property.

"I know this is a big change," Victoria said. "I know this isn't the life you're used to. I don't want you to feel like you're not providing for me or that your work doesn't matter, because it does. You save lives, Eric, and you can't place a price on that."

"Hey." He appreciated her words, but his ego wasn't that fragile. He reached over, took her hand. "So my wife comes with a bazillion-dollar fortune. I can learn to get used to that if I have to. Money doesn't bring happiness, but it sure as hell takes care of a lot of things that do."

Their children would never know the kind of hardship he'd grown up with. That gave him some peace at least.

He turned into the wide concrete driveway and got the first look at their new residence. "Holy fucking …"

Victoria's face lit up like a Christmas tree. "It's beautiful! It reminds me of the house at the Cimarron."

"It's a lot smaller than Jack West's place." That made Eric feel better.

He parked outside the freaking four-car garage—at least he knew there'd be room for his climbing gear—and met Victoria at the side of the truck. "Well, I suppose we should have a look inside."

She gave him an indulgent smile. "I suppose so, since it belongs to us now."

They walked up the sidewalk toward the double front doors, their feet leaving footprints in the dusting of snow that had stuck. Victoria handed Eric the key and stood aside while he unlocked the door. It opened soundlessly, the house dark.

Victoria caught him, held his face between her palms, snowflakes stuck in her hair and lashes. "I want you to know that I would be happy if the two of us spent the rest of our lives living in the cabin. It's not the size of the house that makes it a home. It's the love inside. Marrying you is the best decision I've ever made, Eric Hawke."

He scooped her into his arms, kissed her. "I am the luckiest man alive."

He carried her over the threshold and into their new home, kicking the door shut behind them.

"Hey, where's the light switch?"

Thanks for reading *Slow Burn*. I hope you enjoyed Hawke and Victoria's story. Follow me on Facebook or on Twitter @Pamela_Clare. Join the Scarlet Springs Readers Group on Facebook to be a part of a never-ending conversation with other Scarlet Springs fans and get inside information on the series and on life in Colorado's mountains. You can also sign up to be added to my mailing list at my website to keep up to date on all my releases and to be a part of special newsletter giveaways.

Watch for Book 3 in the Colorado High Country Series coming soon!

Author's Note

If you've read the Author's Note for **Barely Breathing**, you know the Colorado High Country series comes from a very personal place. Yes, the I-Team series was inspired by real-life work I did as an investigative reporter, columnist, and newspaper editor, but the Scarlet Springs stories talk about life in Colorado.

I grew up in a climbing family — rock climbing, mountain climbing, ice climbing — and there is so much family history in **Slow Burn** that my son, reading a draft of it, kept laughing.

Climbing the wrong mountain. If you haven't done this, you probably haven't climbed any 14,000-foot-plus peaks in Colorado. The experiences Hawke describes of twice climbing other mountains when trying to summit Mt. Bierstadt are just two of the instances in which my father and brother climbed the wrong peak. To get a list of all of them would require a spreadsheet, according to my brother Robert, who, by the way, has climbed Mt. Aconcagua, the highest mountain in the Western Hemisphere at 22,842 feet (6,961 meters).

Getting lost. This one made the newspapers. My mother and father had gone out for an afternoon of cross country skiing on New Year's Eve, not knowing that some irresponsible jerk had turned the trail sign around. They ended up getting lost and being benighted on Grand Mesa. In the winter. Now, if you're familiar with Colorado, you're immediately thinking "frost bite," "severe hypothermia," and "body recovery." My father, however, knows a thing or ten about surviving in the mountains. He used to teach mountaineering classes. So the two of them spent a very frigid night out under the stars on New Year's Eve. They met rescuers on their way out the next morning when daylight enabled my dad to find their way back to the parking lot.

Rafting Browns Canyon. Done it. Love it. Yes, I have been one of those people sitting up on the cliffs near Hecla Junction applauding as boats taco— that's what we call it—on Seidel's Suckhole. I have relatives who worked as river guides on that stretch of the Arkansas River. I have a couple photos of myself shooting through Zoom Flume and Widowmaker, and I look like I'm having the time of my life because I am.

Climbing the chimney. What do climbers do on a holiday when they can't really ditch their family and yet feel a pressing need to get vertical? Why, they climb their chimney, of course. One Thanksgiving, my dad and brother Robert disappeared. I found them outside, roped up, and climbing Robert's chimney. I kid you not. I stood there watching for a moment then shouted up to them, "Is this a first ascent? What are you going to name the route?" Which, at least, made me and my kids laugh.

After reading through the draft, Benjamin, my younger son told me he thinks the Scarlet Springs books are ultimately more representative of who I am as a person than the I-Team books because I lived most of my life (until I had to get a job) in the mountains with my family. I hope you enjoy the stories.

And now a word about sex...

As a columnist who covered women's issues for twenty years, I was once publicly tested for HIV/AIDs in order to drive home the message about safer sex to women in my community. In the real world, I take these issues seriously. That hasn't stopped random readers from castigating me for omitting condoms or STI testing from my books. I have, in fact, included at least some mention of both in all of my contemporary novels.

If I choose to omit details about safer sex from a novel, that's because this is fiction. I do not consider it my responsibility in fiction to go into great detail about contraception and STI prevention. We all know what causes these things, don't we? Yes, it's important to model good behavior, but that's not what novels are about. No one expects police dramas to teach safe firearm handling techniques, and heaven help them if they did.

If my books are your only source of sex education, then I strongly urge you to read *A Guide to Getting it On,* written by Paul Joannides and published by Goofy Foot Press. It's hands-down the best book on sex *ever* and includes everything.

Also by Pamela Clare

Contemporary Romance

Colorado High Country Series

Barely Breathing (Book 1)

Slow Burn (Book 2)

Romantic Suspense

I-Team Series

Extreme Exposure (Book 1)

Heaven Can't Wait (Book 1.5)

Hard Evidence (Book 2)

Unlawful Contact (Book 3)

Naked Edge (Book 4)

Breaking Point (Book 5)

Skin Deep: An I-Team After Hours Novella (Book 5.5)

First Strike: The Prequel to Striking Distance (Book 5.9)

Striking Distance (Book 6)

Soul Deep: An I-Team After Hours Novella (Book 6.5)

Seduction Game (Book 7)

Dead by Midnight: An I-Team Christmas (Book 7.5)

Historical Romance

Kenleigh-Blakewell Family Saga

Sweet Release (Book 1)

Carnal Gift (Book 2)

Ride the Fire (Book 3)

MacKinnon's Rangers series

Surrender (Book I)

Untamed (Book 2)

Defiant (Book 3)

Upon A Winter's Night: A MacKinnon's Rangers Christmas Novella (Book 3.5)

About The Author

USA Today best-selling author Pamela Clare began her writing career as a columnist and investigative reporter and eventually became the first woman editor-in-chief of two different newspapers. Along the way, she and her team won numerous state and national honors, including the National Journalism Award for Public Service. In 2011, Clare was awarded the Keeper of the Flame Lifetime Achievement Award. A single mother with two sons, she writes historical romance and contemporary romantic suspense at the foot of the beautiful Rocky Mountains. To learn more about her or her books, visit her website at www.pamelaclare.com. You can keep up with her on Goodreads, on Facebook, or search for @Pamela_Clare on Twitter to follow her there.

Made in the USA
San Bernardino, CA
24 April 2017